TOOTH AND NAILED

☥
ELLORA'S CAVE
ROMANTICA PUBLISHING

An Ellora's Cave Romantica Publication

www.ellorascave.com

Tooth and Nailed

ISBN 9781419956614
ALL RIGHTS RESERVED.
Tooth and Nailed Copyright © 2006 Hannah Murray
Edited by Mary Moran.
Cover art by Syneca.

This book printed in the U.S.A. by Jasmine-Jade Enterprises, LLC

Electronic book Publication September 2006
Trade paperback Publication June 2007

With the exception of quotes used in reviews, this book may not be reproduced or used in whole or in part by any means existing without written permission from the publisher, Ellora's Cave Publishing, Inc.® 1056 Home Avenue, Akron OH 44310-3502.

This book is a work of fiction and any resemblance to persons, living or dead, or places, events or locales is purely coincidental. The characters are productions of the authors' imagination and used fictitiously.

Content Advisory:

S – ENSUOUS
E – ROTIC
X – TREME

Ellora's Cave Publishing offers three levels of Romantica™ reading entertainment: S (S-ensuous), E (E-rotic), and X (X-treme).

The following material contains graphic sexual content meant for mature readers. This story has been rated E-rotic.

S-*ensuous* love scenes are explicit and leave nothing to the imagination.

E-*rotic* love scenes are explicit, leave nothing to the imagination, and are high in volume per the overall word count. E-rated titles might contain material that some readers find objectionable—in other words, almost anything goes, sexually. E-rated titles are the most graphic titles we carry in terms of both sexual language and descriptiveness in these works of literature.

X-*treme* titles differ from E-rated titles only in plot premise and storyline execution. Stories designated with the letter X tend to contain difficult or controversial subject matter not for the faint of heart.

Also by Hannah Murray

Jane and the Sneaky Dom
Knockout
The Devil and Ms. Johnson

About the Author

Hannah Murray started reading romances in junior high, hoarding her allowance to buy them and hiding them from her mother. She's been dreaming up stories of her own for years and finally decided to write them down. Being published is a lifelong dream come true, and even her mother is thrilled for her—she knew about the romances all along. Hannah lives in southern Texas in a very small house with a very large dog, where the battle for supremacy rages daily. The dog usually wins. When not catering to his needs, she can usually be found writing, reading, or doing anything else that allows her to put off the housework for one more day.

Hannah welcomes comments from readers. You can find her website and email address on her author bio page at www.ellorascave.com.

Tell Us What You Think

We appreciate hearing reader opinions about our books. You can email us at Comments@EllorasCave.com.

TOOTH AND NAILED

Acknowledgement

My family and friends put up with me while I was writing this and never once told me to stop whining, so I thank them profusely for that — especially Shannon and Amy, to whom I whined the most. And thanks also to my dog, who gave up way too many evening walks so mommy could write.

Trademarks Acknowledgement

The author acknowledges the trademarked status and trademark owners of the following wordmarks mentioned in this work of fiction:

Ambien: Sanofi-Aventis Corporation France

Avon: Avon Products, Inc.

Buffy: Twentieth Century Fox Film Corporation

Buick: General Motors Corporation

Gap: Gap (Apparel) Inc.

Girl Scout: Girl Scouts of the United States of America

Godiva: Godiva Brands, Inc.

Guinness: Guinness Ireland Group Company

Harp: Guinness Ireland Group Company

Harry Potter: Warner Bros. Entertainment Inc.

Hooters: HI Limited Partnership Hooters Enterprises L.L.C.

Mercedes: DaimlerChrysler AG Corporation Fed Rep Germany

Netflix: Netflix, Inc.

New York Times: The New York Times Company

Red Cross: American National Red Cross, The Federally Chartered Corporation

Red Hot Chili Peppers: Red Hot Chili Peppers Anthony Kiedis, Chad Smith and John Frusciante (all U.S. citizens) and Michael Balzary (Australian citizen) Partnership California

Rice Krispies: Kellogg North America Company

Tiffany: Tiffany (NY) Inc.

Triple A: American Automobile Association, Inc.

Valium: Hoffmann-La Roche Inc.

Viagra: Pfizer Inc.
Volvo: Volvo Trademark Holding AB Corporation Sweden
Wizard Of Oz: Turner Entertainment Co.
Xanax: Upjohn Company, The

Chapter One

"What an absolutely shitty day." Rowan Evans punctuated the muttered words by slamming the front door and walking straight into the living room to fall facedown onto the couch.

From over her head she heard Marvin ask, "Darling, what's wrong?"

Marvin's presence in the house didn't startle her. As her next-door neighbor and best friend, he had a key and often popped over to use her restaurant-grade oven when he was getting ready to entertain. He often lamented that if he'd just started looking for a house a week earlier, he'd have snapped up her cozy little bungalow with the gourmet kitchen. As it was, she'd put in her bid a week before him and snagged the house with the industrial kitchen she never used. He was slightly mollified by the fact his house had a pool and since Rowan was always willing to let him use the kitchen of his dreams, he got the best of both houses. It was a good system—her very expensive oven got some use and she didn't have to order takeout. And from the scents wafting into the room, he was working on Italian night.

She didn't bother to pick her head up but spoke directly into the scarred leather cushion. "My car had a flat tire and I broke three nails changing it."

"Sweetie, why don't you call Triple A for these things? I swear, ever since you took that auto repair course you have delusions of capability."

She twisted her head enough to scowl at him. "I resent that," she mumbled then her head came up in a rush. "What do you have on?"

Marvin grinned. "You like it? It's for Halloween." He twirled in a circle, making the full Fifties-style, red-and-white-polka-dotted skirt billow out around his hairy, muscular legs. Size fourteen pumps in a blazing white encased his bony feet and the whole thing was topped off by a frilly apron in Avon red.

"Fifties theme this year?" she guessed.

He nodded, his artfully arranged dark hair falling over his perfectly groomed brow. "I'm going as Donna Reed and Harry's going to be June Cleaver."

"Cute," she said, "but Halloween isn't for a month. Why are you wearing it now?"

"If I'm going to be Donna, I have to see how it feels to cook in this getup."

"Right. Method drag," she said, and dropped her face back into the couch cushion.

"Sweetie, you're going to smother in all that leather." She could hear the wince in his voice and knew without looking he was once again shaking his head at her choice of living-room furniture.

"Darling, when are you going to get rid of this Italian monstrosity?"

Right on cue. "It's a good couch, Marvin," she mumbled, trying not to drool on the upholstery. "It's functional. I'm not getting rid of it just because it's ugly."

"Darling, you should always, *always,* get rid of both furniture and men when the best thing you can say about either is that they're functional."

It was an old argument and inexplicably cheered Rowan up. She turned her face to the side to grin at him. "That's what you say about shoes."

Marvin waved an elegant, manicured hand. "It's good for everything—shoes, men, furniture..." He frowned. "And it's good for those slacks. What is that—tweed?"

Rowan rolled her eyes. "Bite me, they were on sale."

Marvin was fingering the hem. "Oh Gawd, it's like plastic corduroy. Girlfriend, spend some money on a natural fiber, would you please?"

Rowan grinned and sniffed the air. "I think your sauce is burning, Mary."

"Shit!"

Rowan giggled as he clomped into the kitchen in those ridiculous heels. She heard pots clattering and low murmuring as he talked to the sauce. He always said communicating with the tomatoes and the spices was the secret to great homemade red sauce. Which was why she got her sauce out of a jar with Paul Newman's face on it—it didn't require conversation.

She boosted herself more fully onto the sofa, letting her shoes fall to the floor and curling up fetal style with a sigh. She closed her eyes and was already floating off when Marvin came back in. She felt him sit at the end of the couch and lift her feet into his lap.

"Rough day?"

"You have no idea," she muttered then groaned out loud as he began kneading her toes. "God, that feels amazing."

"You get five minutes and then I have to take the bread out of the oven and finish the sauce."

"I'll take it," she sighed.

"So what happened today besides the flat tire?" he asked.

She laughed without opening her eyes. "What didn't happen? It's like every kid in the room was on speed today. They were just relentless. I wasn't a teacher, I was a referee."

"Sounds pretty par for the course to me," he said. "They're kindergarteners, after all."

"No, this was different. Oh right there on the side, that's perfect," she said as his fingers began kneading her calf.

"I don't see how you work with other people's children all day," Marvin said, and she opened her eyes to see him shaking his head.

"I like the kids," she said, letting her eyes drift closed again. "I like teaching them and helping them discover the kind of people they want to be. I just don't want to have any of my own."

"You'd be a great mom," Marvin protested.

Rowan snorted. "Marvin, you're more maternal than I am."

"This is true."

"I'm happy to have them for a year when they're five or six, help them get started then shuffle them off to first grade. I have a short attention span so that works."

"Short is an understatement. I remember when I tried to teach you how to make paella. You fell asleep before we got to browning the sausage."

"Well, who makes paella with sausage instead of shrimp? It's just not dignified."

"Listen, doll, when you use that stove in there for something more complicated than Rice Krispies treats, then you can talk to me about dignified food. And speaking of, my meal is calling me." He gave her foot a final pat and stood then paused to look down at her.

"Sweetie, you really ought to go clean up. You look like something died on you."

"That's very comforting. Thank you, Marvin."

"Hey, if you want comfort, call a shrink. Me, I tell it like it is."

Rowan grinned at him. "And I love you for it." She curled back up on the couch, closing her eyes. "What's the occasion, anyway? You usually say Italian takes too much time to do it right."

Marvin's voice traveled from the kitchen where, from the scent in the air, he was no doubt taking the garlic bread from the oven. "Michael's coming over."

"Ah. What is this, date number three?"

"Four, actually. I was going to cook for him last weekend but he had that thing in San Jose with his mother so we went out for lunch before he had to catch a plane."

"Slept with him yet?" Rowan grinned at his gasp as he clomped back into the living room.

"That is *such* a personal question."

She chuckled without opening her eyes. "So, that's a no then?"

"That's a no," he said, the huff in his voice coming through loud and clear. "I'm not sure he's interested."

Rowan opened her eyes at that, frowning. "It's your fourth date. He must be interested in something."

Marvin fluffed his apron. "Well, I *thought* so. But when I suggested lunch in bed last weekend instead of lunch at the deli, he turned me down."

Rowan shrugged. "Maybe he's one of those guys who needs to be in a committed relationship to have sex."

Marvin shot her a look. "Darling, that would mean he's straight and a woman."

She laughed. "Well, if Italian night doesn't do it, you can be sure he's not interested. Hell, from the smell of that sauce, *I'd* fuck you after eating it."

Marvin rolled his eyes. "That's a big surprise." He started to say something else but the sound of a car pulling into the driveway their two houses shared had him cursing instead. "Oh please don't let him be early," he wailed, and ran as fast as his pumps would let him to the front window.

When he turned back to her with a raised eyebrow, Rowan sat up. "What?" she asked warily. "That is not a good face."

Marvin cleared his throat. "Brace yourself, darling. Tall, Blond and Delicious is here."

Rowan felt a wave of dread wash over her. "You're kidding. He was supposed to be in Europe for another week! Please tell me you're kidding!"

"Fraid not." Marvin turned back to the window. "He's climbing out of that penis on wheels as we speak."

"Penis on wheels" was Marvin-speak for flashy sports car that served no purpose other than as a declaration of the owner's manhood, and Rowan found herself chuckling at the mental notion of her father's security chief driving around L.A. in a big penis. However, her laughter died in a rush of panic when she heard the steady fall of booted feet across her front porch.

"Tell him I'm not here," she whispered fiercely to Marvin, and slid off the sofa to crouch on the floor where she couldn't be seen from the door.

Marvin gave her a pitying look. "Darling, that's so junior high."

"So fucking what?" she hissed, feeling panic rise into her throat at the thought of having to deal with Jack Donnelly. The knock on the door nearly made her yelp with fright. "Please, Marvin? I just can't deal with him right now. I've had a shitty day, I'm tired and I have it on good authority I look like something died on me. Please?"

She could see he was waffling but it was taking too long. A second knock came and Rowan knew from experience one virtue Jack did not possess was patience. She had about ten seconds before he opened the door himself. He had a key, thanks to her traitor of a father, and if he thought she was in the house hiding from him, he wouldn't hesitate to use it.

"Marvin!"

"All right, fine!" Marvin fluffed his skirt and straightened his apron before striding to the door. He put one hand on the doorknob. "How do I look?" he whispered, and Rowan barely choked back a giggle. He sent her a wink then turned the knob and drew the door open with a flourish as she ducked completely from view.

"Well, Mr. Donnelly! Isn't this a lovely surprise. What brings you by?"

"Marvin." Rowan felt a shiver run over her spine at the sound of his gravelly voice with its yummy hint of Irish accent and ruthlessly suppressed it. "You're looking...interesting tonight."

Rowan heard the rustle of petticoats and crinolines as Marvin, traitor that he was, just couldn't resist twirling in the doorway. "Do you like it? I'm trying it out for Halloween."

"Hmmm." There was humor in Jack's voice now. "Donna Reed?" he guessed.

Marvin sounded as if someone had just handed him Ricky Martin wrapped in bow. "Yes!"

"It's a good costume," Jack said, "but you're missing something."

"I know, I need the wig," Marvin said, and Rowan could picture him patting his hair. "But this is really just a dress rehearsal. Of course I'll do the full makeup thing on the big day."

"I'm sure that would add to the realism," Jack said, the grin evident in his voice. "But actually, I was talking about the pearls. Didn't Donna always wear a strand of pearls around her neck?"

"Gosh, I'm not sure," Marvin said. "I guess I'll have to find out. I bet I can rent some old episodes from Netflix or something."

"Probably," Jack said. "So, can you get Rowan for me? There's something I need to discuss with her right away."

"Oh!" Thankfully Marvin remembered what his role was in this little production and delivered his line. "I'm sorry, she's not home yet. Some parent-teacher thing at school. She said it could run pretty late."

"Her car is in the drive."

Marvin, bless his heart, didn't miss a beat. "I know. I had to drive her to work this morning. She had a flat tire yesterday on the way home and the poor dear didn't have time to go buy a new one. She broke three nails changing the thing too."

"She changed it herself?" Rowan rolled her eyes at the scowl in his voice. She'd be getting a fair lecture about this when her father got wind of it.

"I know, can you believe it?" Marvin's tone was all chummy now, pals having a chat, and Rowan barely restrained herself from throwing a pillow at his head. "Ever since she took that course in auto mechanics she has delusions of capability."

"She's plenty capable," Jack said, the surety in his voice taking her by surprise, "but she never asks for help. Even when she needs it."

That's because I don't need it, she thought, *especially not from you.*

"How is she getting home?" Jack asked.

"Home from where?" Marvin asked, and Rowan bit her lip and prayed he wouldn't blow it.

"From school. You drove her this morning, are you picking her up?"

"Umm…"

Come on, Marvin, think on your feet!

"No, she said she'd get a ride from one of the other teachers. Either that or catch a cab. She didn't really say."

"I see. Well, I do need to talk to her so I'll drive by the school and see if I can catch her when her meeting lets out. If I miss her, let her know I dropped by, okay?"

"Sure, I'll let her know."

"Thanks, Marvin. Good luck with the costume."

"Thanks. Bye."

Rowan sighed in relief as the door closed, followed by the sound of retreating footsteps. She uncurled from her crouched position on the floor and looked up at Marvin. "Thank you," she breathed. "You saved my life."

"I don't get what it is with you two," Marvin said, reaching down to haul her to her feet. "You have this serious love-hate thing happening."

She frowned at him as she brushed the knees of her trousers free of dust, making a mental note to sweep her floors soon. "You're half right—it's a hate-hate thing. No love involved."

Marvin rolled his eyes. "Please. Every time you're in the same room with him you're like a cornered cat, hissing and spitting and scratching. You don't get like that with anyone else, even people you don't like." He turned to walk back into the kitchen.

She followed him and boosted herself onto a barstool. "So? I *really* don't like him."

He lifted the lid off his pot of sauce and stirred. "I don't think so, love. Your normal mode of operation with someone you don't like is to ignore them as much as possible. You're polite, you're civil, but that's as far as it goes."

She shrugged, tracing the grout on the countertop. "That's what I did just now. Ignored him."

"No, you avoided him. There's a difference."

"Semantics."

Marvin went on as if she hadn't spoken. "And this wasn't just passive avoidance, like not crossing the room at a party to talk to him. You actually cowered behind your couch and had me lie for you."

She scowled at the back of his head. "It's been a long day, Marvin. Get to the point already."

"The point, my grumpy friend, is that you hate him just a little too much." He arched a brow at her. "Ever heard the expression 'the lady doth protest too much'?"

"Ever heard the expression 'fuck off'?" she countered, and stuck out her tongue.

"I see we've graduated from junior high and have moved on to high school."

She rolled her eyes at his dry retort. "I don't know why I hate him so much, okay? He just rubs me the wrong way."

"As opposed to rubbing you the right way?" Marvin said then stopped. He turned from the stove, his eyes bulging and his mouth hanging open.

"What's wrong with you?" she asked, frowning. "You look like someone just shoved a broomstick up your ass."

He ignored her jab. "OhmyGod, that's IT!"

"What's it, you moron?"

"You like him!"

"Huh?" Rowan was genuinely confused. "Like who?"

"Jack Donnelly!" Marvin practically squealed. "That's why you act like such a royal bitch around him! You like him and you don't want him to know it!"

Rowan starred at him, ignoring the heat rushing into her face. "You're high, is that it? You smoked a bowl before you started cooking and this is a hallucination."

He just smirked at her. "Pot doesn't give you hallucinations. You're thinking of LSD and don't change the subject."

"As far as I'm concerned, there is no subject," she said. She slid off the barstool, intending to head for the bathroom and peace.

For a man in high heels he moved pretty fast. He was in front of her before she took two steps. "Oh yeah, you like him all right," he crowed. "You're blushing and you're looking at my chin instead of my eyes. You *so* like him!"

Determined to brazen her way out of this conversation, Rowan focused her narrowed eyes on his and folded her arms across her chest. "I don't like him—and by the way, who's in junior high now? I just don't like his style, that's all. He always makes me feel crowded and pushed into a corner."

"Because you like him."

"No, because he has no respect for my personal space. He's always right here," she said, holding her palm six inches from her face. "Right up in my grill, teasing and making fun and generally being a pain in the ass."

"Because he likes you too."

Rowan knew there was truth in that, though she would never tell Marvin. He'd wonder why she didn't just go for it already—after all, Jack *was* Tall, Blond and Delicious—and she didn't know how to tell him she was too freaked-out to act on the attraction. There was always a predatory look in his chocolate eyes—dark chocolate, like the finest bittersweet from Godiva—as if he'd like to throw her over his shoulder and carry her off to a cave somewhere. And even though it made her shiver and tingle in places best left unmentioned, it also filled her with this unreasonable sense of dread. She didn't know where it came from or what it meant, but she was a big believer in not ignoring her instincts. Especially when they were screaming at her to run, lest she be gobbled up like Little Red Riding Hood's grandma by the big, bad wolf.

"No, he doesn't like me too," she said. "Or at all, because there is no 'too', because I don't like him at all. Either. Nobody likes anybody. He just likes to tease me because he knows it bothers me. That's all."

Marvin was smirking now. "I wish you could hear yourself. You sound like the poster girl for denial."

She glared at him. "Don't you have a sauce to finish, Mary?"

"Yes," he said, "and don't think that calling me Mary is going to throw me off track. I'm perfectly comfortable with my well-developed feminine side, so kiss ass. And sooner or later, missy, when I don't have sauce to finish and a hot date who will be here in—" he looked at his watch "—seven minutes, you and I are going to have this discussion."

Rowan watched him pivot on his white heel and head back to the stove. "Not bloody likely," she muttered, determined the topic would never come up again. Aloud she said, "I'm going to go take a shower. Are you going to leave me some sauce?"

"I shouldn't, you're being such a baby."

She scowled at his back. "Are you leaving me some sauce or not?"

He waved at her over his shoulder. "Yes, yes. But you're cooking your own pasta because I don't have time."

She decided not to push him. Besides, she could handle pasta. "Fine," she called over her shoulder as she started down the hall. "Lock the door on your way out."

Without waiting for Marvin to answer, she snagged two towels from the hall linen closet and strode into her bedroom. She shed her clothes as she walked, dropping them carelessly to the floor, just because she knew it would make Marvin's neat-freak fashionista heart cringe. She went into the master bath naked and stared longingly at the garden tub. It had been one of the first things she'd added to the house when she bought it and what she wouldn't give for a long, luxurious soak to ease the strain of the day. But she had a pile of work to get through before school tomorrow. So unless she wanted to be up all night cutting out letters for tomorrow's alphabet lesson, she'd have to forego the bath.

She turned to the separate shower stall, turning on the water with a flick of her wrist and stepped into the needle-sharp spray with a sigh of pleasure. She allowed herself the luxury of simply standing, letting the hot water pound against her shoulders and easing some of the tension knotted there. Tilting her head back, she let it soak into her hair, the dark locks tangled and sweaty from her bout with the flat tire. They unraveled under the pressure, falling past her shoulders to slide down her back in a sleek cascade.

In the quiet solitude of the bathroom, her mind turned back to the conversation with Marvin and she frowned. He didn't know what he was talking about. She didn't *like* Jack Donnelly—the very idea was absurd. The notion that she found him attractive in the slightest way, just made no sense at all.

She sighed. "I can't even lie to *myself* anymore," she muttered irritated, and snagged the bottle of shampoo from the shelf. She poured the creamy liquid right on her head and started ruthlessly scrubbing, digging her fingers into her scalp in an effort to distract herself from thoughts of Jack Donnelly.

It didn't work. As she scrubbed, she thought over what Marvin had said. There was definitely an attraction there—he was the finest-looking thing on two legs. Which was patently unfair since he was also one of the most irritating. Unfortunately her body didn't care that he was constantly taunting her, mocking her and generally making her life a misery. No, she took one look at the six and a half feet of lean muscle, tawny, unkempt hair and laughing eyes the color of bittersweet chocolate, and her hormones sang the hallelujah chorus. When he spoke with that lilting hint of Ireland in his voice, it was all she could do to keep from tripping him and beating him to the floor. Only the knowledge she'd just be one more notch in his already full belt kept her from giving in to temptation.

Well, that and the irrational yet unshakable fear she had of him. She frowned, ducking her head under the spray. It wasn't a fear of him exactly. More like a fear of what he was capable of. He'd never been threatening to her—annoying, yes, but never threatening. Even when he was deliberately crowding her, pushing her temper and invading her personal space, he didn't scare her physically. Somehow she knew he wouldn't lay a hand on her without permission, which was for some reason both aggravating and reassuring. But she'd seen glimpses of him at work, and there was something fierce and lethal about the way he conducted himself.

He was her father's chief of security and therefore in charge of protecting him from the many crackpots and crazies who hated him for his political and social views. She was grateful he appeared more than capable of keeping her dad safe, but she couldn't help but be just a little bit freaked by the stark intensity of his professional persona.

Rowan grabbed the conditioner and squeezed some into her palm. As she worked it into the ends of her hair, she thought about Jack's intensity. It was always there, lurking behind his eyes, like a sleeping wolf. She got the distinct impression he always had a tight leash on his inner wolf and only let it loose in extreme circumstances. She frowned as she rinsed her hair. It was as if he had a mask he wore for the world and kept the real him carefully hidden.

Her hair clean, she squeezed out a dollop of body wash onto a loofah and scrubbed her skin until it glowed. She rinsed and shut off the water, drying herself briskly with the towel and wrapping it around her head before stepping out onto the bathmat. Snagging the second towel from the rack behind her, she wrapped it around her torso, tucking the ends under her arms to secure it.

She frowned into the mirror, her reflection partially obscured by the steam from the shower. "We're going to have to get better at lying," she told herself. "And we absolutely have to get better at avoiding Jack Donnelly." She tried a winning smile in the mirror, sighing when it came out looking like a sickly grimace. Then something else caught her eye and she leaned in to examine her forehead.

"Dammit," she muttered. "That's a pimple." She glared at the offending blemish then stuck her tongue out at her reflection. This day was just getting worse and worse. She sighed again and opened the bathroom door. She took two steps into the bedroom, stopped short and screamed.

Chapter Two

Jack Donnelly raised one tawny eyebrow and tried to control the smirk on his face. "Problem?"

He figured if looks could kill, he'd be lying in a pool of his own blood—what there was of it. Fortunately, he was immune to killing female looks so he lay back against the pillows of her very large bed, laced his fingers together behind his head and enjoyed the very tempting sight of Rowan Evans scrambling for dignity in nothing but a towel.

God, she was every wet dream he'd ever had and then some. Slightly taller than average at five feet seven inches, she was just the perfect height for him to bend over his arm. Her head would tilt back, that silky fall of raven hair would brush over his arm and her creamy throat would be bared to his hungry mouth. Right now though, he could barely glimpse that smooth stretch of skin because she'd unwrapped the towel from around her head and was using it as a cape. She was holding it tight under her chin, almost as if she knew her neck was the object of his attention.

He frowned slightly then dismissed the thought as nonsense. There was no way she could know. And she may have covered her neck but there were still plenty of other attributes he could concentrate on while she struggled to find her voice. In his experience, it didn't take her long to recover so he'd better look while he was able.

There was all that leg left exposed by the skimpy towel. Long and slim, unblemished by the kiss of the sun, her legs were sweetly rounded and were sure to be firm to the touch. He watched the subtle flex and play of toned muscle under the milk white of her skin as she shifted her weight and had to bite back a moan of appreciation.

"What the hell are you doing here?" she screeched, and he winced. Normally, enhanced hearing was a blessing but there were times when it could be a definite curse.

He cleared his throat. "I stopped by to talk to you. Marvin didn't give you the message?"

He watched the blood rush to her face as she realized she'd been caught. Unsurprisingly, she tried to brazen it out. "I just got home—I didn't get a message."

He smiled, a predator's grin that had her eyes widening in instinctive trepidation. He felt a twinge of guilt—he usually tried to temper the beast inside him when dealing with her—but her not-so-subtle attempt to avoid talking to him earlier had him seeing red and he wasn't feeling very generous.

"Really?" he said. "You just got home?"

She tightened her hold on both her towels and lifted her chin. "Just now."

"Funny," he said, holding her gaze as he rose slowly from the bed to stand beside it. He didn't move any closer, seeing her body language go even more defensive. "I stopped by about—" he looked at his watch "—ten minutes ago and Marvin said you weren't home yet."

If possible, her chin went up even higher. "I told you, I just got home."

"How did you get here?" he asked, exaggerated concern in his tone. "I told Marvin I was going to go by the school and look for you there but I decided I didn't want to miss you. So I parked out front and I didn't see anyone drop you off."

He watched her mouth work soundlessly as her cheeks flushed and pressed his advantage. "I didn't see a cab," he continued. "So I'm wondering, Rowan—" he took a step toward her and watched her fight the instinct to retreat "—how exactly you got home."

"You must've missed the cab," she managed, sounding as if she were choking on an onion.

Jack pretended to think that one over as he took another step toward her, eyes locked on hers. He had the brief thought that it was like drowning in a pool of sea-foam green. "No, I don't think so," he said, and continued to close the distance between them. "I don't think I missed the cab. I don't think there was a cab. You want to know what I think?"

He heard her swallow hard and imagined her throat working behind the concealing towel. "I don't care what you think."

He went on as if she hadn't spoken, taking another step that brought him close enough to her to step on her toes. "I think you didn't have a flat tire. I think you were here when I stopped by earlier. And I think you asked Marvin to lie for you and you were hiding behind the couch the whole time."

He watched the shock flash into her eyes and thought she was going to try to fob him off with another lie. She surprised him by shrugging. "I didn't want to talk to you. If you knew I was there, then that much should have been obvious."

He crossed his arms over his chest. "Well, I wanted to talk to you. Or more importantly," he went on when she opened her mouth to protest, "your father wants to talk to you."

Rowan frowned at that. "Then why didn't he just call me? All he has to do is pick up the phone, he knows that."

Jack shook his head. "It's a little more important than that, Rowan. We've got a bit of a security issue and it concerns you. He asked me to come get you, take you back to the house so we can all discuss what's to be done."

She was frowning in concern, her annoyance forgotten. "What's going on? Is Dad okay?"

Her obvious concern for her father's safety had him softening his tone, no matter how irritated he was with her for hiding from him. "He's fine," he assured her. "But he does need to talk to you tonight."

She nodded, distracted enough with worry for her dad's wellbeing that she eased her death grip on the towel around her neck and it dropped to the floor. "I'll get dressed and drive up," she said, turning toward the closet.

Jack bit back a predatory growl at the sight of that elegant sweep of neck and tried to keep his mind on business. "I'll drive you."

She gave him a sardonic look over her shoulder before she disappeared in the depths of her walk-in closet. "I don't think so," she said. "I'm perfectly capable of driving myself. That way, I can get back here later without having to suffer any more of your company."

Jack grinned privately, thinking just how much of his company she was going to have to suffer through over the next couple of weeks, but held his tongue. For the time being at least, the less she knew, the better off he'd be.

* * * * *

An hour later, she climbed out of her ten-year-old Volvo in front of her father's house. High in the Hollywood Hills, it was a sprawling stretch of wood and glass that somehow managed to be modern and traditional at the same time. Rowan had grown up here and usually returning brought back happy memories. But Jack's contention that something was wrong and the fact her father had sent him to fetch her rather than calling her on the phone weighed heavily on her mind, and the usual flood of happy childhood moments didn't come.

She started up the flagstone path, suppressing a flash of annoyance as Jack fell into step beside her. She'd insisted on driving her own car and he'd given in with relative ease. That alone was cause for concern, since in her experience Jack liked to be in charge of everything. His take-charge attitude was one of the things she found infuriating about him. To her everlasting chagrin, it was also one of the reasons she found him so immensely appealing on a physical level. For reasons she'd long ago given up on understanding, dominating men were one of her weaknesses. Unfortunately in her experience, the ones who were dominating in bed were usually dominating everywhere else, so it was pretty hard to find one who didn't want to control every tiny detail of her life.

She'd had enough of that growing up. Simon Evans was a good father and he had raised his daughter thoughtfully, always trying to balance the restrictions the security they lived with had placed on their lives with love and laughter. Most of the time it had worked. But her father was one of the richest men on the planet, along with being one of the most socially active and politically vocal, and there had inevitably been threats on his life.

The result was a life always under scrutiny with someone else deciding when and how things were done. Her dad had done his best to make it as easy as possible—there were tutors when bomb threats made it impossible for her to go to school and scores of indoor activities when she couldn't go outside for fear of sniper fire. Once he'd turned their front hall into a sandlot, bringing in sparkling white sand by the truckload so she could build sandcastles. She grew up always having to check with someone before doing everything so it was no wonder now that she was an adult she didn't like to ask permission for anything.

Except in the bedroom. It was the one area of her life she was able to give up control, to surrender her hard-won independence and just let go. She frowned, thinking it was some cruel trick of the universe that made Jack Donnelly so perfect for her on one level and so absolutely *wrong, wrong, wrong*, for her on the rest of them.

"Penny for your thoughts, darling."

Rowan shot Jack a fulminating look out of the corner of her eye. He was smirking at her as if he could read her mind, the son of a bitch, and she felt a pithy retort forming on her tongue. She swallowed it back, determined not to get pulled into the trap of debating with him. She always lost, which infuriated her. Instead she looked straight ahead, clearing her throat as they reached the massive front door.

"Just worried about Dad," she said, reaching for the doorhandle. As she did, the door swung open from the inside and she smiled her first genuine smile since she'd come home from work.

"Miss Rowan, it's good to see you again."

Rowan smiled with genuine pleasure. "Brooks, how are you?" She crossed the threshold and enveloped the wizened old man in a gentle hug. Frail hands, knotted and curled with arthritis, came up to pat her gently on the back.

"I'm hanging on by a thread, Miss Rowan."

Rowan chuckled and drew back. "Brooks," she said affectionately, "you always say that." She grinned into his rheumy blue eyes.

He let out a cackle that would've done the Wicked Witch of the West proud. "And it's always true, miss." Grasping her hand, he turned on wobbly legs. "Come, your father is waiting for you in the game room."

"I bet he is," she muttered, trailing behind her father's aging butler and leaving Jack to follow behind. "Brooks, what's going on? Why's Dad holding court up here like a ruling dictator?"

"No one tells me anything, miss. I just work here."

Rowan rolled her eyes behind his back. "Oh please, Brooks. You know all, see all, hear all. Dad doesn't even buy a new pair of jockey's without your knowing it."

He cackled again. "He's wearing boxer briefs now, miss. Says they're more comfortable."

She stifled a snort. As they approached the closed door of the game room, she drew to a halt, laying a hand on Brooks' elbow. "Brooks." She waited until he turned to look at her. "Tell me what's going on."

He shook his head, his smile fading into serious lines. "He's keeping them quite close to the vest on this one, miss. I'm afraid I don't know much. But I've never seen him so worried."

Rowan sighed. "I guess I'd better find out then."

Brooks nodded. "I'll be in the kitchen if you need me, miss."

She squeezed his frail hand. "Thank you, Brooks."

He bent his regal, balding head and pressed his lips to the back of her hand. "Anything for you, miss."

She smiled at his retreating form then turned back to the door, drawing a deep breath. She could feel Jack's presence at her back. "You want to give me some idea of what's going on or do I go in blind?"

She started when he suddenly moved around to stand in front of her. He looked at her with quiet watchfulness and the serious expression in his eyes somehow added to the ball of dread forming in her stomach.

"He wanted to tell you himself," he said, his eyes searching hers. "But I can tell you that he's very concerned for your wellbeing and for once in your life maybe you could do as you're told instead of being so bloody stubborn."

"Excuse me?" she said, acid dripping from every word. She felt the ball of dread turn to something much more dangerous as he rolled his eyes at her.

"Don't get your knickers in a twist," he drawled mockingly. "I'm just suggesting you listen to the advice of those who know better, instead of going off half-cocked on your own."

Rowan hissed out a breath. "Maybe you should just let me talk to my father and keep your opinions to yourself."

"Ah, but you're forgetting, love. This is a security matter and as such falls under my purview."

"I don't care if it falls under the purview of the fucking attorney general of the United States. Get your insulting ass the fuck out of my way. I want to talk to my father."

He shook his head. "Tsk, darling. Language. One would think you weren't a lady, hearing you speak that way."

She narrowed her eyes. "One would think you were British, hearing you speak that way."

Now his eyes narrowed and he opened his mouth to retort. He was cut off however by a shout from behind the door.

"Dammit, Jack!" Her father's voice boomed like thunder from the other side of the door. "Let the girl through! We don't have time for you two to dance around each other for a couple of hours."

"So there." Rowan stuck her tongue out at him.

"Careful," he admonished, eyes riveted to her mouth. "You stick it out like that, I'm going to assume you want me to do something with it."

"Keep dreaming," she muttered. She opened the door and tried to squeeze past him into the room. He didn't move, just kept that chocolate gaze steady on her face as she struggled to walk by without touching him. But he was a big man and she wasn't exactly tiny, and the doorway just wasn't wide enough for her to make it through unscathed.

She turned slightly, angling her hips and shoulders to move through the narrow space. As she was moving, walking practically sideways, Jack suddenly took a deep breath, expanding his chest, and in the diminished space, her breast brushed against the hard, muscled wall of his torso. Rowan narrowed her eyes at him, silently cursing him for the deliberate action. She knew there was no way he could have missed the shiver that raced over her skin at the contact or the sudden protrusion of peaked nipples through her T-shirt. But damned if she'd give him the satisfaction of reacting.

She turned away from him, moving farther into the room. Her face broke out in a bright smile as she headed toward her father's open arms. "Hi, Dad."

"Baby girl!" He folded her into his burly arms, lifting her off her feet and swinging her around in a circle. He set her down then held her at arm's length. "Look at you, girl! You're just as pretty as ever—the picture of your mother."

She smiled. "You always say that."

Simon simply grinned at her. "And it's always true." Suddenly Simon frowned, bushy black brows meeting over his nose. "Now, what's this business about you changing a flat tire by yourself?"

She turned, pinning Jack with a glare. He grinned back, unrepentant. "It was nothing, Dad. I know how to change a flat tire."

Her father's frown didn't ease. "You should've called someone. The auto club, me or even Jack here. He'd have changed it for you."

She managed a tight smile, thinking it'd be a snowy day in L.A. before she called Jack for help on anything. "Dad, I can change my own tire. Besides," she hurried on, forestalling the tirade she knew was brewing, "by the time anyone got there, I'd have had the tire changed twice over."

He harrumphed, clearly not happy. "Still," he grumbled. "Next time, you call me. Hear?" He pinched her chin and she grinned.

"Sure, Dad," she agreed, both of them knowing next time she'd do exactly the same thing.

"Okay then." Parental concerns laid to rest he turned to the bar. "Drink, honey?"

She shook her head. "No, I've got to drive home."

"Jack didn't drive you?" he asked, turning to frown at her.

"No, I drove myself. Dad—"

He shook his head and poured himself a scotch. "So independent," he said. "You've got your mother's stubbornness as well as her good looks."

"Dad!" She waited until he turned back to face her. "What's going on? Why did you send Jack to get me and what's with all the cloak and dagger?"

Instead of answering her, he looked over her head to where Jack still lounged in the doorway. "Give us a few, will you, lad?"

Rowan heard Jack shift behind her but she didn't take her eyes off her father's face. His usually ruddy complexion was pale and his normally impeccably groomed raven locks were disheveled, as if he'd been plowing his fingers though them in agitation.

"I'll just head to the kitchen then, see if I can nag Brooks into giving me a spot of supper." Jack's voice was tense, almost brittle, without its normal hint of laughter. She felt the hair on the back of her neck rise.

She didn't wait to hear the door close behind her. "Dad, you're seriously freaking me out. What the hell is going on?"

He shifted his eyes to hers and she saw with some alarm the sheen of tears. "Baby, I'm so sorry about this."

"Sorry about what? Dad, come on. Sit down over here and tell me what's going on." She led him to a leather club chair, eased him onto the seat. The fact he didn't fight her coddling alarmed her as much as the tears. Simon Evans wasn't a man who allowed himself to be led.

She snagged the ottoman, pulling it close so she could sit and grasp her father's hands. "Now. Tell me what's going on. Jack said something about a security problem."

Simon nodded, clinging to her hands and blowing out a breath. "Yes. Have you seen any of the local news lately?"

She shook her head, keeping her eyes steady on his. "No, you know I never watch the news. Too depressing."

"Right." He nodded. "Well, if you had been watching, you'd know that Stephen Job and his group of fanatics are stepping things up."

Rowan frowned, struggled to remember. "Stephen Job. Isn't he that fanatical preacher? He's got a little cult of followers, right? Call themselves the Army of God."

"That's them." Simon shook his head, incredulous disgust stamped on his features. "They use religion as a weapon, an excuse to harass and intimidate anyone whose beliefs aren't in line with theirs."

She flipped through her mental files, recalling some of the causes the Army of God had trumpeted over the years. They picketed abortion clinics, held book-burning demonstrations. They'd staged a sit-in outside a Muslim daycare center a few years ago, which had turned violent. That incident had attracted serious law enforcement attention but the investigation had discovered one person had caused the trouble and the group at large had escaped censure. They had continued with their campaign of moral cleansing, always being careful to stay within the bounds of the law. They targeted strip clubs, adult bookstores, public libraries and religious institutions that didn't conform to their own narrow views.

"Okay, they're nutjobs. This isn't exactly news, they've been around for what, ten years or so? So why is everyone worried all of the sudden?"

"Well, you know my political views aren't exactly in line with their teachings."

Rowan shrugged, not understanding. "So are the political views of half the nation. More than half the nation. So what? They're nut jobs."

He grinned briefly at the sneer in her tone then once again grew serious. "Well, nut jobs they may be, but they're getting to be pretty dangerous ones. They've stepped up their rhetoric over the last few weeks and they've decided I make a pretty handy target."

Rowan blinked in surprise. "Why you?"

He shrugged. "They've never been happy with my views on, well, on practically everything. I funnel a lot of money into political candidates and social causes that dismiss them as crackpots and religious zealots. They don't like it."

She frowned slightly. "But, Dad, none of this is news. Why all the urgency now?"

"Jack thinks they've decided they can't touch the politicians themselves so why not go after their most vocal and influential supporters? We're not really sure, honey. But they're really getting aggressive and more and more crazy. Now they're saying I'm a devil worshiper and I'm trying to seduce the population at large into being my followers."

Rowan let out a choked laugh. "You're kidding." She looked into her father's sober face. "You're not kidding. Surely nobody believes that bunk?"

"Of course not. At least no one who has any kind of influence or power. Army of God is too much of a fringe element—even the most conservative politicians aren't going to align themselves with these guys. But they are making some fairly serious threats and not just against me this time. Rowan—" he clasped her hands tighter "—they're talking about coming after you."

She started to laugh that off, but the shadow of fear in her father's eyes had her choking back the laugh. "Dad." She gave his hands a squeeze. "I'll be okay. I'm smart and I'm fully capable of defending myself. I'll be fine."

"Rowan. They're lunatics. They're not going to play fair, they're not going to give you a chance to get away if they do come for you. And the threats they're making…well, they're pretty specific. I need to know that you're safe. I can't deal with this if I think they're going to come after you, use you to get to me."

"What do you want me to do?"

He took a deep breath, his crystalline blue eyes steady on her pale green ones. "I need you to go away for a little bit while I deal with all of this. I'll send some of my security team with you to keep you safe so I can work with the authorities on this and put these people away."

Rowan winced. She hated living with security—it was the main reason she didn't live with her father anymore. It made her stomach clench and skin crawl just thinking about having people with her all the time, watching her every move. It nearly drove her crazy as a child—only her father's efforts to make life as bearable as possible had kept her from climbing the walls.

It was on the tip of her tongue to refuse, to demand they find another way. But one look at the worry and fatigue in his eyes stilled the protests. She sighed. "How long are we talking about here?"

"A week, maybe two at the outside," he hastened to assure her. "The authorities have a few ideas on how to draw them out, get them to make a mistake."

She frowned. "Why does that sound like you're setting yourself up as bait?"

"Don't worry, honey. I'll have the best security possible. The FBI's coordinating with the locals on this."

"No offense, Dad, but the Feds haven't done much to stop this guy yet. Forgive me if I don't really put my faith in them."

He grinned at her, the smile lighting his face and erasing the lines that fatigue and worry had drawn on his features. "Me neither, baby. That's why I brought in Jack."

"Well, good." Rowan sighed in relief. For all his many annoying, irritating, heinous qualities, Jack was the best when it came to personal security. "If Jack's running the show, then I won't worry."

"I'm very glad to hear you say that, baby. Because Jack won't be guarding me—he'll be guarding you."

For one stunned second, Rowan simply gaped at her father, paralyzed. Then she shot to her feet in a rush. "Like hell he will!"

Chapter Three

ಬಿ

"Now, baby, just calm down," Simon began in a placating tone.

"No, Dad. Forget it. No way, no how. I am NOT spending two weeks in protective custody with that Irish playboy!"

He sighed. "Don't you think that's a little harsh?"

Rowan crossed her arms over her chest and scowled. "I'm not spending one minute with him protecting me and that's that."

"Darling, such venom! Anyone just overhearing would think you didn't like me very much."

Rowan whirled. Jack had slinked back in the room at some point and sat comfortably slouched in a recliner that flanked the big screen TV.

"Nobody's talking to you, Rent-A-Cop." She didn't miss the way his eyes narrowed at the dig but she was too incensed to care. She swung back to her father, prepared to dig in her heels. Jack's voice had her swinging back in his direction.

"Simon, why don't you give me a moment with your delight of a daughter." He merely raised one eyebrow when she hissed at him. "Perhaps I can convince her to be more cooperative."

Rowan held her tongue until her father closed the door behind him. As soon as she heard the snick of the latch, she exploded. "What the hell are you playing at, Jack?"

He merely stared at her, eyebrow raised. "Rowan, you're becoming overwrought. Perhaps you'd like a drink to calm yourself?"

"No, I do not want a drink." She all but snarled it as he rose slowly out of the chair. She narrowed her eyes as she watched him stretch to his full height, knowing the deliberateness of the gesture was meant to intimidate. Had she been less angry, it might have worked.

"Well, I do." He sauntered over to the bar, turning his back on her as he fixed himself a drink, and infuriating her even more in the process.

The second he turned to face her again, she let fly. "If you think that convincing my father there's some kind of danger from a religious nut is going to be enough to get me into your bed—"

"Stop right there." His eyes had gone flat and cold, his voice harsh enough to send chills racing over her skin. "Your father is one of the best friends I've ever had and I take threats to him and his very seriously. Don't flatter yourself into thinking I'd make all this up just to get you under me."

Rowan subsided, properly chastened. "I'm sorry, that was uncalled for. I know you're loyal to him and I'm grateful for it."

He inclined his head. "Apology accepted." His dark eyes glittered at her from above the rim of the glass as he sipped his scotch. "Of course, I'm not so foolish as to let an opportunity slip past."

Rowan threw her hands into the air. "I give up!"

"Really?"

She narrowed her eyes at his suddenly enthusiastic expression. "No."

"Thought not," he said. "That would've been too good to be true."

Rowan swallowed hard as he advanced on her. She barely refrained from taking a reflexive step backward, only the knowledge that it's what he expected her to do kept her from it. "What're you doing?"

He rolled his eyes. "Jesus, Rowan. I'm not going to make you my love slave or whatever hideous scenario you're imagining in that fertile mind of yours." He set his glass on the coffee table and spread his arms wide in a gesture intended to put her at ease. Funny how it didn't. "I just want to talk about the plan your father and I have come up with."

"Fine." She watched as he sat in the chair her father had just vacated. Somehow, with him in it, the oversize club chair looked like doll furniture.

"Rowan." She pulled her eyes from the mass of his torso filling the chair to his face. He rolled his eyes at her, pointed to the couch. "Sit down."

She sat, struggling to appear comfortable and relaxed. Tough job, considering her muscles were so tense they quivered. He knew it too—he always did. The son of a bitch.

"So." She crossed her legs, met his gaze with a bravado she was far from feeling. "What's with the Army of God and why does Dad think they're serious enough to actually do something?"

His gaze flickered over the length of her thighs encased in worn denim that stretched with her movements, but his voice when he answered her was serious. "The main reason is that they've changed leaders in the last six months. And the new guy is a nut."

Rowan frowned, momentarily distracted from the tension being near him produced. "Right. Stephen Job. He wasn't always in charge of the Army?"

Jack shook his head. "No, he was always with them but his vision didn't quite gel with the aspirations of the rest of the leadership. He's not interested in having political power—he believes what he's preaching is gospel truth and he's made it his mission to convert the masses. And those he can't convert, he'll eliminate."

She snorted out a laugh. "Come on, Jack. You don't have to be so melodramatic."

"Rowan." He reached out, snagged her hand in a firm grip. "Six months ago, the leader of the Army of God, who also happened to be Stephen Job's father, died in a house fire. When they found the body, his hands and feet had been staked to the floor of his bedroom with railroad spikes. He'd been disemboweled and doused with accelerant."

"Ew, Jack." She glared at him and snatched her hand back, rubbed it against her suddenly uneasy stomach. "Do you have to be so graphic?"

"Honey, I'm not trying to shock you here. I'm trying to make a point—this guy is so focused on his religious vision, he killed his own father for not sharing the same beliefs."

"How do you know he killed his own father? If that were true, he'd be in jail."

"He'd only be in jail if they could prove it and they can't. And the reason I'm sure is because at the elder Reverend Job's televised funeral, his son delivered the eulogy. And it mainly consisted of listing the reasons why dear old dad had been a sacrifice to the cause, to show the world what judgment awaited them if they didn't become believers. He said that his father's sin of disbelieving was now forgiven and whoever had killed him had saved his soul."

"Oh gag." Rowan made a face. "Okay, he's dangerous. And I can see the wisdom of maybe going away for week or two." She saw the satisfied gleam come into his eyes and hastened to add, "But I don't see why I have to go away with *you*."

"Because your father trusts me to keep you safe. And he won't be worried about you—he'll be more alert and focused on his own safety and on catching the good reverend."

She let out an inelegant snort. "He wouldn't trust you so much if he knew you wanted to bend me over the first available surface."

He grinned, the smile moving over his face slowly, eyes taking on a sinister gleam. "Darling, have you been reading my diary?"

Rowan could feel her face burn with mortification and cursed her glib tongue. She stiffened as he slid smoothly out of the chair and barely resisted the urge to shrink into the sofa cushions as he came closer.

He braced one hand on the arm of the couch, the other by her shoulder, effectively caging her in. She kept her head resolutely lowered, refusing to look into those eyes that she knew would now be glowing with hunger and triumph.

"Of course, I don't keep a diary so you couldn't have been reading it." His voice rumbled right in her ear and she fought to control the shudder that rolled over her flesh. "You're not psychic, unless you've been keeping big secrets, so I doubt you have any actual mind-reading abilities."

Rowan swallowed hard, the sound loud in the hushed silence of the room. He chuckled. "So nervous, Rowan." He dragged a blunt fingertip down the line of her throat, raising gooseflesh while she fought to remain still. "I wonder why?"

She kept silent as he shifted, stretching across her body to murmur in her other ear. She nearly whimpered as the motion dragged his heavy sweater over the thin cotton of her T-shirt and her nipples grew diamond hard. He blew gently on her ear, and this time she couldn't contain the shudder.

"Now, where was I?" he whispered. "Ah yes—I remember now. So, if you haven't been reading my diary," his nose brushed against the heated skin of her neck as his teeth delicately nipped her lobe. "And you haven't any psychic powers..." he laved the lobe with his tongue and she nearly felt her eyes roll back into her head at the incredible heat that pooled low in her belly.

"Then one does wonder how exactly do you know that I'd like to bend you over the first available surface? Unless of course—" he gave her earlobe one last flick before moving back "—you've been having the same thoughts."

Her head snapped up at that, a harsh retort on her lips. She bit it back with difficulty, knowing that all he needed to launch a full-scale attack at this point would be a denial of what was painfully obvious to both of them. She narrowed her eyes, struggling to maintain her even breathing as he kept her within the cage of his arms, looming over her.

She had to swallow twice before she could speak. "Since that is exactly what you've been thinking," she managed to squeak out of her tight throat, "give me one good reason why I should trust you."

He smiled at her, a slight quirking of the lips that told her he knew exactly what she was up to. But he moved back, settling into the chair once again, and she drew a deep, steadying breath.

"Because I say you can." He quirked a brow at her scoff. "What, you don't believe me?"

"Not especially, no."

"I promise I can protect you, Rowan."

"Against a bunch of religious fanatics? Yes, I'm sure you can. The question is, who's going to protect me from you?"

"Do you need protection from me?" At her arch look, he chuckled. "Point taken. But you don't have to worry about me, darling. I promise, I won't take what isn't freely given. All you've got to do is say no."

Rowan sat forward, incredulous. "I've been saying no for a year and a half and I don't see you letting up any!"

"Ah, but you haven't really been all that convincing. When you are—" he picked up his glass and toasted her with it "—I'll let up."

She folded her arms across her chest and glared at him. "You know all that bunk you read in romance novels where the heroine says no but really means yes? I've got a newsflash for you, Jack. When I say no, I mean it."

"And I've a newsflash of my own for you, darling. You haven't said no. You just haven't said yes."

Rowan opened her mouth to argue then closed it on a snap. He was right, she realized. She'd evaded, sidestepped and avoided his advances and attentions for nearly two years, but she'd never come right out and said no.

She was still wrestling with that in her mind when she felt something being pushed into her hand. She blinked, looked down to see the tumbler full of amber liquid then up into Jack's impassive face.

"Have a drink, darling, while we work out the details."

She grimaced at the glass and set it aside without drinking. "Fine. So you're going to spirit me away for a while. Are you thinking of your place in Big Sur?"

Jack picked up the glass and put it back in her hand, curling her fingers around it. "No, Big Sur's too close. The Army of God has their main base of operations in California, so we need to get you out of the state."

She frowned at the glass, set it aside again. "Okay, that makes sense. Vegas, then?" He kept an apartment there.

He shook his head. "Still too close. Your father and I agreed that we want you as far away as we can get you." He pushed the glass back into her hand again.

"Dammit, Jack! I don't want a drink—I just want you to tell me where we'll be headed for this little forced vacation."

"Darling, trust me when I say you'll want the drink when I tell you where we're going."

Rowan went still. "Why? What aren't you telling me?"

"Take a drink first, love, and I'll tell you."

"Fine." She drew the glass to her lips, grimacing in distaste at the bite of the scotch. "God, I hate scotch." She took a large gulp, wincing as it burned her throat. "Now," she wheezed, "where are we going?"

"Ireland."

Rowan sputtered, eyes watering as she coughed up scotch. "Ireland?" she gasped, still choking for air.

"Yes, Ireland. Land of leprechauns and Guinness." Still seated, he stretched out an arm to pat her on the back when she continued to cough. "All right there, darling?"

She glared at him as she tried to get her spasming throat under control. "No!"

He frowned. "No, you're not going to be all right?"

She shook her head. "Not what I mean," she gasped. He got up, and out of the corner of her eye she saw him pouring a glass of water. When he brought it back to her, she snatched it out of his hand and gulped it down with relief.

"Now, that's better isn't it?" he drawled when she'd finished. At her answering glare, he gave an exaggerated shrug. "What?"

"I'm not going to Ireland. Forget it."

"Oh that's what you meant by no." He took the empty water glass back to the bar then turned to lounge against it. "I'm afraid I have to insist, darling."

"Jack, in case you hadn't noticed, we're in the United States."

"I had noticed that actually. What about it?"

"Between the United States and Ireland there's this big body of water called an ocean."

"Wait, don't tell me," he pressed a finger to his temple as if deep in thought. "The Atlantic, right?"

"Don't be a smart-ass. You know I don't fly and I sure as hell don't fly over oceans. You're just going to have to figure out some other place to stash me for a couple of weeks because there will be no flying."

"Rowan, it's perfectly safe," he began, but she cut him off with a wave of her hand.

"I know all the statistics about it being safer than driving, blah, blah, blah. I don't care. God did not give me wings, man was not meant to conquer the sky. I'm not flying."

"Sweetheart, I don't think you understand." He strode back over and sat next to her. "I'm not giving you a choice."

The calm, easy way he said it somehow made the words themselves all the more harsh. "Don't you tell me what to do, Jack Donnelly. You may be in charge of security around here and you may be the finest-looking thing on two legs, but I'm not getting on a plane with you and that's final!" Her voice rose until she was shouting at the end.

"Never say never, darling." His voice sounded as if it was coming from far away and she frowned.

"Why do you sound funny?" Her voice sounded tiny to her own ears and she blinked as her vision wavered.

"Do I sound funny?" She could hear the laughter in his voice but her vision was blurred so she couldn't see him. She shook her head to try and clear it, pushing herself up to stand, and the room took a sickening turn.

She felt herself begin to fall and flung out a hand to catch herself. It landed on something solid and instinctively she curled her fingers around it to hold on.

She heard a sharp intake of breath then Jack's voice calling out for help. He sounded a little distressed and she struggled to right herself to help, tightening her grip for leverage. She heard a hoarse shout, had a brief, blurry view of Jack's face twisted with pain and everything went black.

Jack heaved a sigh of relief when he felt Rowan go limp, though her grip on his dick remained uncomfortably firm. He lowered her gently to the couch, propping a beaded pillow under her head before gingerly uncurling her fingers from around his aching cock. He drew a deep breath, trying to keep the nausea at bay. Jesus, she had a grip like a teamster, and trust her to grab hold of the one truly vulnerable part of his body.

He studied her limp form with a faint smile. She was going to be seriously pissed when she woke in Ireland—he'd be lucky if she didn't come at him with a hatchet when she came to. He reached down to brush an errant lock of baby-soft hair off her flushed cheek. She looked like a fairy princess under a spell. But he'd wager that unlike a fairy princess, when Rowan woke up, she'd do it swinging.

He glanced up as the door opened and Simon peeked his head around the corner. "All clear?"

"Yeah." He brushed his hand over her cheek once more before rising with some discomfort and walking to the bar. "She's out like a light."

Simon walked over and looked at his child with naked worry on his face.

"She's going to be all right, Simon. I promise you that."

His friend nodded, bent to press a kiss on her forehead then straightened. "I know she will be, Jack. I can count on you for that."

Jack glanced back at him as he pocketed the bottle of liquid sedative he'd slipped into her scotch. "Then what's worrying you, friend?"

Simon sighed, plowing an unsteady hand through his hair so that it stood in raven spikes. "I don't like drugging her."

"You know it was the only way, Simon. She'd never have gotten on that plane without someone carrying her on and she'd have made herself sick with worry the entire trip. This way, she'll wake up already there and the worry will be over."

"She'll be angry."

Jack gave a low laugh. "Oh yes, she'll be right pissed. Rather looking forward to it actually."

"That's another thing I'm worried about." Simon waited until his old friend turned to face him. "I don't want you taking advantage of her."

"Simon."

"No, just listen to me. She's vulnerable right now. She'll be worried about me and she'll be worried about being away from her job for so long—I just want to make sure anything that happens between the two of you is what she wants."

"Dammit, Simon." Jack paced to the window, staring out at the glassy surface of the swimming pool and the glittering city beyond until he was sure he could speak without snarling. "I'd never hurt her."

"I know that, Jack." Simon's quiet voice had him turning from the window. "I know that," he repeated. "But I also know you want her. You have for a long time. And if you wanted to, you could make that happen, with or without her conscious consent."

It was Jack's turn to plow his fingers though his hair in frustration. "It wouldn't mean anything then, don't you see? She has to want me as much as I want her or it's no good." He turned to fully face his friend. "And she does want me, Simon. But she's afraid of it, for whatever reason."

Simon nodded his head slowly. "Yes, she is. I don't know if it's you, that she senses what you are on some elemental level or if it's something else entirely. Whatever it is, I want your word if she says no, you'll respect that."

Jack's eyes narrowed. "You know, that's the second time tonight someone's called my personal integrity into question in just that way."

Simon searched Jack's face for a moment then nodded. "Okay then. Brooks is having the car brought around—the plane's waiting at the airport."

Jack swallowed the bitter words on his tongue and nodded. He turned, scooped Rowan up into his arms and strode out the door.

Within ninety minutes, they were in the air.

Chapter Four

Rowan was having the best dream. She was floating on a cloud made of marshmallow fluff with little tiny chunks of fudge swimming around. She could reach out and scoop up a handful and nosh to her heart's content anytime she wanted. She smiled, snuggling down farther into the cloud. She drew a deep breath, eager for the scent of chocolate and sugar, and instead drew in the unmistakable scent of a peat fire.

She frowned. There were no peat fires on marshmallow clouds. She breathed in again, and this time, along with the scent of smoke and turf, she caught the scent of furniture polish and wool.

"That's not right," she muttered, and the sound of her own voice brought her crashing back to reality.

A reality that apparently consisted of a wool blanket, a peat fire producing too much smoke and a headache the size of Montana. She winced, raised a palm to her head and nearly jumped out of her skin when she heard, "You're awake then, darling."

Rowan kept her eyes closed, her brain racing to make sense of what had happened. The last thing she remembered, she'd been arguing with Jack in her father's game room. He'd handed her a glass of scotch, insisted she drink it. Insisted, she realized now, because otherwise how would he drug her?

She kept still, orienting herself to her surroundings as best she could without her sight. She was lying on something, probably a bed, which was sinfully soft and blissfully comfortable. She refused to give him credit for it. She could smell the fire, the wool in the blanket draped over her and the faint scent of an industrial cleanser just under a pleasant layer of vanilla.

She wasn't given a lot of time to puzzle out where exactly she might be. Intermingled with the scents of wool, peat, vanilla and cleaner was the unmistakable tang of Jack's aftershave. And it was coming closer.

Rowan could hear Jack moving, felt him getting nearer the bed. She carefully kept her expression confused, even though her clarity was rapidly returning. She let out a whimpering moan and shifted slightly, opening her eyes just a slit so she could track his approach.

The traitorous son of a bitch looked concerned, his brow furrowed with it as he drew close. He laid a broad palm along her right cheek. "You feeling all right, darling?" She shifted, let out a fretful moan, and his palm shifted to brush her hair back.

"Jack?" she muttered, blinking her eyes as though trying to wake.

"I'm right here," he crooned, and his palm slid off her forehead to brace along side her hip as he leaned over her. Clearing the path of her right arm.

"Jack," she murmured, keeping her eyes slitted just enough to see his face. "I can't…" she let her voice fade away on an exhausted sigh, fluttering her hands as though she hadn't the strength to lift them. Predictably, he shifted closer.

"What is it, Rowan? What do you need?"

He was so close now she could smell mint and cigar on his breath. Somehow, it pissed her off even more. "Just this," she gritted out, and swinging from her shoulder, plowed her fist full in his face.

He reared back from the blow, instinctively grabbing for his bleeding nose as he did and she planted her foot in his solar plexus and kicked out, using his own backward momentum to send him tumbling head over ass off the foot of the bed. She had kicked free of the blanket and was on her feet almost before he hit the floor.

She stood over him, fists clenched at her sides. "Get up, you son of a bitch, so I can hit you again."

Jack sat up with a shake of his tawny head, shifted to his feet in one smooth moment. "I wouldn't if I were you," he cautioned. His voice carried a faint nasal quality, a result of him pinching the bridge of his nose to stem the flow of blood. She noted with disgust it was already slowing and wished she'd hit him harder.

"Give me one good reason why not?" she hissed, already picturing her foot planted between his legs this time.

Jack narrowed his eyes. "Because if you do, I'm going to turn you over my knee and paddle your little butt, that's why."

Rowan couldn't help the shudder that shimmered through her at the silken threat in his voice but she resolutely held her ground. "You drugged me, Jack. It was a dirty trick."

Jack took his hand away from his face, the blood flow from his nose slowed now to a trickle. "Well, how else was I to get you on the plane?"

Her eyes went big and round. "Plane? You put me on a plane?" She whirled, found a window and dashed to it. She stared, mouth agape, at thatched roofs and cobblestone streets and lush, green hills that rolled out for miles in the fading twilight.

"Where the hell are we?"

"Welcome to Slane, County Meathe, Ireland." She turned from the window to see him wiping his face with a square of linen. He folded his arms and grinned that devil's grin at her.

"You actually drugged me and put me on a plane," she whispered, growing angrier by the second. "I'm going to twist your balls off."

He tsked disapprovingly even though he couldn't help a manly wince at the image. "I told you where we were heading, darling. And it isn't polite for a guest to speak to her host in such a manner."

"A guest? A *guest!?*" Her voice rose incredulously. "I've been drugged and kidnapped by a deranged lunatic — with my father's help apparently — and plunked down in a..." she looked around at the luxuriously appointed bedroom. "What is this place anyway?"

"My flat."

"Your flat." She stared at him. "Fabulous — that's just fabulous. Plunked down in a deranged lunatic's flat in Ireland."

He laughed, a deep chuckle that vibrated out of his chest and seemed to streak straight to her nipples. "You make it sound as though I've brought you to a beheading." He turned to place the soiled handkerchief on the bedside table. While his back was turned, she scowled down at her nipples and tried to push them back in. It didn't work.

She dropped her hands quickly to her sides as he turned back, but from the look of lazy amusement on his face, she had a feeling he knew exactly where her hands had been. She scowled, determined to have it out with him here and now. "I don't appreciate being drugged or tricked."

He sighed heavily and sat on the edge of the bed. "Look at it this way, darling. If I hadn't drugged you, you'd have fought me tooth and nail all the way to the airport. And again when I put you on the plane, and again when I'd have had to truss you up to keep you from killing me."

"Bet your ass," she muttered. He merely lifted a brow and continued.

"Whereupon you'd have gotten even angrier, on top of being terrified of the flight, and we'd both have had a very unpleasant thirteen hours. At least this way, you got some rest and I got to relax without worrying I'd have to call for an ambulance upon our arrival. For both of us."

"So drugging me was for convenience?" She glared at him. "If this explanation was meant to placate me, you've missed your mark. I couldn't give two damns about your comfort. I do however care that you hijacked me without regard for my feelings."

"Darling, you weren't exactly being cooperative when I tried to discuss it with you rationally."

She raised one raven brow. "You drugged the scotch even before you told me where we were going. You never intended to give me a choice or a chance to come around to the idea on my own."

He shrugged, unrepentant. "Seemed the most expedient way to get you where you needed to be. I didn't want to spend a lot of time debating the issue with you."

"Well, that's just too damned bad, Jackie," Rowan snarled, taking perverse satisfaction in his wince at the nickname. "It's my life, my body and my flaming head that hurts like hell! What'd you slip me, anyway?"

"Just a sedative, nothing dangerous. Your head probably hurts more from not having eaten in several hours—with the time change, it's been almost a full day since we left L.A." Jack watched thoughtfully as she rubbed her temple, as though to erase the ache that lingered there. "So is that what you're angry about? Not that you're in Ireland but the method that brought you here?"

"I don't like having my choices taken away."

He nodded, his eyes thoughtful as he studied her expression. "I can see you don't. All right then. I promise not to do it again."

She stared at him, eyes intent on his for so long that he began to wonder if she'd forgive him that easily. Things were going to be pretty difficult if she continued to hold a grudge, however justified it was. And it was justified—he'd have ripped the arms off anyone who tried to do the same to him. It hardly mattered her safety was at stake—she was an adult and deserved to be informed of what was happening.

"I mean it, Jack." Her voice was quiet now, her eyes steady and somber. "You don't make any more unilateral decisions. You tell me what's going on, what the options are."

He nodded slowly. "All right. But you have to promise in return to be reasonable about things. And if we have to move in a hurry, then you listen to me without question. If somehow Job or his ilk track us here, I don't want either of us gunned down in the street because we were debating whether to flee by train or car."

"Fine," she agreed. "I'll defer to you on the security measures since you're the expert." She drew a deep breath. "I'm sorry if it seems like I'm overreacting. But I need to be able to participate, to know what's going on. I'm not an imbecile and I won't be treated like one."

Jack rose from the edge of the bed, walked toward her until they were only a few feet apart. "I know you're not an imbecile, darling, and if that's how I made you feel, then I apologize. I was just trying to avoid a big ugly scene." He tried a tentative smile. "You're quite capable of peeling the paint off a car with that temper of yours once it gets going."

Rowan remained sober but her eyes took on an amused twinkle. "You'd do well to remember that, Jack. Because if you ever presume to make my choices for me again, I'll do more than peel paint. I'll cut out your heart with my nail file and fry it up for breakfast."

He winced, rubbed at his chest reflexively. "Duly noted."

"Good." She gave a brisk nod then turned on her heel to what she assumed was a bathroom. "I assume you brought some clothes for me to wear?" she asked, glancing back over her shoulder.

He nodded. "Marvin put a bag together for you. Your father called him, asked him to throw it together."

Marvin. Well, she'd deal with him later. "Good because I sure as hell am not walking around in this outfit for the next fortnight." She continued into the bath. "And by the way, I'm starving. Can we go out, get some food?"

"Sure." He waited until the bathroom door closed behind her then breathed a heavy sigh. It was going to be an interesting two weeks.

*****

"So, tell me more about this Army of God business."

They were settled at a booth in the local pub, having a pint while they waited for supper. Jack was drinking Guinness, and while the building of the drink had fascinated Rowan, one sip had her grimacing in distaste. She preferred to drink her beer not chew it, she'd informed a laughing Jack and ordered a Harps. The lighter brew suited her palate and she took a long sip while she waited for Jack to answer.

He studied her. "What do you want to know?"

She shrugged. "Well, Dad said they'd been making threats—specific ones—against me. What are they?"

Jack shook his head. "He doesn't want you to know that, Rowan."

She huffed out a frustrated breath. "Jack, I'm a big girl. I can handle it. And even if I can't," she hurried on as he started to shake his head again, "I need to know so I'm prepared for it. I can hardly participate in my own protection if I don't know what I'm being protected against."

"You've got a point," he conceded reluctantly. "But I don't like going against your father's wishes on this. He specifically asked me not to tell you."

"And you promised me to not make any more decisions for me. I need to know, Jack." She laid her hand over his on the scarred tabletop. "Please."

"You know, I'm starting to hate when you do that." He drained the rest of his beer in one swallow. "Okay, you

Tooth and Nailed

deserve to know what's going on. What's your father told you?"

"Just that they were talking about coming after me, nothing specific."

"Right. Well, the gist of it is—" he broke off as the waitress brought her food, the plate piled high with steaming French fries and sandwiches that looked like enough to feed an army.

Rowan sighed with pleasure as the plate was laid in front of her. "God, that looks amazing." She beamed at the waitress. "You've saved my life."

The server, a curvy sprite of a girl with curling red hair and dancing green eyes, grinned back at her. "You're welcome, miss. If you've a need for anything else, just give a shout. My name's Shannon." With a wink, she moved on to the next table.

Rowan inhaled deeply, drawing in the tantalizing aroma of roast beef and onions. "Tell me what this is called again?" she asked, even as she picked up half of the enormous sandwich and prepared to take a bite.

"Bookmaker's sandwich. Beef, onions, horseradish...good?" He grinned as she moaned around a mouthful of food, her eyes all but rolling back in her head as she savored the flavor of it.

She swallowed. "It's heaven. You sure you don't want any food?"

He shook his head. "I ate while I was waiting for you to wake. I'm fine."

She shook her head, taking another bite of sandwich. "Suit yourself." She looked up to find him watching her with that predatory gleam that made her insides go all squiggly.

Rowan swallowed hard and pushed her plate to the middle of the table. "French fry?" she offered desperately.

He snagged a potato from the plate, never taking his eyes off her. "In Ireland we call it a chip, darling." He popped it into his mouth, hummed in satisfaction. "Tasty."

Rowan was saved from a response by Shannon arriving with a fresh round of drinks and she took the opportunity to try to settle her scattered system. With one look, he had her all atwitter. Her heart was pounding, her skin felt tingly and too tight, and if she didn't figure out a way to bring her raging hormones under control, she was never going to be able to resist the seduction she knew was coming.

As soon as the waitress had stepped away again, she rushed to fill the conversational void. "You were going to tell me about the Army of God and their threats."

He raised one sardonic brow, amusement on his face. He knew she was trying to evade the growing tension at the table and she wondered if he'd let her get away with it.

"The Army of God," he began, and she breathed a sigh of relief that he wasn't going to push her, "is threatening to harm you in order to get to your father."

Rowan scowled at him. "Duh, Jack. Come on, stop sugarcoating it. I though we were going to be honest with each other."

"Darling, I wouldn't be throwing the honesty stone if I were you, living in your little glass house. You can't even be honest about your own feelings."

She pointed a finger at him. "That's entirely different and you know it. We're not talking about giving in to hormones here, we're talking about my life. I want to know exactly what was so horrible I had to leave my job and fly halfway across the world to escape it."

He folded his napkin, watching her across the table. She kept her eyes steady and square on his, and finally he nodded. "Fine then. You want to know?" He placed the napkin on the table and folded his arms across his chest.

"The Army of God, or more specifically Stephen Job, is threatening to kidnap you and cleanse your soul of the sins of your father. According to the phone call they made to your father, they plan to do this by ritual torture, gang rape and burning you at the cross." He raised a brow. "Honest enough for you, darling?"

Rowan sat frozen for long moments, the picture his words painted swirling around in her head and making her nauseous. She concentrated on evening out her breathing, willing the enormous sandwich that had tasted so delicious to stay in her stomach. If it came back up, she'd never be able to eat another one again.

When she was sure she could speak without losing her supper all over the table, she cleared her throat. "Well. I'd rather you didn't let him do that, if it's at all possible."

He silently cursed himself. Her cheeks had gone porcelain white, her pupils dilated with shock. "I'm sorry, I shouldn't have said that."

She shook her head, the motion jerky and abrupt. "No, I asked you to be honest."

"Well, you didn't ask me to be a flaming ass about it," he muttered. He stared at her for a moment then surged to his feet, digging a few bills out of his pocket and dropping them on the table. "Come on, let's get some air." He held out a hand.

She stared at it for a moment then placed her hand in his. She let him pull her gently to her feet, felt him drape a protective arm around her shoulders, and soon found herself shepherded out of the bar and out into the starry night.

They walked in silence for a while, the only sound the click of their feet on the cobblestone street and the music and laughter drifting out of open windows. Rowan looked up, enchanted by the sheer number of stars hovering in the blackened sky and tried to quiet her rioting thoughts.

"You all right?" She turned her head at the quiet question to find Jack watching her soberly.

She shrugged. "I'm a little scared, honestly."

"Good."

The stark statement had her head whipping around in shock. "What?"

"If you're scared, you'll be careful," Jack explained, eyes steady and serious on hers. "I shouldn't have said it to you like that, Rowan, but I can't protect you if you insist on being foolish. I need you to know this is serious, not just a prank by a harmless lunatic."

"Believe me, I know it now." They walked on in silence for a moment. "I guess I just got used to the harmless lunatics. Dad's had so many of them come after him for one reason or another and they mostly turned out to be nothing. I guess I just figured this was the next one in line."

Jack shook his head, steering her down the side street leading to his flat. "Not the case this time, darling. This one's dangerous, which is why tucking you away was imperative. I've friends here still, friends I can count on to lend a hand if the going gets rough. Besides," he grinned at her. "It's the perfect opportunity to get you all to meself."

Rowan rolled her eyes, her good humor partly restored by the normalcy of his flirtatious tone. "I knew you had ulterior motives."

"Naturally, I've made no secret of them."

"Yeah, well don't expect to get lucky with me, Rent-A-Cop. I'm not that easy."

"I never thought you were," he said, "and is it necessary for you to call me that? Makes me feel as though I should be working at the mall, scolding teenagers for loitering near The Gap."

She grinned at him. "You could ride around in one of those little golf carts and carry a clipboard!"

He stared at her, the look of horrified shock on his face so comical that she burst out laughing. The longer he stared at her, the harder she laughed until she was holding her aching sides and struggling to stay on her feet.

"It's not that funny," he grumbled, and let go of her elbow. She gave a startled yelp at the sudden lack of support, pinwheeled her arms twice and went down hard on her backside, still giggling like a loon.

Every time she got herself under control, she looked up, saw the miffed expression on his face and started laughing all over again. Finally after her third bout, she figured she about had it beat.

"You finished?" he asked, and she risked looking at him. He was staring down at her, one eyebrow cocked in that way he had, and though she continued to giggle, she managed to keep it in check.

"I think so," she sighed, wiping her streaming eyes. She held up her hands. "Help me up?" He grasped her fingers and unceremoniously hauled her up. She let out a startled squeak as she flew into the air as easily as if she were made of marshmallow fluff. She landed solidly against him, her feet dangling about a foot in the air as his arms banded around her like steel.

She gulped, the laughter fading. He was holding her high against his chest, her face even with his, and the look in those dark chocolate eyes had her heart skipping a beat then pounding a heavy rhythm in her chest.

"Um, Jack," she began, and that was all she managed to eek out before he swooped in.

His mouth descended on hers lightning fast and she froze, braced for a heavy assault. But he merely rubbed his lips over hers lightly, and the contrast between his hard embrace and the gentleness of the kiss threw her off balance. His tongue flickered out to taste the inside of her lower lip then to the corners then retreating again. His teeth nibbled lightly, tasting but not taking.

He grasped her hair in one hand, used it to tilt her head to one side and she moaned in anticipation. But he didn't deepen the kiss. Instead he continued the tender assault on her mouth, kneading her skull and twining her hair around his big hand. Rowan moaned, lost in the sensations of his mouth nipping at hers, of his hand cradling her head and twisted to get closer. He held her in place easily, his superior strength not even challenged by her struggles, and suddenly the long months of resisting him, of denying herself that which she so desperately wanted, caught up with her in a rush and she'd had enough.

She moved her arms from where they were braced on his shoulders, grasped his head in both hands and bit his lower lip. Hard. He reared back, eyes narrowed so they were slits of inky black. He flicked out his tongue, catching the droplet of blood that seeped from his torn lip. He growled, a low rumble that slithered over her skin like a rough caress, and the desire pooling in her belly turned into something sharp and fierce at the sound.

"If you're going to kiss me," she hissed at him, "then quit fucking around and do it."

She barely had time to catch the flare of triumph in his expression before he slammed his mouth down on hers. She moaned in relief at the contact then stopped thinking period as he devoured her, using lips and teeth and tongue to eat at her mouth until her head spun and her blood boiled.

She felt him shift and move, felt something hard press against her back, and dimly realized he'd backed her up against one of the buildings lining the street. He pulled his hand from her hair, his arm from where it had been wrapped around her hips, and she felt them working at the fastenings on her blouse. He fumbled for a moment with the tiny mother-of-pearl buttons then with a curse, simply hooked his hands in the open neckline and yanked.

Buttons flew, clattering on the cobblestones, and Rowan gasped as he tore his mouth from hers. The narrow street was lit with only a street lamp at both ends and standing as they were in the shadow of the building, she could barely see him. But she could feel the heat of his eyes on her flesh. She didn't have to look down to know her breasts were spilling out of the cups of her bra, the nipples barely concealed by the sheer lace, and she felt rather than heard another growl rumble up in his chest.

She gave a brief thought to the fact they were standing on a public street then his mouth latched on to her flesh and she ceased thinking at all. He dragged his tongue along the upper swell of her breast, first one then the other, then grasped the delicate lace between the cups in his teeth and tugged. It broke clean, the cups falling away to hang by their straps, and his mouth was on her nipple, hot and wet. He wasted no time on preliminaries, simply pushed the aching peak to the roof of his mouth with his tongue and sucked hard, and Rowan felt herself sliding down the slippery slope to orgasm.

She whimpered at the sensation, sparks going off behind her eyes as they drifted shut. They popped wide open again when he gripped her thighs in both big hands and tugged them apart. Reflexively her legs wrapped around his hips for balance and he wedged his hips into the opening, grinding the thick ridge of his erect cock right where she needed it most, and she cried out shrilly as the orgasm slammed into her without warning.

It seemed to go on forever, the shuddering convulsions prolonged by his voracious mouth at her breast and his hips grinding against her pulsing cunt through the layers of cloth still separating them. Gradually the shudders slowed, fading into the occasional tremor, and only then did he lift his mouth from her aching nipple.

Her eyes had adjusted somewhat to the dark and as she watched his head come up, her breath caught at the look of him. His eyes were all but glowing, the pupils a flame inside the black pool of his irises, and the snarling desire reflected there made her womb clench all over again. Then he licked his lips, drawing her eyes to his mouth and she froze.

"Oh my God," she breathed, her horrified gaze locked on his teeth. His very long, very pointy, very sharp-looking teeth. "What the fuck are you?"

Chapter Five

Jack's expression, so open and full of naked desire only moments before was suddenly like stone. "What do you mean?" he asked in an odd, toneless voice.

Rowan pushed at his shoulders, panicking when he resisted. But after a long moment, he stepped back, releasing her just as quickly as he'd grabbed her only moments before. She slumped against the building, feeling the rough brick snag the delicate fabric of her blouse and bite into her skin as she struggled for understanding.

Unable to look him in the face, she looked down and a wave of appalled embarrassment swept over her as she realized her clothes were in tatters. She grasped the edges of her bra and tried to pull them together over her exposed breasts for several minutes before she realized the clasp had been destroyed. Frustrated tears welled in her eyes and she gave up, simply pulling the edges of her blouse over her chest.

"Rowan," he said quietly.

"What?" she asked, keeping her eyes on the ground in front of her.

He cleared his throat, but when he spoke, his voice was still strained and tight. "Are you okay? Did I hurt you?"

"I'm fine," she managed in a voice that only shook a little. A few moments passed in tense silence then, "What are you?"

"Just a man, Rowan."

Her head came up, eyes narrowed as righteous indignation flooded though her. "Bullshit. *Just men* don't have fucking fangs."

He sent her a rueful smile, careful not to show any teeth. "Okay, maybe not just a man. But I am a man, fully human."

Her eyes widened. "Fully human," she managed. "As opposed to what, half human?"

"As opposed to not human."

"What the hell are you talking about, not human?" She held up a hand before he could answer. "You know what, I don't even want to know. I can't handle that right now." She crossed her arms tighter over her chest, acutely aware of her state of undress.

"We should get out of the street," he said, eyes dark and unfathomable as he stared at her in the faint light from the moon. Some of her trepidation must have shown on her face because he shoved his hands into his pockets. "I won't touch you again," he promised quietly. "But I really don't want to give you the explanation you deserve out here in front of God and everyone."

She stared at him for a long moment then slowly nodded. "Okay," she agreed.

They started walking slowly toward the apartment, Rowan being careful to keep a good arm's length between them. She shivered, chilled by the night breeze now that her blood had cooled.

Blood. She shivered at the thought, her mind still struggling to wrap itself around what she'd seen. She knew what fangs looked like—she watched *Buffy* reruns. She'd just never actually seen them on a person before, at least not one who hadn't gone through extensive body modifications to get them. Jack's fangs were not a product of repeated dental visits or fake. Fake fangs didn't just appear and he hadn't had those extended eye teeth when they'd left the restaurant.

She shivered again, this time from more than the cold. She was an intelligent person, she had a fucking master's degree, and she knew what those teeth meant—what they *had* to mean.

Tooth and Nailed

"Stop thinking so hard," Jack said quietly, causing her head to whip around to face him. He was watching her with a quiet intensity. "You're smart, you know what you saw. I'll answer all your questions as soon as we get to the flat."

She turned back to the path in front of her. She must not have as good a poker face as she thought if he could read her that easily, she mused.

"Your poker face is fine."

Rowan stopped dead a few steps from the stairs leading to his apartment. *Oh my God, he's actually reading my mind!*

Jack grimaced. "Sorry," he said, turning to face her, "but you're thinking so loud it's like you're shouting in my head. I can't not hear you."

Rowan felt her temper flare. "Well *try!*" She stomped past him, up the stairs to the apartment door then had to wait impatiently for him to unlock it. She tapped her foot, letting her temper build and getting a good head of steam—it might be easier to get through the coming conversation if she were pissed off.

When he finally got the door unlocked, she swept through the door ahead of him, going straight into the kitchen and getting a beer out of the refrigerator—thank God he didn't do the whole warm beer thing that was so popular here. It might be cowardly and she would probably be better off stone sober, but she'd already had two pints with dinner so what was one more bottle? She popped the top, took a long pull and turned back to the living room with remarkably false bravado.

"So," she said, "you're a vampire."

He laughed, startled. He ran his hand though his hair in a nervous gesture. "Well, that's certainly blunt."

She shrugged. "You said I was right."

He grinned ruefully and some of the tension eased out of his muscles. "So I did. Yes, I'm a vampire."

"Right." Rowan nodded, taking another sip of her beer. "So what the hell does that *mean*?"

He sat down on the couch. "Let's start with something easy. Give me all the myths about vampires you know and I'll tell you if they're true or not."

Rowan frowned a little—he was acting so normal it was getting hard to hang on to her anger. "Fine," she huffed, and crossed the room to sit in a chair opposite him. "Let's see. Vampires drink blood, they need to sleep on their native soil and they burst into flames in sunlight."

"True, false, kind of true."

She frowned. "You kind of burst into flames in sunlight?"

He shrugged. "Let's just say I tan fast."

She blinked at that. "Okay. But you do drink blood."

"Yes."

She grimaced. "Do you have to?"

He chuckled. "Pretty much."

"Why?"

He shrugged again. "I'm not really good at making my own anymore."

Rowan's eyes bugged out as she suddenly remembered one other myth about vampires. "Oh sweet baby Jesus, I made out with a dead guy!"

"Actually, we prefer the term 'undead'," he said, and roared with laughter at the nauseated look on her face.

"Ugh," she managed.

Jack was holding his sides and howling with mirth. "You look like you just swallowed a spider!"

"Are you dead?" she demanded, and he reined in his laughter with effort.

"Technically no," he said, still chuckling quietly. "I was turned before I died."

"Turned," she said. "You mean someone else made you a vampire?"

"That's how it works," he explained, and leaned forward, his elbows on his knees, to explain. "Think of it like a virus — it's transmitted from one person to another in a certain way, under certain circumstances."

"How?" she demanded, her curiosity overcoming her initial squeamishness at the idea.

He grinned at her. "C'mon, you watch *Buffy* reruns."

She narrowed her eyes at him. "You stop reading my mind!"

"I wasn't. Honest," he said when she glared harder. "Everyone — especially women in their thirties — watches that show. It's been off the air for years, but for some reason people love it."

"It's just good television," she agreed.

He rolled his eyes. "Right. Anyway, that's one thing the stories get right. You become a vampire by having one feed from you—"

"Drink your blood," she said, and he nodded.

"Drink your blood. Then you feed off them and the circle is complete. But that's a simplified view. It's actually a little more complicated than that."

She rubbed her fingers over her temples, suddenly confused. "How do you mean?"

"The circumstances have to be right too. Human's have a natural immunity to whatever it is in our blood that makes us what we are — that's why there are so few of us compared to the rest of the population. Best we can figure there has to be some kind of weakness in the body already — an illness or an injury — to make the transformation complete."

She sighed. "I'm getting very tired."

"Like I said, it's complicated. There's a lot we still don't know."

She frowned. "What, is there like a lab full of vampire scientists somewhere trying to figure out the hows and whys of it all?"

"Actually, there are several," he said mildly, and she did a double take.

"Where?"

"Long Beach, actually. Also London, Paris, Prague, Budapest and Vancouver." He chuckled when her jaw dropped.

"Long Beach. That's weird," she decided. "So, what have they figured out?"

He shrugged. "They're still doing basic research into transmission and transformation."

"Transformation?" she asked. "You mean what happens to your body when you become a vampire?" He nodded, and she chewed her lip thoughtfully, mind racing. "So what does happen?"

Jack grinned. "More curious than mad now, are we, darling?"

"Oh I'm sure I'll get back to mad," she assured him. "It's just fascinating is all."

"Indeed," he murmured, a spark of something lighting in his eyes as he watched her.

When he didn't say anything else, she shifted restlessly. "The transformation?" she prompted.

"Right." He cleared his throat. "The details are fuzzy on my own transformation since I was unconscious when it took place, but basically something happens on a molecular level. Bones become more dense, muscles become thicker, stronger. The need for basics like food, water, even air becomes almost miniscule. The aging process is slowed so it's almost infinitesimal."

Rowan struggled to understand. "But you're not dead."

He shook his head. "No, but one of the things they can't figure out is why we don't appear to make our own blood anymore. It's why we have to feed, to replenish the supply."

"Yeah, that is sort of odd—that it would strengthen you and slow down the aging process but not allow you to make your own blood."

"One of the theories being tested is that the process is slowed down just as the aging process but to such a slow rate so as to be impossible to survive without regular infusions."

"Infusions." She raised a sardonic brow. "You make it sound like a medical procedure, like dialysis."

"It's not that different. It's not," he insisted when she continued to look skeptical. "It's necessary for survival and there is a network of blood banks all over the world. I keep a supply in the freezer and thaw a packet each day. Which reminds me, don't eat the blue packets in the freezer."

She made a face as if she'd just tasted something foul. "Don't worry, I won't. What do you do if you don't have a freezer handy?

"We can get it in powder form as well and mix it with water. Think of it as a vampire protein shake."

"Doesn't it skeeve you out?"

"Skeeve?" he asked.

"You know," she said, impatient. "Gross you out."

He shrugged. "It's a little inconvenient, but one does get used to it. The major advantage is it makes surviving without feeding off humans possible."

She started. "You don't feed off humans?"

Jack shook his head. "Not as a rule, not anymore. There was a time when it was the only game in town. But this is the twenty-first century and it's considered bad form to go pillaging. Besides, how long do you think it would be before we were discovered and hunted down, exterminated, if we went around biting people all the time."

"Good point," she conceded. "So the blood banks stock blood. Is it human blood? Where does it come from?" She suddenly had a horrible thought. "That's not where my Red Cross donation goes, is it?"

He chuckled again. "No, darling. I call them blood banks because it's just simpler. What they are actually, are manufacturing sites for synthetic blood. There are at least two in every country, sometimes more. It's not actually synthetic blood either, it's more like a serum that gives our bodies the boost it needs to make more."

Rowan frowned, oddly deflated. "So what, vampires don't drink blood anymore at all?"

"Sure we do. Just not for survival. It's more for…recreation."

She blinked, the rough, intimate sound of his voice gliding over her like a rough caress. "What is that? Are you flirting with me?"

He grinned at her, unfazed by the panicked edge to her voice. "Yes, I think I was."

"Well knock it off!" she shrieked. When he just continued to grin, exuding sexual charisma and charm, she decided to distract him with more questions. "Tell me about the mind-reading thing."

"I can't actually read minds," he explained. "It's more like I can read emotions. Anger, fear." His voice dropped. "Arousal."

She ignored that. "But before, you picked the words—I mean the *exact words*—right out of my head."

"If the emotions are strong enough, the effect is amplified and I get more specific impressions."

"You can do it with everyone?"

"In theory," he said. "I don't notice half the time actually, unless I stumble across someone who's experiencing some extreme emotion."

She frowned. "Why, if you can do it with everyone?"

He shrugged. "I had to learn to block other people's emotions or I'd have gone crazy."

She narrowed her eyes. "Then why aren't you blocking mine?"

"I have to have some leverage with you," he explained, and she felt her temper go nuclear.

"Excuse me?" she said, her voice barely audible, she was so angry.

He must've known she was mad—he was a fucking mind reader after all—but he wasn't fazed. "At first, I didn't know if you knew I was a vampire or not and that's why you didn't want to be with me."

"Wait." She held up a hand. "You thought I might know you were a vampire. Why would you think that?"

"Your father knows."

Rowan's mind boggled at the thought. "My father knows?"

Jack nodded. "We had an...incident...in the first few months I worked for him. The assassination attempt in Sacramento."

She nodded. "I remember."

"The assassin was another vampire. When the police shot him, he played dead until they left then tried for your father again. I had to fight him, hand to hand." He shrugged. "He figured things out for himself after that."

"Ew."

"It wasn't pretty," he said dryly. "Anyway, I thought he might have told you. But he hadn't, and after that I would just kind of check in whenever I saw you, to see if I could get a glimmer of interest from you."

The thought that he'd been fishing around in her mind while she was fantasizing about him was so potentially humiliating that she forgot about her father for a moment. "You were trying to see if I wanted you?"

He nodded.

Her face was starting to feel warm. "I see."

Jack stood up. "Don't you want to know what I found out?"

"No, not really," she said, shaking her head so hard she whipped herself with her own hair.

"Coward," he chided gently.

"Damn skippy," she said. She frowned when he took a step toward her. "What're you doing?"

"Walking," he said, taking another step.

"Smart-ass." Having him loom over her was making her more nervous so she stood to put them on even ground. It didn't help too much. "You're crowding me again."

"Am I?" he said, one tawny brow quirked in question as he stopped in front of her, his toes nudging hers.

"Yes," she said, fighting the urge to turn tail and run into the bedroom. "You're always doing that and it drives me crazy."

"Well then we're even, because the way you keep pulling away from me—when I know bloody well you want me as much as I want you—drives me crazy."

Rowan forced herself not to flinch away when his hand came up to stroke her cheek then had to force herself not to lean into the caress. He leaned down to speak directly into her ear.

"We both know I could have you naked and begging me to fuck you in no time," he whispered, his breath washing over her ear and making her shiver despite herself. "That orgasm on the street wasn't nearly enough to take the edge off. I can smell the desire on you, simmering below the surface. It wouldn't take much—a kiss here—" he brushed his lips over her earlobe " —a lick there." He swiped his tongue up the side of her neck.

"You'd beg me to sink my cock into you and before I was done, you'd be begging me to sink my teeth into you too."

She swallowed hard. "It wouldn't mean anything," she managed.

"I know," he said, and dropped his hand from her face.

"What?" she said, stunned. She'd thought for sure he was going to press his advantage. It wouldn't have taken much to push her over the edge, and even though a part of her would have absolutely regretted it in the morning, she was a little disappointed.

"It doesn't mean anything unless you want it too." He picked up his head and waited for her to meet his eyes. His gaze was serious and direct. "I know you want me, but you don't want to want me. Right?"

"Ah...it's a little more complicated than that."

"Sure it is. You don't like losing control and around me you feel like you don't have any."

Rowan felt her face getting hot. "I'm not wild about this mind-reading thing you do."

He chuckled, the sound full of gentle humor. "I know. But this was a problem even before you knew I was tapping into your head—and remind me to ask you about that plum pudding fantasy sometime." He grinned at her outraged gasp then went on. "You don't like feeling out of control."

Rowan was still struggling with knowing he'd been privy to one of her most unusual and most sensual fantasies. "That's not exactly news," she muttered. "Everyone knows I don't like to be managed. I had enough of it as a child. But I'm an adult now and I don't have to put up with it anymore." She knew she sounded like a petulant child but she couldn't seem to help it.

"I don't want to manage you," he began, but stopped at her scoff of disbelief.

"Oh please, Jack. You're managing my entire life right now! I got put on a plane—against my will—and flown to a foreign country. I assume I can't do much, since I'm supposed to be hiding out from a homicidal maniac who wants to literally crucify me. And none of this is my idea."

He sighed. "You've got a point."

"And frankly," she went on, "the idea that you can just dip into my thoughts any old time you like, well, that freaks me the hell out! It makes me feel vulnerable and off balance, out of control. Having someone being able to read your thoughts and feelings...well... It makes me feel like...like..." she cast around for the right phrase.

"Like your choices are being taken away?" he asked quietly.

"Yes." She slumped in relief that he understood. "Exactly."

"Fuck!"

Rowan started. He'd been so quiet and gentle until now, the violence contained in that one word took her aback. He turned to pace away from her, dragging one hand through his hair in a gesture of frustration. He stopped with his back to her, his body tight with tension.

She shifted awkwardly from foot to foot, not knowing what to do. Her instinct was to go to him, offer comfort, but how could she do that since he was what *she* needed comfort from?

Nevertheless, the long silence was making her very uneasy. "Jack?" she ventured tentatively, and his shoulders tensed even further. Then he seemed to make a conscious effort at relaxing them and turned to face her again.

"Rowan, I'd never hurt you." His voice was low, his tone intent, and she knew he meant it.

"I know that," she said, and she did. No matter what he was, he was an honorable man and she knew he'd rather cut off his own arm than cause her pain.

"But you're still afraid."

"Jack, it's not that I'm afraid you'll hurt me." She looked down at her feet. "I just don't like feeling so out of control. You have all the advantages, all the knowledge. I feel like I'm being carried along by the tide."

She risked a peek at him. He was studying her thoughtfully now, the frustration and anger of a moment ago replaced by speculation. "What?"

"I've been trying to get you into my bed for a year and a half."

She rolled her eyes. "I know."

"I'm not going to try anymore."

"What?" She stared at him, mouth agape, and he grinned.

"Nope." He said, his voice disgustingly cheerful despite the arousal that was evident by the erection straining the fly of his jeans and his fully extended fangs. He grinned at her, those fangs gleaming in the overhead light. "If you want me, you're going to have to seduce me."

Chapter Six

☙

"If you want me, you're going to have to seduce me!" Rowan mimicked, seething. She was in the worn football jersey she used as a nightgown, pacing the floor of the room he'd given her and working herself into a fine temper over the night's events.

He'd dropped his little bombshell then, while she was still stunned speechless, hustled her into the bedroom with a kiss on the forehead and a cheery goodnight. Her lip curled in to a sneer at the memory. He got her all worked up, made her come on a *public street* for God's sake, told her he was a vampire then patted her on the head like a child.

She sat down on the bed with a huff and ran frustrated fingers through her hair. Goddamn him, he'd been right—the panting, clenching climax in the shadows of a deserted street hadn't even taken the edge off. Her pussy still pulsed, aching to be filled, and her nipples were still diamond hard. She'd expected him to bring her back here, spread her out like a Thanksgiving feast and eat her alive. Instead, he'd made it her choice.

The unexpected chivalry of the gesture had her completely off balance, which, come to think of it, was probably part of his plan. "Bastard," she muttered, and got back up to pace.

Jack was an accomplished seducer. She'd seen plenty of it in the time he'd worked for her father. He loved women, and while he was with them, he was completely focused. Attentive, considerate, charming. He took them to dinner, to shows, to the hot spots in L.A. In the work he did for her father, he came into contact with a lot of high-profile names and he wasn't above exploiting those glitzy connections to show a lady a good time. But eventually the novelty wore off, at least for him, and within a few weeks, a month or two at the most, he'd be ready to move on. The woman was always left satisfied, but she was always left.

Rowan paced harder, recalling a particularly ugly scene she'd witnessed during an impromptu visit to her father's house for dinner. Jack was there discussing some bit of company business with her dad and doing his best to drive her crazy when Brooks had come into the dining room and announced Mr. Donnelly had a visitor. Jack hadn't even had time to inquire who when a strung-out, sobbing mess of a woman had stumbled into the room.

She winced as she recalled the pity and sorrow that had welled up in her as she watched. Jack had taken control of the situation immediately, guiding the distraught and weeping woman to the terrace off the dining room, his low voice soothing as he pulled her out of earshot.

Rowan would have liked to believe that she was just a friend in need, come to him for aid, but she knew better. She knew the woman, at least through social circles, and knew Jack had broken off a two-month relationship with her only a few weeks before.

She hadn't stayed to see the outcome but made excuses of a headache and an early teachers' meeting the next morning, leaving as quickly as she could. She knew her father hadn't bought the excuse but he hadn't pressed her. She'd gone home and crawled into bed, ridiculously close to tears, and had determined then and there she wasn't going to be one of Jack Donnelly's casualties.

Which didn't do anything for her current state of arousal. She stopped at the window, looking out on the quiet village, the blanket of stars covering it, crossing her arms over her chest. The scrape of soft cotton over her oversensitive nipples had her swallowing a groan. What was she going to do?

* * * * *

Jack lay naked on the king-sized bed in the master bedroom, covered only by a thin sheet. He stared at the ceiling and wondered for about the hundredth time in the last half hour what the hell he was doing.

It had taken all of his willpower to not grab Rowan, shove her down on the bed or whatever flat surface was available and have at her. Giving her the choice of whether or not to finish what they'd started in the shadows of Ms. McGilley's Millinery Shop had been an impulse, one he was now bitterly regretting.

He stared down at his cock, which showed no sign of subsiding any time soon, and the thought of Rowan only a thin wall away nearly had him rising to his feet to go get her. He knew she'd let him — she was just as frustrated as him, if not more. Hell, he could smell the arousal on her from here and the thin walls of the flat did nothing to hide sound of her pacing in the next room.

No, she wouldn't turn him away tonight, but there was more than just a quick fuck at stake. He made her skittish — not physically. Most people were intimidated by his size — six feet six inches and two hundred and forty pounds tended to get people's attention. But she'd never shown any signs of being afraid of his greater strength and size. She wasn't afraid of him as a man either, although he knew their sexual chemistry made her nervous. Hell, it made him nervous — he'd never been with a woman who'd affected him so quickly.

No, it was the sexual connection they shared and the possibility of a more meaningful emotional connection that had her running scared. And frankly, he couldn't blame her. Were the situations reversed, he imagined he'd feel the same. He had a huge advantage over her that she hadn't even realized until tonight, and he knew the knowledge he could get inside her head was going to be one more obstacle — a big one — in his way.

He shifted, trying to find a more comfortable position on the bed as he thought over their conversation in the street. He couldn't actually read her mind, not in the way that most frightened her, but his senses were particularly sharp when it came to reading emotion. If she lied to him, he'd know it by the telltale quickening of her pulse, as easy for him to read as a neon sign. He knew when she was aroused, when she was angry, when she was happy or sad. She couldn't hide what she was feeling from him, which in some ways was worse than if he were able to read her thoughts. One could control thoughts to a certain degree but emotion was much harder to regulate.

He shifted again, grimacing as comfort eluded him. He was lying on the finest Irish linen but he was so painfully aroused that his skin was ultrasensitive and it scraped at his flesh like burlap. He finally gave up, propped his hands behind his head and decided to count the cracks in the plaster ceiling to pass the time. God knew he wasn't going to get any sleep, not with the woman of his dreams in the next room, fairly marinating in her own juices.

He was going to leave the choice up to her if it killed him. Which felt like a distinct possibility at the moment. He sighed and started counting cracks.

He was doing a fair job of distracting himself and had counted four hundred and sixty-seven cracks when the hairs on the back of his neck suddenly stood on end. He paused in his examination of crack number four hundred and sixty-eight, muscles coiling and waited. Something had alerted him, a slight noise in the hall, and he prepared to leap from the bed. Then the scent caught his nose and he paused in mid spring. Warm and musky with an underlay of spice and the faint floral of lingering perfume. He'd know that scent anywhere.

"Rowan?" he called softly, and again heard the soft shuffling sound that had first alerted him.

There was a long pause and then, "What?"

He frowned. "What are you doing in the hall?"

"Couldn't sleep."

"Are you hungry?"

"No."

"Thirsty?"

She laughed faintly. "No."

"Lonely?"

He watched the doorknob turn slowly, the glow of light from the hall edging into the room as the door opened. "Can you make me a promise, Jack?"

He didn't hesitate. "Anything that's in my power to do."

"Good." The door opened wider and he saw her. She was backlit by the hall light, the generous curves of her body outlined clearly in the soft glow. She was wearing some oversized jersey from an American football team as a night rail. The soft fabric draped her lovingly, hugging every curve and ending at the tops of her thighs, and even from the bed, he could see her trembling faintly. Her face was in shadows though, and he strained to read her expression.

She walked into the room, closed the door at her back and without the competition of artificial light, the moon caught her in its beam and lit her face. He saw the trepidation in the depths of her eyes, in the hard swallow that drew his eyes to the elegant column of her neck. But he also saw the arousal in the frantic pulse beating there, in the quickness of her breathing. And he smelled it on her. The scent of her need, which had been taunting him all night, had been faint and fleeting through the barriers of wood and plaster. But now, in the same room, it nearly made him swallow his tongue.

He struggled to focus on her face. He knew this was an important moment—she'd come to him after all. But he was having a hard time remembering that over the beating of his own blood. He swallowed hard and managed after a couple of attempts to speak.

"What promise is it you need from me, Rowan?"

He watched her draw a deep breath. The large shirt she was wearing rose with the motion, thrusting her breasts forward and raising the hem of the shirt a tantalizing inch higher on her thighs. His eyes nearly crossed trying to keep track of both movements. Still, he managed to keep his ears open for her response.

"I need you to promise me that I can be in charge."

He frowned, disappointed. They'd been over this, security was his area. If there was any danger, he needed to be able to count on her to follow direction.

"Rowan, we've discussed this. I know you're not happy about having to be here, away from your job, your friends. And taking orders from me. But it's necessary for your safety."

She stared at him, and for a moment he was afraid she'd burst into tears. He blinked—startled when she laughed and shook her head. "No, that's not what I mean."

"I don't understand."

She rolled her eyes. "I know you've got to be in charge generally, Jack. I don't really like it but I accept it. That's not what I meant."

He was confused. "You've lost me, love."

She was fiddling with the hem of her shirt, giving him flashes of silken thigh and the shadows between them. He struggled to concentrate when he saw her mouth moving. "I mean, I need for you to promise me I can be in charge in *here*."

It took him a minute to understand what she meant. The realization when it came nearly knocked him sideways with lust. "You mean the bedroom?" She nodded and he swore he actually felt the majority of his blood drain to his lap. "All the time?"

She shrugged, meeting his gaze squarely. "Well, most of the time. Especially the first time."

"Okay." He waited a beat. "Do you mind telling me why?"

"Well, I ought to get to be in charge of something. And it was your idea, anyway."

He shook his head. "I certainly don't remember that."

"Sure you do." She smiled at him then, a faint half smile that only women seem to be capable of. "Remember? You said it was my call. You weren't going to seduce me, I would have to seduce you. I can hardly be the seducer if you're the one calling the shots."

"Wait a minute." Jack could quickly feel the situation spinning out of his control and he wasn't sure he liked it. "I'm not a lie back and take it kind of man, Rowan."

She cocked her head. "I'm not a lie back and take it kind of woman, Jack."

He watched her carefully. Her eyes were bright with mischief and desire, her body language fairly shouting confident sexuality. But there was just a hint of vulnerability to the set of her mouth, a shadow of insecurity in her eyes. For whatever reason, she felt she needed to be in control of the situation, and if that's what she needed to finally give in to the attraction between them, Jack wasn't fool enough to quibble the point.

He reached back for a pillow, folding it and propping it on the headboard then relaxed against it. He linked his fingers behind his head and smiled slowly. "Show me what you've got, sweetheart."

Rowan shivered in anticipation. She knew he wasn't the type of man to give up control easily, especially in the bedroom, and the idea that he was going to let her hold the reins had her nearly giddy with anticipation. Since it wasn't a role she normally held either, it also had nervous butterflies dancing in her stomach. But the anticipation overrode the butterflies and she watched him settle back on the bed, his long body laid out in a symphony of shifting muscle and bone, and licked her lips. This was going to be fun.

Now that she'd given herself permission to give in to the attraction she felt for him, she felt free to enjoy him to the fullest. She was so absorbed in watching him, when he spoke she jumped a little, startled.

"Do you need a hand getting started, darling?"

Her eyes darted to his face to find him watching her with sensual amusement, one corner of that fabulous mouth kicked up in a half smile that turned her knees to jelly.

She gave him an answering smile. "Just taking inventory." She tapped one finger against her lips thoughtfully. "I think for starters, you can keep your hands where they are. No moving them without permission."

He quirked an eyebrow, the amusement still plain on his face. "Yes, ma'am."

She grinned, enjoying the little thrill of power. "Good boy," she purred, and watched his eyes narrow slightly. Ah, he wasn't as comfortable in the subservient role as he pretended. Goodie.

"Now then." She strode forward, putting an extra swivel in her hips as she approached the bed's massive footboard. She barely held back a giggle as his eyes tracked the movement and the sheet draped over his lap tented a bit more. Oh she was going to enjoy this.

She leaned over from the waist and braced her hands on the footboard. Eyes on his, she licked her lips. "Move your feet apart." He complied immediately, sliding them apart so they pointed at the corners of the bed. She watched his chest move as his breathing deepened almost imperceptibly. His face remained the same, still showing that lazy amusement, but his eyes were blazing black fire at her.

She reached forward and grasped the sheet in her fist. "This isn't really necessary, I don't think." She began gathering the fabric in her fingers, inching it lower and lower along his body. She nearly swallowed her tongue when his abdomen was fully exposed. The muscle there was rippling, either a reaction to the tickling sensation of the sheet being dragged across his skin or lust, she didn't know which. But the sight of that skin, smooth but for the slender ribbon of hair narrowing down from his navel, nearly had her abandoning her plans for a torturous seduction and pouncing on him then.

With a hard swallow she knew didn't go unnoticed by her captive, she continued dragging the sheet downward. When the sheet caught on his erection, she gave a slight tug, pulling it loose and allowing his cock, fully erect, to spring free. She continued gathering fabric, but her eyes never left that column of flesh pulsing in time with his heartbeat.

Rowan finally finished gathering the sheet to the bottom of the bed, reaching to both sides to fully uncover his feet then resumed her braced position against the footboard.

"Well," she said softly, not bothering to try to disguise the desire in her voice. "Someone looks ready to play."

There was a hard flush on his cheeks and the muscles in his arms were bunched with tension. Still, his voice when he spoke was smooth, his face still lazily amused. "It's your game, darling."

She tilted her head and smiled, power and lust mixing into a heady cocktail. "Yes, it is, isn't it?" With that, she straightened, reached one hand over her head. She grasped the neck of her jersey and pulled it smoothly over her head, tossing it to the far corner of the room. She shook back her hair, placed her hands on her hips and smirked at the strangled gasp that escaped his lips. "Game on," she said softly.

She stood still, allowing him to explore her body with his eyes as she knew he was aching to do with his hands. She wasn't physically perfect but she worked out regularly and had good muscle tone, and if the blazing heat in his black eyes were any indication, he wasn't noticing any flaws.

Rowan could feel his eyes on her like a physical presence and lifted her hands to trace over her own skin as he watched.

She slid her hands under her breasts, heavy with desire, and lifted them in her palms. She stroked the already hard nipples with her thumbs, shivering as sensation raced over her skin. She watched as he shifted on the bed, his cock lengthening even farther under her gaze and she shivered again.

She let her hands flow down over her belly, his eyes following the movement. She stroked over her hips, down her thighs, using the barest of touches. She was arousing herself unexpectedly with her actions—the act of performing for him while he was helpless to do anything but watch was erotic in a way she hadn't expected. She enjoyed the touch of her own fingers on her skin, the anticipation sweet. She allowed her fingertips to glide down her flanks and then trail back up the tops of her thighs, stopping at their apex.

She paused there for long moments, her fingertips just resting on the top of her bare mound. She smiled as he shifted again, muscles bunching and tightening in a silent display of tension. "Are you uncomfortable?" she inquired politely, biting back a grin as he glared at her.

The lazy, amused look was gone, replaced by fierce eyes and unsmiling lips, and she could see the fangs in his mouth lengthening as his desire grew. "Someday," he growled, his voice deep and harsh, "I'm going to pay you back for this."

She laughed softly. "Oh baby, I haven't even started." With that, she widened her stance, opening herself up to his gaze and dipped one hand between her legs.

"Mmmm," she purred, feeling a surge of female power as he peeled his lips back in a snarl. "My pussy is so wet and hot," she whispered, and shivered as she dragged her hand back, catching her clit and playing with it for a moment. She knew he could see her clearly enough, despite the relative darkness in the room. She was so wet she knew without looking that her juices would be glistening on the bare lips of her cunt. She kept herself waxed smooth and without the impediment of hair, could feel the warm liquid trickling past her pussy lips to anoint her thighs as well.

He was practically vibrating as she played with herself and she drew out the moment, working herself dangerously close to orgasm as she toyed with him. She saw him gather himself as if to move and she stopped. "No moving."

She watched him with trepidation, certain he was going to ignore the directive and lunge at her, but he didn't. He didn't look happy about it but he settled back on the pillows, this time reaching over his head and clamping his hands on the top rail of the headboard. His cock was bobbing in the air now, dark red and pulsing with his heartbeat, and she licked her lips, suddenly nervous. There was only so far she could push this man so perhaps it was time to move this show along.

She pulled her hand from her cunt and raised it to her lips. Eyes on his, she delicately licked the thick cream from her hand. His lips peeled back in a growl, his fangs gleaming in the faint moonlight as he watched her taste herself.

"I'm so sorry." She widened her eyes in mock apology. "I'm being so selfish. Would you like to taste?" She walked around the bed, stopping by his shoulder. The bed was so wide she had to lean over just to get close to him, her breasts swinging forward. She cautiously extended her fingers toward his lips and waited.

For a heartbeat she thought he was simply going to grab her and drag her underneath him and she braced herself to leap away. Instead, he extended his tongue, curling it around her fingers and sucking them into his mouth. She gasped as the sharp edge of his fang caught her skin, scratching it. She pulled her hand free reflexively, noted the scratch along her index finger. It was barely more than a paper cut, tiny beads of blood appearing along the torn flesh. Suddenly his head lifted from the pillow and he sucked her finger back into his mouth. She saw his eyes flare as the combination of her cunt juice and blood hit his tongue and he began sucking hard, cleaning her fingers thoroughly of the juice that coated them and drawing more blood from the cut.

Rowan moaned at the blatant sensuality of the act, felt herself drowning in the sensation his mouth on her fingers evoked. With an effort, she pulled her hand free.

"Ah, ah, ah," she scolded, backing away from the bed. "My game, remember?"

Jack licked his lips. "I remember," he rasped, and once more relaxed against the pillows.

"I must admit, you've been better about this than I expected you to be." She tilted her head in question. "Why'd you agree to this, Jack? Was it because it was the only way to get me into bed?"

He shook his head. "No. Sooner or later I'd have gotten you here on my terms."

She rolled her eyes at the arrogance of the statement but didn't let herself be sidetracked from the question. "Then why?"

"Because you asked me to. Because you needed me to."

Rowan blinked back sudden tears at the tenderness in his voice. "Well then," she managed, her voice choked with unwanted emotion. "I think you deserve a reward."

With that, she crawled up on the bed, slid between his sprawled legs and in one smooth motion, took his cock in her mouth to the root.

He hissed, hips surging up in an instinctive thrust and she hummed around him. He was big, stretching her mouth wide, and with delight she began a slow, heavy up and down suction that had him growling.

She worked him steadily, curling her tongue around the sensitive head of his cock on the upstroke, taking him all the way to the back of her throat on the downstroke. He was flooding her mouth with pre-come, the dark, erotic taste of him making her head spin and her cunt flood with renewed moisture. She felt his hands tangle in her hair, and though she knew she should stop and make him move his hands back, she couldn't make herself do it. His fingers were tugging on the strands reflexively as he guided her movements and the sharp little pains were making her even wetter.

She moaned around him, loving the feel of him, the taste of him against her tongue. She slid one hand to his balls, cupping them gently. They were drawn tight against the base of his cock, heavy and full, and she knew if she didn't stop in the next few moments, she'd be drinking his come.

As darkly appealing as the idea was, she wasn't about to let it happen. Her pussy was drenched, pulsing with the need to have him deep inside her, and she wasn't about to let the opportunity to finally have him pass by. With a final swirling lick of her tongue, she pulled her mouth off him with a soft pop. She gripped him in her fist, lazily stroking his cock as she watched him.

Jack was breathing heavily, his chest heaving with the effort. He was watching her, his hands now clenched in the sheet at his sides. His eyes were burning into hers and she felt as though he could see right past her outer defenses to the vulnerable woman underneath. She dropped her gaze in self-defense, but the sight of her small, pale hand wrapped around his dark cock didn't calm her racing heart.

She forgot her fear, forgot she didn't want to be vulnerable to this man, and concentrated only on the delicious erection that more than filled her hand. He was weeping pre-come steadily now, bubbling at the tip and flowing down the shaft to soak her hand. She slid her hand slowly from root to tip, marveling at the way the flesh seemed to ripple under her touch. He was hot and hard, and suddenly she couldn't wait another minute to have him.

She rose to her knees in a rush and straddled him, lifting herself high as she gripped his cock her in hand, positioning him at her opening. She was fairly dripping with juice, her inner thighs soaked with it, and she couldn't resist sliding the mushroom-shaped head of his cock through the valley of her pussy. Her breath caught as she dragged him across her clit and Jack growled in response. Her eyes flew to his, staggered at the restrained violence in the sound. His face was flushed, his eyes glowing bright red and his entire body was tight and tense. He looked ready to pounce.

She froze, poised over him as a thought suddenly occurred to her. "Jack, condom."

He understood immediately. "I'm clean," he rasped. "My body doesn't tolerate disease and it's doubtful I can get you pregnant."

"Oh good," she said, "and I'm on the Pill anyway." He brought her attention back to the matter at hand when he growled.

"Darling, I know I said this was your show," he said. His lips were peeled back in a snarl and she could see his fangs, fully extended. "But if you don't fuck me in the next ten seconds, I'm taking over."

Somehow the ultimatum, combined with the obvious signs of his arousal brought her back under control. Deliberately, she slid him once again through the syrupy wetness at her cunt, smiling to herself as he arched, instinctively trying to lodge himself inside her.

She silently counted down the seconds, all the while tormenting him by dragging his cock along her dripping cleft until she got to ten. Then she leaned forward slightly, arching her hips so he was right at the perfect angle. She leaned even closer, whispered, "Eleven," and slid down.

Jack shouted hoarsely, his hips arching hard so that her knees came up off the mattress. She cried out, releasing her grip on the base of his shaft to brace her hands on his ribs and gravity forced her fully down on his cock. She keened loudly, bright lights and colors exploding in her head as her cunt clenched down on him hard in sudden, unexpected orgasm.

Jack gritted his teeth, barely managing to hold off his own satisfaction as he watched her face contort in pleasure. Her cunt was gripping him like a slick, hot fist and he wanted to come inside her more than he wanted his next breath. But he resisted, urging her pleasure along with short, sharp thrusts of his hips. His cock barely shifted inside her she was gripping him so tight, but he knew the added friction would prolong the spasms he could feel racking her womb.

He distracted himself from the almost blinding need to come by focusing on her face. He'd never seen anything as lovely as Rowan lost in passion. Her head was thrown back, eyes closed. Her mouth was open, little mewing whimpers escaping her lips with each spasm of her cunt. Her milky white throat was bared to his gaze and he could see the pulse that beat there in rhythm to the contractions milking his cock. He felt his fully extended fangs ache at the sight, his flared nostrils catching the sweet tang of the blood beating beneath her skin. Combined with the scent of her arousal, it was intoxicating and he redoubled his efforts to hold back.

Finally her contractions slowed and she brought her head forward on a sigh. She opened her eyes, licked her lips as she watched him.

"Hmmmm," she murmured. "That was nice, but I'm glad you didn't join me."

Jack arched one tawny brow. "And why is that?" The answer better be damned good, he thought, or she was going to find herself flat on her back in less time than it took her to come the first time.

"Because," she breathed. She rose up on her knees, pulling almost completely off him before sinking back down to engulf him fully. "Now I get to do it again."

Jack growled. He wrestled briefly with the idea of flipping her onto her back and simply having his turn. Then she brought her hands up to her own breasts, pinching the pretty pink nipples and twisting them, making herself moan, and he gave up. He placed his hands on the tops of her thighs for balance, gave one brief prayer of thanksgiving that the shop downstairs was closed and began thrusting up to meet her.

Within moments he could feel his balls tighten even farther, the tight, hot clasp of her pussy pushing him to the brink, and with a shout of completion, he arched hard and began coming. Rowan squealed, lifted off the bed and impaled fully on him once again, feeling her cunt contracting as she came with him. Her head flew back and once again the pulse in her neck drew him like a lodestone. He gritted his teeth hard, knowing she wasn't ready for that, pricking his own lip with the edge of his fangs in an effort to hold back.

When it was over, Jack lay sprawled on the bed, legs still akimbo, arms spread wide. With a throaty moan, Rowan slid down weakly on top of him, her head nestling in the notch of his shoulder. Jack brought his arms up around her, lazily stroking her back.

They lay there for long moments, panting for breath until finally Rowan broke the silence. "You didn't bite me."

Chapter Seven

Rowan could've cheerfully bitten her own tongue off. His hands paused in their lazy stroking of her back and she held herself as still as possible. She hadn't meant to say the words out loud but the haze of great sex was still clouding her brain and she'd spoken without thinking.

After a long pause, his hands resumed their gentle glide up and down her spine and he spoke. "I wasn't aware you wanted me to." His tone was lazy, amused, and for some reason got her hackles up.

She braced her hands on his shoulders and pushed up so she could look him in the face then scowled at the hank of damp, tangled hair obstructing her view. She blew it out of the way and scowled at him. He looked amused and satisfied. "What's that supposed to mean?"

He shrugged, the motion nearly dislodging her hands. "You made it clear you were calling the shots, darling. I figured if you wanted me to take a nibble, you'd have said so."

That gave her pause. She was still astonished he'd let her take command as he did, although she had the sneaking suspicion she wasn't nearly as in charge as she'd seemed to be. She frowned at him. "I thought you would. I thought that's what you meant earlier when you said you only drink from humans for recreation."

He quirked a brow. "I did mean that."

"So why didn't you do it? You know—"she waved her hand vaguely " —the biting thing."

"Because you're afraid of it." He patted her on the ass. "Be a love and get my fags from the table there, would you?"

Rowan huffed out a breath, but shifted over to reach the bedside table for the pack of cigarettes and lighter that rested there. She handed them to him, sliding off his chest to lie at his side while he lit one and took a long, satisfying drag. "I didn't know you smoked."

He blew out a lazy stream of smoke, propped himself higher on the pillows. "Only occasionally. So—" he took another drag, blew it out "—you wanted me to bite you?"

She bit her lip. "No."

He chuckled and flicked ash into the porcelain dish on the bedside table. "You lie so badly, darling. It's charming."

"Stupid mind reader," she muttered.

He chuckled. "Look, Rowan. The 'biting thing', as you so quaintly put it, can be a very sensual experience. That's why some of us still like to do it. It's why I still like to do it. But it's like any other sensual experience—if you aren't in the mood for it, if you're not aroused, then it's just somebody biting you. It won't work."

She rolled her eyes. "In case you didn't notice, I was turned on. So again—why?"

He sighed. "Because you didn't tell me you wanted me to. And I don't think you know if you want me to. And you're deliberately testing me to see if I'm going to do something to go back on my promise."

Rowan grinned at him. "Caught. In any case, I can safely say you've earned your ladies' man reputation."

He grinned back. "Does that mean you're one of my ladies now?"

She stuck her tongue out. "Don't hold your breath, Fangityville Horror."

He winced as he stubbed out his cigarette. "Lovely, now she's got whole new material to come up with nicknames."

She giggled and reaching her hands up to the headboard, indulged in a long, luxurious stretch and a jaw-cracking yawn.

"God, I'm tired. It's almost dawn, I better get back to bed." She started to swing her legs to the floor.

Jack reached out, snagged her arm. He caught her off balance and used her own momentum to swing her back into bed, and in a blink had her pinned underneath him.

"What're you doing?"

"That was my question." He raised an eyebrow. "Is there any reason you can't sleep in this bed?"

"Um. No, I guess not. But I was looking to actually *sleep*."

"Well, contrary to another popular belief, I'm capable of sleeping with a woman without jumping her every second."

Rowan snorted. "That's not what your ladies say."

Jack wrapped his arms around her and rolled so she lay sprawled on top of him. "Good night, darling."

Rowan snuggled in, her cheek against his chest. "G'night, Fangityville."

Jack chuckled. "One day I'm going to get even for that one."

She yawned. "Promises, promises." And with his chuckles ringing in her ears drifted to sleep.

* * * * *

Rowan was jerked out of a dream about a giant wheel of brie several hours later when her tailbone hit the floor and her head hit the leg of the nightstand. She cursed, seeing stars and struggling to wake. She sat up, wincing as she rubbed her head and peered up over the edge of the mattress. Jack was sprawled over the mattress diagonally on his stomach, arms and legs akimbo. His face was buried in her pillow and he was snoring loud enough to wake the dead.

"Well, good morning to you too," she grumbled.

Since he didn't seem to be close to waking, she left him snoring and went back to her room for a hot shower. She took her time, letting the heat and steam wash away the last of the travel fatigue and stress. She noticed that he had her brand of shampoo and conditioner waiting for her, still in their packaging. Her favorite brand of body wash was there, along with a brand-new loofah sponge. He'd obviously gone to a lot of trouble to make sure she'd be comfortable there.

She soaped leisurely, letting her mind drift over the events of the last day. Even though the immediate problem of spending time with Jack in close quarters was resolved—at least for the time being—she now had the whole new issue of him being a vampire. The thought was so daunting she put it in the back of her mind and thought instead of the mess her father was in.

She wasn't sure she believed the Army of God was as big a threat as everyone seemed to think. After all, her father had been known to overreact when it came to her safety. She grimaced at the showerhead, recalling a particularly embarrassing incident in her seventh grade year. The bodyguards her father insisted she keep with her at all times had mistaken a member of the school hockey team for a sniper—apparently a hockey stick looked like a long range rifle to an ex-Marine—and they'd taken him down on the front lawn of the school. They'd fractured two of his ribs, his parents had sued and she'd had to change schools.

Rowan frowned, picked up the bottle of shampoo and poured a generous amount into her palm. She didn't know much about current events, she barely paid attention to the news as a rule, and she'd been so busy lately with one thing or another that she hadn't even bothered to check in with the world at large for longer than usual. As she worked the fragrant suds into her hair, she tried to recall everything she knew about the Army of God and the Reverend Stephen Job.

Unfortunately she tended to tune out the crazies and weirdos so she didn't know much. She knew he was overweight, mostly bald and a pompous jackass, but that described half of the population of L.A. She stuck her head under the spray, closing her eyes as suds sluiced down her face. She picked up the conditioner, working it in as she tried to recall more details. She thought she remembered something about him publishing some manifesto on the web recently, some kind of manual he'd written for the damned masses of humanity to redeem themselves.

She rolled her eyes, cursing when conditioner dripped in them. When they'd stopped stinging, she finished rinsing her hair then shut off the water. She dried herself briskly, wrapped herself in her own robe, which she found hanging on the hook behind the door. Looking around the bathroom, she noticed her own cosmetic bag sitting on the vanity and gratefully made use of the moisturizer.

She emerged from the bathroom feeling refreshed, the hot shower having revived her considerably. She found her clothes unpacked and hanging in the closet, and dressed hurriedly in a clean pair of jeans and a tank top. She combed her hair out to let it dry naturally then left the bedroom. She peeked in on Jack, snorting out a laugh as she saw him still sprawled across the bed.

She was starving so she padded into the kitchen to forage for food. Aside from all the little packets of stored blood in the freezer she wasn't about to touch, there was beer, bottled water and one sorry little apple in his fridge. "Geez, you'd think he'd go shopping for me," she muttered. She took the fruit, wandering around the apartment as she ate. She hadn't had much of a chance to look around the day before and she took her time now.

Situated above a tobacco shop it was small but charming with pine floors and arched doorways and windows. The walls were painted a creamy white throughout. The paint looked textured but it was uneven in spots, and when she ran her hand over the wall she realized it was because the walls were plaster instead of sheetrock. There were bookcases built in, covering an entire wall in the living room, the dark wood a pleasing contrast to the white walls. A closer look at the shelves yielded a surprisingly eclectic taste in reading material.

There was an entire library of Irish history there, along with lots of popular fiction and a smattering of romance novels, which had her brows rising in interest.

The furniture looked new and was modern without being over the top. The sofa was leather, a creamy butterscotch color. She ran her hand over it, noting the supple softness of the leather. The other chairs in the room were upholstered in the same buttery leather with pillows in a soft sage color tucked into the corners.

She realized as she looked around that the entire room was decorated to soothe. Soft textures, neutral colors, it all combined to create a sense of calm she was sure was deliberate. The bedrooms were the same way, she recalled. The same creamy walls with wood furniture and muted tones for the bed linens. This was obviously a haven for Jack, a place for him to be at ease.

Rowan swallowed the last bite of apple and went into the kitchen to throw it away. The room reflected the same quiet tone as the rest of the flat, with pale sand-colored countertops and simple stainless steel fixtures. She felt comfortable here, she realized. Comfortable and at home, and wasn't that a scary thought?

Shaking that thought loose, she found the trash under the sink and threw away the apple core. She turned on the faucet to rinse her hands, thinking again over what Jack had said about Army of God and their plans for her. It was frustrating to not be able to recall much about them or their methods. Her father was always warning her that her penchant for ignoring the world around her would come back on her one day. The irony of that statement wasn't lost on her.

"Well, I need information," she muttered to herself, turning off the faucet with a flick of her wrist. And the best way to get it was the Internet. She headed for her bedroom, curious to see if Marvin had packed her laptop.

She found it on a closet shelf and the apartment was setup with a wireless Internet connection. Within ten minutes Rowan was sprawled on her stomach on the living room floor with a bottle of water, looking at the Army of God website.

Jeez, they were creepy. The website was like an homage to hate and there didn't seem to be anyone immune from their wrath. The homepage had a list of "spiritual enemies"—they stopped short of using the word target—who the righteous followers of the Army were to help "educate" in the name of God. Rowan shook her head. It never ceased to amaze her the lengths some people would go to, to justify their own evil.

She noted several film stars on the site—apparently they cursed and had sex too much in their movies. Several national bookstore chains, along with independent stores in every major city in the country were listed, along with restaurants, dance clubs, bars and sports teams. There was a list of "disapproved" television shows, a section on churches that weren't holy enough and of course, a list of local and national politicians who stood in the way of their vision. And her father's name was at the top of the list.

She read through the dossier they'd composed on him, astonished at the detail. They had her mother's death noted and even had her parent's wedding picture next to the text. She traced a fingertip gently over her mother's smile, a pang in her chest. God, some days she missed her so much. With a sigh of regret, she turned to the text. They listed all of his political campaigns, his voting record in the California house, the various charities he contributed to or raised money for. There was so much information there was a second page. She clicked the link, taking a sip of water, and nearly choked when the page loaded and she saw her own face grinning back at her.

The picture was a recent one, taken at a charity softball tournament a few weeks ago. She'd agreed to play when someone else had backed out at the last minute. She was standing on third base in the shot, grinning like an idiot. She'd hit the ball hard, had barely stretched what should have been a double into a three bagger, and the photographer from the local newspaper had caught the gleaming triumph on her face.

It had been a great moment but looking at it now with the caption reading "Second Generation Evil", she felt slightly ill.

She quickly scrolled through the rest of the page, sickened but not really surprised to find it was mostly about her. They chronicled her childhood in cold, merciless terms, calling the private education she'd received "brainwashing" and every little incident was laid out in stark detail. The time she'd put a frog in Mr. Palmer's meatloaf was noted as the first sign that the devil lurked within her soul.

"They wouldn't say that if they knew Mr. Palmer," she muttered to herself, reading quickly through the rest of the page. Hell, they even had her prom picture, the one of Tommy Mulvany and her standing out by the pool, both of them looking eager and uncomfortable in their formal wear. Rowan giggled at the sight of the corsage on her wrist—Tommy was of the opinion that bigger was better, so she was wearing a huge arrangement of roses and baby's breath on her arm. He'd told her, with not a little pride, that it had had to be special ordered, and like a giddy girl in the throes of puppy love, she'd thought it the most beautiful thing in the world.

She shook her head. The picture was captioned "Getting Set to Dance with Satan". How any person could look at those two clueless young people and see anything nefarious was beyond her comprehension.

Unwilling to read any more, Rowan rose from the floor, carrying the water bottle back toward the kitchen. She was putting it on the counter next to the sink when she heard the noise. Thinking Jack might be waking up, she turned to head down the hallway, determined to give him shit for kicking her out of bed. She froze as she heard the noise again, this time clearly coming from the hallway outside the front door to the apartment.

"Shit," she whispered, frozen in momentary indecision. She could try to wake Jack but the front door was between her and the hall, and someone had just slid a key into the lock and entered the apartment.

Rowan went with instinct, pressing her back against the kitchen wall and sliding as soundlessly as possible along the wall until she reached the doorway. She had a view of the front window and doorway but she couldn't see anyone. Whoever had come in was out of her line of sight. She held her breath and risked a quick glance into the room, taking it in, in a heartbeat and then pulling her head back into the shadows quickly, her blood beginning to boil. The intruder was crouched over her laptop, his back to her, likely reading through the website she hadn't bothered to minimize. Since he faced away from her, she risked another longer look.

He had a cap of fiery red hair and was dressed in jeans and a black sweater, worn sneakers with the laces trailing the floor on his feet. The sweater was bulky, she couldn't tell if he had any kind of weapon tucked into his pants but she could see that he wasn't holding one. His hands were busy on her keyboard, opening the files she kept on her laptop, and she clenched her fists.

She knew she should stay put, see what he did after he finished violating her privacy, but her temper was getting the best of her and rational thought went the way of the dodo. She *hated* it when people snooped into her private property. It was rude and wrong and it just pissed her off.

Riding a wave a self-righteous anger that obliterated her natural caution, she swung into the doorway. "What the *hell* do you think you're doing?"

At her snarl, the man's head snapped up, surprise stamped on his face. He opened his mouth to speak, coming out of his crouch and reaching one hand to his waist. Rowan didn't think, just reacted, spinning and kicking out. The back kick caught him in the chest rather than the jaw as she'd intended—he stood faster than she'd anticipated and he was tall!—but it knocked him back a full two steps and gave her time to reset.

She went into a crouch, balanced on the balls of her feet, anticipating an attack. Instead, he held up both hands. "Easy, lady. I was just taking a peek. No harm done."

She'd straightened slightly at the gesture of surrender but his words had her seeing red again. "No harm? That's my personal property, you pig!"

"Well, if you didn't want anyone taking a look, why'd you leave it lying about for anyone to see?"

"It wasn't lying about for anyone to see," she hissed through clenched teeth. She was going to wipe that quirky little grin right off his face. "I want an apology."

He quirked one fiery brow. "For takin' a peek at your little machine? I don't see where the trespass occurred, love, but if it'll ease your unreasonable female temper, then I apologize most humbly." He swept his arm out, bowing from the waist in mock deference and it snapped the final thread of her temper.

With a shriek, she launched a double front kick, catching him square in the chin and sending him flying back. He crashed into the coffee table, sending it splintering into a dozen pieces. Rowan ducked as a table leg came flying past then whirled at the muffled grunt that sounded behind her.

She winced as she saw Jack standing there naked as the day he was born with a bright red mark on his forehead from where the table leg had caught him.

"What the bloody hell is going on here?" he bellowed. He looked past her to the semi-conscious man lying in the debris of what used to be his coffee table. "Deacon?"

"Aye," the man on the floor groaned and sat up. "Fuck me, it feels like me head flew off and hit the wall."

"Looks like she caught you good, mate." Jack walked past Rowan, paying no heed to his nudity and caught the man by the hands to haul him to his feet. "It's good to see you, lad," he said, and pulled him into a hug.

While Rowan looked on, confused, the man called Deacon hugged him back. "Same goes, Jack, though I could've done without the kamikaze greeting from your woman." He slid a side-glance at Rowan.

Jack grinned. "She's a fierce one, she is," he agreed.

"Hello?" Rowan crossed her arms over her chest and glowered at the pair of them. "Somebody better be giving me an explanation pretty damn quick or I'll start knocking heads again."

"See?" Jack said to Deacon before turning to Rowan. "Don't be getting upset, darling. This is Deacon O'Rourke, a good friend. I asked him to pop by."

She lifted a raven brow. "Well, you might've warned me he'd be 'popping by'. I thought he was one of the good reverend's friends."

Deacon laid a hand across his heart, wincing. "You wound me, love. To think I'd fall in with that lot of lunatics and zealots."

In spite of herself, Rowan softened at the boyish charm dancing in his green eyes. "Well, how was I to know? I come in and find you rifling through my hard drive. Which you still haven't apologized for, by the way."

"I certainly did."

She shook her head. "Sarcasm doesn't count."

"T'wasn't sarcasm, love. Truly, I apologize for the intrusion. I thought Jack had got himself a new toy and wanted to take a peek is all."

"Well, it was rude."

"I know, darling, and you've my solemn pledge I'll not be doing such a thing again." He was openly grinning at her now, fairy lights dancing in his eyes. "Will I be forgiven?"

Rowan rolled her eyes, feeling like an idiot now that her temper had cooled. "Yes, you're forgiven. Just lay off the charm or we'll be swimming in it soon."

Jack threw back his head, laughing at the genuine shock that came over Deacon's face at her words. "She's a feisty one all right," he chortled, and slapped his friend on the back.

Rowan made a face at him. "Shouldn't you—" she waved a hand at his nude form "—put some clothes on or something?"

Jack grinned at her, apparently unconcerned about his state of undress. "Well, I was going to see if I could tempt you into a quick tussle but seeing as we've company, it would probably be in poor taste."

"Would I get to watch?" Deacon asked, face bright with anticipation.

"No," came the joint answer from Rowan and Jack, and Deacon's face fell in exaggerated disappointment.

"Well, if I can't watch, then it would definitely be rude," he declared.

Rowan chuckled, amused. Jack gave her a sour look then turned to his friend. "Help yourself to whatever's in the fridge, mate. Back in a sec." But instead of turning down the hall to the bedroom, he began walking toward her.

He had the strangest look on his face, intent and purposeful. Confused, she opened her mouth to ask him what was wrong. The only thing that emerged from her lips was a muffled squeak as he fisted a hand in her hair and took her mouth.

This was no gentle wooing or even a kiss of hunger or desperation. It was a marauder's kiss, his tongue thrusting past her teeth and sweeping into her mouth with unmistakable dominance. Rowan could feel the edges of his fangs pressing against her lips. She moaned, her hands coming up to grip his bare ribs as her brain went fuzzy and her blood began to heat.

Then, as quickly as it had begun, he was pulling away. He nipped her bottom lip hard enough to sting and she yelped, her eyes flying open to stare at him in shock. He was looking at her with fire blazing out of his black eyes, his mouth grim.

He started to say something then seemed to change his mind. His eyes softened and he leaned forward to press a gentle kiss on her stinging lip. "Back in a moment."

Rowan watched him turn and walk out, one hand pressed to her mouth. When he disappeared around the corner, she looked over at Deacon. He watched her with a speculative gleam in his eye and amusement in his face.

"Well," he said, rocking back on his heels. "I can't wait to hear this story."

* * * * *

Jack dressed quickly in jeans and a pullover sweater, cursing himself all the while. He shouldn't have kissed her that way, not when she was just beginning to feel comfortable with him. It was bound to make her wary. He cursed himself again, jammed his feet into boots then just stood in the mirror, looking at his own reflection.

Of all the vampire myths out there, the stupidest to his mind was the one that said they didn't cast a reflection. Although there were times when it would've come in handy, it simply wasn't true. He mulled that over while he looked at himself. Part of his problem was he wasn't sure how much to tell Rowan about the realities of being a vampire. He'd given her the basics last night and popular culture did get a few facts straight. But the reality was a bit different.

He sighed. He'd known she wasn't trying to flirt with Deacon. The boy was a charmer and she'd simply been responding with genuine enjoyment. But he'd watched her smile at him, laughter in her pretty green eyes, and he'd quite literally seen red. He'd never before done that with a lover. Oh he didn't tolerate cheating and didn't cheat himself, but usually he and his current lady knew they were only together for the enjoyment of each other's company and once their mutual enjoyment wore off, they'd go their separate ways with no hard feelings. But somehow with Rowan, he just couldn't look at the situation casually.

Perhaps it was the inherent danger of the situation. After all, it was his job to protect her. That must be it—he wasn't feeling possessive out of anything other than concern. He scowled at himself in the mirror. "And if you believe that one, I've a bridge in Brooklyn to sell you," he grumbled. He raked an unsteady hand through his already unkempt hair. "Face it mate," he told his reflection, "you're stuck on the girl but good."

His possessiveness didn't have a damn thing to do with protecting her or the danger or the phases of the moon. He was in love with her, he brooded, and damned if he knew what to do about it. He glared darkly at the closed bedroom door as female laughter drifted in from the kitchen. The first thing he was going to do was stake his claim.

Jack walked into the kitchen, his mood immediately brightening as he saw Deacon standing at the sink, arms folded, and Rowan seated at the small dinette. On the opposite side of the room.

"Well, getting acquainted?"

Rowan sent him an arched look he pretended not to notice. "Yes, Deacon was just telling me you've called him in as reinforcement for the duration of our little 'vacation' here in Slane."

Deacon flashed a grin. "Glad to be of service, darling. Jack and I, we go back a ways."

"So I take it you know his little secret?"

"What, that the man's a blood-sucking fiend? Known for years." He grinned, ignoring Jack's warning growl.

"And it doesn't bother you?" she asked.

Deacon shook his head, still grinning. "As long as he doesn't take it in his head to take a nibble of me, it's no matter. In any case," he continued, "I'm happy to be of help while you're here, so anything I can do to lend a hand, you just consider it done."

Rowan propped her chin on her fist. "Can you go grocery shopping? There's nothing to eat here."

Deacon blanched. "Shopping? Can't I do something a bit more manly for me first task?"

Jack chuckled, pleased to see Deacon off balance. "Not to worry, Deac. We'll head out for a bite and get the grocery shopping done on the way back."

Rowan brightened. "Real food? That I don't have to cook? Count me in. But," she cast a dubious glance at the one window in the room. "It's still daylight. I don't think I've ever seen you out in the day. Isn't that a bit dangerous for you?" she asked Jack.

Jack shrugged. "It's fairly overcast and I'll take a melanin tablet. I'll be fine." At her blank look, he shook his head. "Melanin tablets help keep me from burning. They're not a cure all but they help. I didn't explain that?"

"Nope." She shrugged. "Somehow I get the feeling there's a lot you didn't explain. You can catch me up over food—it'll keep my mind off the fact that someone's trying to kill me."

Jack sighed at the grim look that came over her face. He held out a hand. "Come on then, darling. We'll have a spot of breakfast, I'll explain all about melanin tablets and sun exposure. And then we can discuss how to keep you safe for the next fortnight."

* * * * *

It was the local pub again, for in Ireland, she was told with some pride and not a little bit of haughtiness, the pubs never close. This time instead of the bookmaker's sandwich, she had a mountain of fried potatoes and eggs and sausage that the waitress had proclaimed to be fresh off the farm. Rowan decided she didn't really want to know how fresh and concentrated instead on shoveling it in as Jack explained more about the practicalities of being a vampire.

"So you can't produce the melanin yourself, right?"

Jack handed her a napkin. "Right. The pills only replace it on a temporary basis. Makes life just a little less complicated."

Rowan thought that was pretty damn cool and said so once she'd swallowed. "What else?" She waved a hand. "Last night we covered drinking blood, native soil and sunlight. What about crosses, holy water and garlic?"

His dark eyes twinkled with amusement. "Holy water just makes me sneeze. As for the cross," he reached into the neck of his pullover, tugged on the chain to show her the tarnished bit of rough metal that he wore on it. "My mother's. I can wear it without turning to ash so I guess there's one more myth debunked."

"And the garlic?"

"You can never have too much garlic to my way of thinking."

She grinned at him. "Good to know. I'd hate to accidentally kill you by kissing you after eating Italian food. Food!" She pointed at his plate of sausage and eggs. "You can eat regular food too?"

"Sure," he said. "I can still taste it, still digest it. It just isn't enough to keep me alive anymore. For that, I need the blood."

Rowan winced. "Right. The blood. Bet that took some getting used to."

He chuckled at the look of mild distaste on her face. "Well, you could say it's an acquired taste. But it's not so bad. Beats dying and it's a lot better with the synthetics. It's a lot easier for a single guy to get food than it used to be."

"So how does the—" she waved a hand vaguely "—blood versus food thing work?"

Jack shrugged. "It's pretty simple. I can digest food but my body doesn't absorb the nutrients the way yours does. I can't replenish red blood cells on my own so I have to take them in from an outside source. Used to be a vampire had to feed at least once a day and that meant feeding on humans."

Rowan swallowed. "Ick."

He grinned. "That's an understatement."

Deacon cleared his throat. "Not that I'm not charmed by this lovers' banter," he began, "but am I here for decoration or to talk strategy?"

Rowan swallowed a forkful of potato. "Do we even have a strategy?"

Jack shot her a look. "Yes. Our strategy is to keep you out of sight for as long as possible and draw as little attention to ourselves as possible."

She pointed her fork at him. "Sounds to me like you're planning on keeping me cooped up in that box of an apartment for the next two weeks and you can just forget it, Fangy. I may be stuck in Ireland and I may be stuck with a couple of bodyguards but I'm not going to be doing nothing."

Jack crossed his arms over his chest and looked down his nose at her. "Now how did I know you were going to be difficult about this?"

Rowan laid down her fork and mimicked his pose. "Don't get all big on me, Chitty Chitty Fang Fang." She ignored Deacon's choking laughter and narrowed her eyes on Jack. "I'm not afraid of you so don't think you can intimidate me into doing what you want."

Jack's look was sardonic. "Believe me, I don't think that. I'm just not that lucky."

"I'm not trying to be difficult." She ignored his inelegant snort and plowed on. "I'll take reasonable precautions, I'll defer to you in matters of security and all that—" she waved a hand "—nonsense. But I won't be shut up like a bird in a cage. And if you try, I'll make your lives a living hell."

"Why are you including me? I'm just along for the ride, like you."

Rowan ignored Deacon's affronted dismay and concentrated on Jack's face. His expression hadn't changed. "I mean it, Jack. You can't lock me up and just expect docile acceptance." She tried to keep her voice steady and firm but the desperation and fear that he'd do just that leaked through.

"Not to worry, Rowan. I'm not so blind to your nature that I'd assume you'd go along with such a plan. And since neither am I a glutton for punishment, I won't be attempting to make you. But there will be rules and I expect you to follow them."

Rowan sighed quietly in relief. As long as he wasn't planning to force her to stay inside for two weeks she'd be fine. "What're the rules?"

Jack watched her carefully while he ticked them off. "Rule number one—you don't go anywhere without Deacon or me. Which means, if you have to run to the chemist for an aspirin, you do it with one of us in tow.

"Rule number two—if anything happens, if we come under attack or we run into some of the good reverend's henchmen, you do what I say, when I say it. That's very important, Rowan. If I'm to be responsible for your safety as I promised your father I would be, then you need to trust me enough for that."

Rowan nodded. "I already promised and I meant it. If anything happens, you're in charge."

Jack nodded. "Okay. Rule number three—no communication of any kind with anyone. Which means no email, no phone calls, nothing that can be traced back to you. That means your father, Marvin, friends, coworkers—they're all off-limits."

"Oh but—"

"No one, Rowan." His eyes went hard, his face implacable. "I'd rather you didn't have your computer at all, but I'm willing to let you keep it as long as you agree on this point. Push me on this one and you *will* find yourself locked up in the apartment and the laptop gone."

Her hackles automatically rose at the dominant tone and she was about to argue when a thought occurred to her. "I just logged on to their website—could they trace me from that?"

He frowned. "Why did you do that?"

"I wanted to see what they were saying about me, about Dad. Call me crazy, but when someone's trying to kill me, I'd like to know why."

He sighed. "We should be all right. The connection here is secure and scrambled—you wouldn't have been able to connect if I hadn't already coded your laptop for it. But even so," he said as she opened her mouth to argue, "emails are a different issue and not negotiable."

"Then if it's secure, email shouldn't be a problem."

"Don't push it, Rowan."

"Fine. I won't contact anyone."

He didn't trust the mutiny in her expression. "I'm not trying to control you, darling. Just the situation. The fewer people who know where you are, the safer you're going to be."

"I said fine, didn't I?" she grumbled, resentful.

"Yes, but do you mean it?"

She sent him a baleful glare. "You know, you have to trust me a little too. I promise, no contact."

He watched her for a moment then nodded, satisfied. "Okay then, I think that covers the rules. Anything else we'll take as it comes."

"Okay." She picked up her fork again, dug back into the potatoes. "So is the charmer going to bunk in with us at the apartment?"

Deacon grinned. "Hear that, Jack? I'm a charmer."

Jack grinned back and lit a cigarette from the crumpled pack he pulled from his pocket. "That's because she doesn't know you yet, lad. To answer your question," he said to Rowan, "no, he won't. He's got a flat just up the street so he's close if and when we need him."

"Besides," Deacon rolled his eyes, "I think I might very well lose my sanity if I have to listen to the two of you...how do you Americans put it? Ah yes...'knock boots', through those thin walls."

Rowan snorted out a laugh. "Prude."

He glared at her, his handsome face ruddy with annoyance. "Bite me."

Rowan dissolved into giggles, pointed at Jack. "Sorry, that's his department."

Jack sent both of them a look of mild reproach. "Children, please."

"Sorry." Rowan got her giggles under control. "So, what now? Sightseeing, shopping, jazzercise?"

Dark eyes flashing, he chuckled. "Actually, I was thinking we'd go back to the apartment and knock boots again."

Rowan pretended to mull the idea even as she felt her pussy clench and her nipples peak in anticipation. "I dunno. I think jazzercise will burn more calories."

"Yes, but can it give you multiple orgasms?"

"Well, it never has before. But there's always a first time."

"You should always go with a sure thing." Jack quirked an eyebrow, blew smoke in a lazy curl. "Trust me on this."

"Well, you have proven yourself adept in this area previously."

"Okay, I'm officially feeling like a voyeur now." Deacon stood, laying a few bills on the table. "You'll ring if you need me." He clapped Jack on the back, sent Rowan a wink and a flashing grin and slid out the door.

Rowan eyed Jack. Her blood was pumping at the heat flaming in his gaze and she could feel her skin tingle as her arousal grew. He watched her with equal intensity, his cigarette now sitting forgotten in the ashtray at his elbow.

"So." He leaned back in his chair, posture deceptively calm and relaxed. "Jazzercise or boots?"

She pretended to ponder the question for a moment. God, he was sexy. All wild tawny hair and flashing dark eyes. His cheekbones were flushed, the skin pulled tight across his face, and when she glanced at his hands she saw he had the table edge in a death grip, his knuckles white. She felt a surge of feminine power burst through her as old as Eve and gave him a slow smile.

Without speaking she laid her napkin aside then pushed back from the table. She moved slowly, sliding her chair back into place before turning to walk to the door. She laid her hand on the polished brass doorplate, cast a look over her shoulder. He hadn't moved, was still in the same deceptively casual position. She flashed him a grin. "I'll race you." And pushed out the door and bolted into the street.

Chapter Eight

Rowan ran down the road as fast as her legs would carry her. She'd barely cleared the threshold of the pub before she heard the crash of Jack's chair overturning. She hadn't paused to look, just kept running. She knew she was fast—she'd run cross country in college and still held the record for stolen bases on her high school softball team—and if she were racing any human, she'd have a better than fair chance of winning. But this was Jack, who while not strictly an immortal—he'd explained as much to her last night—was about twenty times stronger and faster than the average mortal.

She saw the corner of Jack's street just ahead. Not wanting to slow down more than absolutely necessary, she put a hand on the corner of the building, used it to slingshot herself around the corner and pounded down the street. She could hear Jack behind her, his boot heels ringing on the cobblestones. He was close but she didn't want to risk turning to see how close since it would only slow her down.

She saw the tobacco shop and picked up speed, the blood pounding in her ears as she heard the footsteps behind her speed up as well. She dug into her pocket for the door key he'd given her earlier, flying on adrenaline as she pounded up the stairs to the apartment. Jack was right behind her, she could feel his breath on the back of her neck, and she put on a burst of speed, slapped her hand on the apartment door a split second before Jack's broad palm did the same.

A hard hand on her shoulder spun her around, her back hitting the door. His hand came up on either side of her head, effectively caging her in. She looked up into flashing black eyes, her breath coming hard and fast, adrenaline still singing through her blood. "I win," she panted.

Jack was breathing deep too, but not because the run had tired him out. He could smell the arousal on her—she was so hot he was surprised she hadn't soaked through her slacks. His dick was so hard he could hammer railroad spikes with it and it was all he could do not to pin her against the door and slam into her. "I let you win," he growled.

She grinned, eyes snapping. The thrill of the chase had whetted her appetite and she was seriously considering taking his pants down right there on the landing. "I still won."

"Now what?" he rumbled.

She raised a brow, a little surprised he was still going along with the idea of her being in charge of the sex. She could see how worked up he was, his lips were peeled back over his fangs and his cock looked as though it might burst past his zipper any second. She licked her lips. That bulge was calling her name.

"Now," she breathed, reaching behind her and fitting her key into the lock by feel, "I'm going to have sex. You can join me if you want."

She twisted the knob, the door swinging open under their combined weight and she tumbled backward into the room, stopping when her knees came up against the arm of the couch.

Jack slammed the door behind him and began tearing at his clothes. "I want."

Rowan toed off her sneakers, whipped the jacket off her shoulders and the tank top off her head. Her breasts bounced free, the nipples already pinched tight in excitement. She fought with the waistband of her jeans, her suddenly nerveless fingers fumbling with the buttons.

"I'm ahead of you," he rumbled, and she looked up. Her mouth went dry and her pussy flooded when she saw he was naked, his cock standing out from his body. The tip was already slick and it seemed to throb in time with his heartbeat.

She was so focused on looking at him she forgot about undressing. Until he growled, "Rowan, get out of those jeans."

She fumbled once again at the button fly of her pants. Her fingers felt like they were five times their normal size, she couldn't make them work. She fought the stiff fabric, nearly sobbing in frustration when she heard a muffled, "Fuck this," and her hands were being pushed out of the way.

Jack grasped the waistband of her pants in both hands and yanked hard in opposite directions. Brass buttons went flying, her gasp of surprise nearly drowned out by the sound of rending fabric. In a flash, he had her panties and jeans in a bundle around her knees.

She had a brief flash of his face, hard and intent, eyes glowing red, before she found herself bent backward over the arm of the couch. With her head buried in a cushion and her legs dangling over the edge of the sofa, she gasped, "What're you doing?"

"I'm having sex," he growled. She felt the searing heat of his breath wash over the damp folds of her cunt an instant before he clamped his mouth over her clit.

She screamed, her back arching hard at the sudden lash of sensation. He was ruthless, using teeth and tongue and lips to drive her crazy. Her head was thrashing on the cushion, her hands clinging desperately to the arm of the couch. She was moaning incoherently, unknowingly begging for release, and suddenly the tension burst free and she screamed his name as she came.

The shudders had barely faded when she felt him slide one large hand between her legs. With her panties and jeans still around her knees, she couldn't move them very far apart and he had to wedge his hand in. She felt him slide the tip of one broad finger through the lips of her pussy, opening her slightly, then push deep inside with agonizing slowness.

She was swollen, sensitive from the climax that still shimmered through her and she groaned aloud at the sensation. He felt huge, his one finger rasping over delicate tissue and curving to unerringly finding her G-spot. "Christ, Jack," she gasped. Suddenly her vision was full of him, eyes blazing with lust as he bent over her.

"Feel good, baby?" he rumbled in her ear, and she swallowed another moan at the dark velvet of his voice. Suddenly she couldn't wait to have him and began working her legs, trying to move the bundle of her pants and underwear farther down so she could kick free of them.

He realized what she was trying to do and bent to help, using his free hand to shove and tug at the hopelessly twisted fabric. Finally he just wedged his foot in the crotch of the jeans and shoved them down hard, and once they were around her ankles, she managed to kick free.

Immediately, Rowan lifted her legs, wrapping them around his waist. Grasping his shoulders for leverage, she lifted herself up. He straightened with her, wrapping his arm around her back to support her weight, the motion pushing her farther onto the finger he still had buried deep inside her. They moaned together as her inner muscles clamped down on him, pulling him deeper.

"Jesus, Rowan," he rasped. His eyes were practically black with lust, his breath soughing in and out of his lungs. "I don't think I can wait much longer to fuck you."

She wiggled a little on his finger, clenching and releasing her cunt in rhythmic pulls. His eyes darkened even more, his fangs coming out fully. She felt heady with power, knowing that this strong, powerful man was reduced to raging hormones and baser instincts because of her—her head swam with the knowledge. "What's stopping you?" she breathed, and watching his eyes, flicked her tongue over the tip of one fang.

With a growl that made her ears ring and her pussy clench, he yanked his hand from between her legs, wrapped both arms around her and spun around. When they stopped twirling, she found herself sitting astride him on the couch.

His hands were clenched on her hips, raising her up, and she reached down with one hand to steady his cock and hold it in place. He held her suspended over him for a moment, poised to slide into her. She was so wet she was dripping onto him—she could feel her own moisture coat her hand as she held him there.

She whimpered and wiggled in his grasp, trying to wrest free to impale herself. She slid her hand from his cock to grasp both his forearms for more leverage but he held her firm. "Dammit, Jack! What're you waiting for?"

"Look at me, Rowan," he commanded. Her eyes flew to his and the moment green met black he brought her down hard, sliding deep with one smooth motion, impaling her on his thick cock.

She screamed at the piercing sensation, flinging her head back and gasping for breath as she saw stars in her vision. He was huge, and in this position there was no impediment to him driving all the way to the core of her. With her pussy still swollen and sensitive from her first orgasm he felt even bigger and she struggled to bring her rioting nerve endings under control.

Jack was struggling himself to keep from lying her back on the couch and fucking her brains out. Knowing she was still tender from last night and the promise he made were the only things holding him back. The way the walls of her cunt shivered around him as she fought to adjust to his cock were making him crazy—he wasn't sure how much longer he could hold out. And the way her neck was arched was making his baser instinct surge, pushing him to bite her, mark her, make her his so no one could ever take her away from him.

Finally she brought her head up to look at him, gasping for air, and he clenched his teeth to keep from pounding into her. Her hair was damp with perspiration and clinging to her face and neck. Her face was flushed, her eyes heavy-lidded and slumberous with arousal, and it was all he could do to keep from sinking both cock and fangs so deep into her she'd forget what it was like to not be full of him.

"Jack," she moaned, eyes drifting nearly shut. She peeled her fingers from the death grip they had on his forearms and slid them up her torso to grasp her breasts. She squeezed the tender flesh, pulling and rolling the nipples and feeling the corresponding shivers in her pussy. She saw him throw his head back, felt him clench her hips hard enough so that she knew she'd have bruises in the morning and started to move.

She dragged herself up, up, up his cock until just the head remained buried within her clasping walls then slowly impaled herself again. She was so sensitive she could feel the broad head of him tunneling through her flesh. It felt so good she did it again, as slow as she could manage. She was hovering right on the brink of orgasm, could feel the tension gathering in her belly, but she wanted to prolong it as much as possible so she kept her movements slow and deliberate. She continued to play with her breasts, squeezing them and pulling and tugging and twisting the engorged tips. It wound the tension tighter without pushing her over the edge, and she knew by his moans and groans he was enjoying watching her pleasure herself.

She lost track of time as she fucked him, keeping the pace slow and easy. Her skin was sheened with sweat, her breath coming in panting gasps. She could hear him moaning on every thrust but it was faint and distant, so lost was she in her own pleasure.

She could feel the orgasm begin to bloom inside her and struggled to keep it at bay for just a little longer. She didn't want to stop moving, didn't want to stop the delicious friction that was making her feel so good. She slowed her pace, trying to prolong the pleasure just a little longer and it proved too much for Jack.

"Fuck this!"

Her eyes flew open at his shouted oath. She stuttered in her movements, taken aback at the look of him. His eyes were black, the dark iris almost swallowed by the pupil and glowing with an eerie light. The skin of his face pulled taut over his cheekbones flushed a dark red and his fangs were fully extended. She stared in awe for a split second at the picture of sensual danger he presented and unbelievably felt herself grow even wetter at the sight.

But then he grasped her hips even tighter, taking control of her movements from her and began thrusting heavily, bringing her down hard to meet each wild surge of his hips. She screamed, her hands clenching on her breasts so hard they'd leave marks and she felt all the gathering tension in her body tighten and explode in a burst of color and light.

He continued thrusting, pushing her orgasm higher and harder until she was sobbing with the force of it. The spasms seemed never-ending, rolling through her with the force of a freight train, and she felt the edges of her vision dim as they went on and on.

She heard Jack's muffled shout, felt him tense and hold himself deep within her as he began coming and the feel of him pulsing inside her set off another round of spasms in her cunt. Her muscles were milking him dry, keeping them both in a state of suspended orgasm for what seemed like hours. Finally, the spasms slowed and the tension seemed to leak out of her like air from a balloon and she collapsed, exhausted, against his chest.

"Jesus Christ," she gasped.

"I know," he panted, still struggling with the mad desire to sink his teeth into her.

"If every race had ended like that, I'd never have quit the cross-country team."

Startled into laughter, he wrapped his arms around her and chuckled. "What am I going to do with you?"

She picked up her head and grinned at him. "Gimme a few minutes and we'll race again."

His eyes took on that feral gleam she was coming to recognize and his fangs, which had begun to recede, lengthened again. "Few minutes?" She squealed as he surged to his feet, grasping his shoulders frantically for balance. He bounced her once, driving his still hard cock deep into her and she shuddered from the impact.

He grinned into her startled eyes. "I don't need a few minutes. Do you?"

She fought to keep her eyes from rolling back in her head as he started walking down the hall toward the bathroom. "Apparently not," she managed, and gave up trying to hold off the pleasure.

* * * * *

Four hours later, after having had each other in the shower, the hallway and the kitchen counter, they were both famished. Jack suggested a trip to the local grocer but Rowan had wheedled and cajoled until he finally went down to the pub to pick up dinner. She suspected he only did it to stop her nagging, but she appreciated the gesture anyway.

They sat comfortably hunched over bowls of thick beef stew and hunks of soda bread at his tiny kitchen table. He was wearing jeans but no shirt—she couldn't imagine what the waitress down at the pub had thought when he walked in like that—and she had on his shirt but no pants.

"So." Rowan swallowed a bite of stew and eyed him speculatively. "What're we going to do for the next two weeks?"

He shrugged and took a drink of the dark mix in his glass. She was drinking Harp, he was having his vampire protein shake. It bothered her a lot less than she'd thought it would. After all, the man had to eat, right?

"Besides make love like minks on Viagra, you mean?" He grinned as she stuck out her tongue at him. "Well, I've got a bit of work to do here and there while I'm in town. I need to keep an eye on your father's security team, check in with them from time to time. Make sure the team here in Slane is doing what it should."

"And what will I be doing while you're out handling all your manly business?"

"Well, quite a bit of it can be done from right here." He gestured to his laptop sitting on the counter. "It'll only be necessary to venture out to check on things a few times a week."

She nodded, spooning more stew. "So what will I be doing while you're in here handling all your manly business?"

"Cooking, cleaning, taking care of your man like a good Irish wife?" He arched a brow at her. "No?"

She gave him a fiercely sweet smile. "Only if you like arsenic in your food and nettles in your boxer briefs."

He grimaced. "Well, perhaps we can find something else for you to do."

Rowan pushed back her empty bowl with a satisfied smile. "Good. I can get some work done."

"What kind of work can a kindergarten teacher possibly do outside the classroom?"

"Well, if I still have a job, after disappearing with no notice for several days—"

"Better plan on it being several weeks," he interrupted, and she scowled.

"Fine. If I still have a job after disappearing for several weeks with no notice, I'll need my lesson plans. Which I didn't have time to get from my house, since I was drugged and on a plane."

"You're not going to let me live that down, are you?"

She shook her head. "Not in this lifetime. Anyway, I can try to work on my lesson plan and project list for the year. It'll give me something to do."

"You can't get in touch with anyone from the school."

She shook her head again. "No, I know I can't, I'm not talking about that. I'm just talking about getting online and downloading last year's lesson plans from the school's system. I can log in to the network from any Internet connection."

"You can't do that," he said, and held up a hand when she opened her mouth to protest. "Hear me out. Even though the access is secured, if you log on to the school's network, someone could trace the IP address. Chances are good they wouldn't be able to trace it back here, but given enough time, equipment and expertise they might."

"Oh come on! How far do you think these people are going to go to try and find me?"

"I don't know, but I'm not willing to risk finding out. No email."

She sighed. "Well, I should at least be able to use it to look at sample lesson plans online. Then I can just do my best to recreate my own."

When he frowned, she rolled her eyes in exasperation. "Oh Jack, please. It's not like they're going to be able to monitor every single person online looking at lesson plans. Do you know how many children in the United States are homeschooled? And I'll use your laptop instead of mine. I'm sure you've got some security hoodoo voodoo on it that makes it safer."

His lips twitched before he once again schooled his features into stern lines. "That security 'hoodoo voodoo', as you so quaintly refer to it, is important. If I need the laptop, I don't want you giving me grief about interrupting your search for toilet-training books."

She sniffed. "Shows what you know. Kindergarteners are already potty-trained. Well, most of them. There is this one kid in my class, Clarence Walker? He seems to think it's a grand conspiracy of some kind so he's still in diapers. He's five, can you imagine?" She shook her head. "His poor mother."

Jack winced and cleared his throat. "Back on topic. No bitching or whining if I need the computer when you're using it."

She held up three fingers in the Girl Scout pledge. "Scouts honor. But I reserve the right to bitch if you just want it to download porn."

"Darling, I'd let you watch it with me."

Rowan tore off a hunk of soda bread and pitched it at his head. "Pig."

He snatched the bread out of the air and with lightning speed, pitched it back at her. She opened her mouth and caught it deftly between her teeth, chewing smugly when he blinked in surprise. Then she squealed, almost choking on the bread when he scooped her out of the chair and over his shoulder.

"What're you doing?" she managed to get out around the laughter. Her head was hanging down below his waist, only his arm clamped around her knees keeping her from tumbling headfirst to the floor.

"Just occurred to me—I ought to be putting such a talented mouth to better use."

She muffled a laugh. "Really? Like this you mean?" she purred, and clamped her teeth into the firm muscle of his backside.

Her reward was a string of curses in Gaelic and a sharp swat on the ass. "Watch it, Rowan. I just might take that as an invitation to do some biting of my own."

Rowan opened her mouth to retort then squealed again as she went flying through the air, landing with an "Oomph" on her back in the middle of his wide bed. Panting, she pushed herself up on her elbows. Whatever clever retort she'd been planning died on her tongue as he started shucking his jeans with lightning speed. The feral gleam in his eyes, coupled with the gleaming fangs bared by his grin had her gulping in a devastating combination of fear and arousal.

"No biting," she managed to choke out as he strode naked toward the bed. She thought of how she must look, sprawled on the mattress with her elbows under her, pushing her breasts high. Her legs were sprawled and as she watched, he snagged an ankle in each brawny hand. He yanked, pulling her flat and dragging her forward so that the shirt she wore slid up past her hips.

He licked his lips, his eyes leaving hers to take in the smooth lips of her cunt, still swollen and sticky from their earlier lovemaking. "If I'm not going to bite," he rumbled, "I'll just have to be content with licking."

Rowan's head fell back on a gasp as he snaked his tongue through her sensitive flesh in one long swipe that ended with a quick flick on her clit. She reached down to weave her fingers through his hair, holding him in place. "Maybe this won't be so bad after all," she managed then her eyes rolled back in her head and she gave herself up to the singular pleasure of being devoured by Jack Donnelly.

Chapter Nine

Two weeks later, she was pacing the flat and wondering just how she could ever have thought being with him would be anything but nerve-rackingly, hideously annoying.

The first few days hadn't been too bad, she mused. She'd been worried about her dad, yes. But she knew Jack's team was the very best and she knew he loved her father almost as much as she did. He'd do anything in his power to keep him safe so she'd allowed herself to quit fretting about him. It was hard not being able to contact him in any way but she accepted the necessity of it.

Then there was the sex. The sex, she mused as she paced into the kitchen and back out again, was nothing short of amazing. The man was incredibly inventive in bed. Of course when a guy had been around as long as he had, he picked up a few skills here and there. And while Rowan didn't really care to dwell on just how he'd obtained his panache in the bedroom, she could certainly appreciate the result. She still wasn't quite sure how he'd managed to convince her to let him use a banana as an impromptu sex toy but the results had been worth it. Even washing the sheets after hadn't dampened the glow of the experience.

She'd even managed to get some work done. Working on her lesson plans for the year had been frustrating and depressing at the same time. Even though whoever they'd gotten to substitute teach for her had undoubtedly made up their own, she wanted to be ready when she got back to work. She missed her classroom and the kids in it more than she thought she would, and the very real possibility she wouldn't have a job to go back to was a major downer. But she'd gotten it all done and it had kept her mind occupied for a while.

The problem now was she had nothing to do. Nothing except pace, watch television—if she never saw another football match in her entire life, it would be too soon—and fuck. The fucking was fine, but she couldn't do it twenty-four hours a day. Jack might be able to go all night but being a mere mortal, she needed a little recovery time. And even though she got out occasionally during the day with Deacon, he had his own life to live and couldn't be available all the time. Which left several hours in the day with nothing to fill them except sheer, mind-numbing boredom.

On her third tour through the apartment, Jack looked up from the laptop. "Rowan, you're making me dizzy. Something bothering you?"

When she only hissed at him, he raised an eyebrow and shut down the computer. "I'd say that's a yes."

"There's nothing to do!" She threw her hands up in the air. "I'm bored out of my mind sitting around this apartment."

"I can think of something we could do." He wiggled his eyebrows at her.

"Ugh, I'm so not fucking you right now."

He blinked. "Well, ouch."

"Oh don't give me that wounded look. You know very well you're Senor Studly in the sack—I come screaming every time, you are a god among men." She paced to the window. "But no matter how many orgasms I have, I'm still stuck in this apartment. A prisoner with no one but you and Deacon for company. And it sucks."

He grimaced. "Don't say sucks to a vampire."

"Fine, it blows then."

Jack sighed and set aside the laptop. "Rowan, you knew it would be like this. You knew you wouldn't be able to contact anyone."

"Yeah, well. That doesn't make it blow any less." She turned from the window, pleading in her eyes. "Couldn't we just go out for an afternoon? A few hours? Honestly, Jack, I'm not trying to be difficult. But I've got a major case of cabin fever going on here and I'm afraid I'm going to start throwing things if I don't get out for a while."

"You've been out. We've been to the pub for supper, Deacon took you out for a spot of shopping the other day."

She rolled her eyes. "Grocery shopping isn't shopping. And it's been three days since I've been any farther than the front door."

He rose to join her at the window. He wrapped his arms around her waist from behind and set his chin on her head. They watched each other in the reflection of the window. It was overcast, the sky a dreary gray that only added to her melancholy mood.

"I'm sorry I haven't seen how unhappy you are," he murmured.

She sighed. "I don't mean to be a pain in the ass. Really. I know you're doing your best to keep me safe while the FBI and the team back in L.A. work to find Job and put him away. But I hate this kind of confinement. I hated it when I was a kid, when I had bodyguards following me everywhere. It was horrible, Jack, and I swore I'd never let my life be controlled like that again."

"I know, love. But I'd rather you be safe and unhappy than put yourself at risk."

She spun in his arms, desperate pleading on her face. "I know. But surely there's something we can do, something that won't put me in too much danger. I've got to get out for a while, for an afternoon. A few hours. Please, Jack. I don't know how much more of this I can take."

Jack looked down at Rowan. He hated to see her as unhappy as she was, as unhappy as she'd been these last two weeks. Being cooped up with very limited and supervised outdoor activity didn't suit her, and the strain was beginning to show. He sighed. "Rowan, I promised your father I'd keep you safe."

"I know." She lowered her eyes. "I know you did and I understand. Still sucks though."

"Yes, it does." He frowned when she moved out of his arms, walking across the apartment to the kitchen. "Are you all right?"

"Yeah, I'm fine." She turned and gave him a wan smile. "I'll just fix something for a snack."

"If you're hungry, we can go out and get something to eat. Get out of the apartment for a while."

"Nah, I'm sick of the pub. I'm not hungry for a full meal, anyway." She shrugged and opened the fridge.

Jack sighed, dragging a hand through his hair in agitation. He moved out of earshot from the kitchen and pulled out his cell phone. He punched in a number, watching the slump of Rowan's shoulders as she pulled plates out of the cupboard.

"Deacon, it's Jack. Yeah, I'm going to need your help with something, mate."

* * * * *

Making a snack had taken all of five minutes and she'd excused herself to take a shower as soon as she'd cleaned the kitchen. She worked lather into her hair, feeling sorry for herself. She didn't want to be, but she couldn't seem to shake the melancholy that had settled over her in the last few days. It made her feel like a petulant child to be broody and whiney when all Jack was doing was making sure she was safe.

But she couldn't help it. It was a knee-jerk reaction, one left over from a childhood full of bodyguards, restrictions and "necessary precautions" that made going on a school fieldtrip more complicated than a military operation in the Middle East.

She could resent Jack—in fact, had resented him in the beginning. But it was hard to stay mad at a guy who was just following his loyalties. His devotion to her father was driving him in this and she could only be grateful her father had such a fierce and loyal friend. Also, multiple orgasms tended to mellow a girl. Besides, she was getting to like him. He was funny, entertaining and not as big a hard-ass as she'd always thought him to be. Although he really did hate the nicknames she'd been using ever since she discovered his blood-sucker status. She grinned as shampoo dripped into her eyes. That was really fun.

But all that aside, she was going stir-crazy. Maybe she'd get Deacon to find a bookstore for her today. There was bound to be something available to read that would hold her interest for more than a few minutes. Maybe she could find the latest JD Robb.

She was deep in thought, making a mental list of thing to have Deacon look for at the bookstore, when the shower curtain was suddenly wrenched aside. She spun, choking back the scream on her lips when she saw it was Jack.

"Christ on a crutch, Jack!" She shoved soapy hair out of her eyes. "You scared the shit out of me. What's the matter with you?"

"You want to get out of the apartment?"

Rowan blinked. "Huh?"

Jack grinned at her. "I said, do you want to get out of the apartment?"

"Yes!" She frantically wiped more soap out of her eyes. "Are you kidding? We're going out? And not to the pub?"

Jack pulled a towel off the warming rack. "Here. Dry off and get dressed. Deacon and I will be in the living room."

She stood there, water streaming over her face, the towel in her hand getting soaked, for a full thirty seconds after the bathroom door closed behind him. Then she scrambled, rinsing the remaining shampoo out of her hair as fast as the water pressure would allow. She ditched the towel he'd handed her for one that was still dry and was in her clothes and headed for the living room in record time.

She skidded to a stop in the doorway, panting for breath. Deacon and Jack turned to look at her, both men fighting back grins at her wet hair and hastily put together appearance.

She looked expectantly from one to the other. "Well? Where're we going? What're we going to do? When do we leave?"

Deacon chuckled. "In a rush, love?"

Rowan grinned. "Damn right. So what's the deal?"

Jack extended a hand to her and she automatically crossed the room to take it. "First of all," he said as he began redoing the buttons on her shirt she'd missed in her haste, "we need to go over the rules."

She rolled her eyes, impatient. "I know the rules, Jack. Stick with you and or Deacon, scream like hell if anyone tries to snatch me and try to blend in."

He finished fixing her blouse. "Good. Now, we're going to be in a large crowd so it's extra important you stick with me. Deacon will be there as backup but I don't plan on letting you out of my sight the entire time we're there. But just in case we do get separated, we'll have a fixed meeting point. If anything happens, you'll go there, call me on the cell and wait." He tugged her chin up to look into her eyes. "You'll wait for me, Rowan."

"Yes, Jack. I'll wait for you. Cross my heart, hope to never have another multiple orgasm again. Just tell me where we're going!"

He fought back a grin at her enthusiasm. "We're going to a concert."

Rowan clasped her hands together. "Great. Let's go."

"Whoa, wait a minute!" Jack managed to get a hand on her elbow before she swung out the door. "Don't you want to know who, where?"

"As long as it's not the two of you, in this apartment, I don't care." She grabbed his restraining hand and tugged. "Let's go."

Jack rolled his eyes at Deacon. "Should be an interesting afternoon."

The younger man grinned. "This was your idea, mate."

"Less talking, more walking." To ensure they both complied, she reached out and snagged Deacon's belt in her other hand and yanked them both out the door.

Chapter Ten

"Slane Castle?" Rowan turned to gape at Jack. "We're going to a concert at Slane Castle?"

He frowned at her. "You don't like Slane Castle?"

"Don't be a jackass," she murmured absently, completely absorbed in the massive structure in front of them. "This is so cool." She turned in a slow circle. "You know, a friend of mine who works in advertising got to do a shoot once when the Red Hot Chili Peppers did a concert here. Well, she didn't get to do the shoot," she amended. "It was the art department. I guess their tour manager liked one of their photographers, had him take some still shots of the concert and she showed them to me. It looked amazing. But it sure as hell didn't do it justice."

Jack looked around, taking in the castle with her. "I guess it is pretty striking." He turned to find her staring at him. "What?"

"You have no idea how cool this is, do you?" She held up a hand when he started to speak. "No, how could you? You grew up with this stuff. It's old hat to you."

Jack shifted, vaguely uncomfortable with the idea he'd become jaded. "I grew up with rioting in the streets and an unstable government."

She sighed, eyeing him sadly. "That's my point, Jack. Even with all the trouble, you had this—" she spread her arms to encompass the enormity of the castle courtyard "—around you."

"Yeah, well." He shrugged. "It's all a matter of perspective, I guess. I think L.A. is pretty neat with its museums and entertainment and all the different people who live there."

"Right. Perspective." She looked around. "When did we lose Deacon?"

"When you were gawking at the portcullis. He's taking up post on the other side of the stage." He held up a two-way radio. "We'll stay in touch with this."

Rowan rolled her eyes. "Take the poker out of your ass, Jack, and try to have a little fun."

He rolled his eyes at her and shoved her forward with a hand on her back. "Shut up, Rowan, and hand the nice man your ticket."

She grinned at the fresh-faced freckled youth taking tickets at the turnstile. "Thanks."

Jack shook his head in sympathy when the boy, red to the roots of his hair, had to be nudged twice to take the tickets from the couple behind them. "Do you have to do that?" he demanded, guiding her into the crowd.

"Do what?" Her head was whipping around, trying to take in everything at once.

"Smile at impressionable young men. It gives them ideas." He watched her whirl around for another minute then clamped his hand on her head to hold it still. "Calm down, will you? You'll break your neck and save Job the trouble."

"Sorry." She beamed up at him. "It's just so cool. I'm *outside*. Around people other than you and Deacon."

"That sound you hear is my ego deflating."

She laughed. "You'll get over it."

He opened his mouth to respond but the crowd suddenly erupted in a roar, cutting him off. He turned, keeping Rowan tucked firmly to his side. The stage, which had gone dark after the last warm-up act had finished, was suddenly lit up again and the emcee was striding toward the center mic.

"Are they starting?" She practically shouted to be heard over the screaming throng.

He nodded, pulling her close to talk directly into her ear. "Stick with me."

Rowan rolled her eyes. "I will, I will." She bounced on her toes, trying to get a better view of the stage. She craned her neck then dropped back to her heels in frustration. She was just too short and the crowd was too thick.

She turned to look at Jack. "Kneel."

If she hadn't been so focused, she'd probably have enjoyed his look of pure astonishment more. "Excuse me?"

She poked him in the ribs. "Kneel down, I want to get on your shoulders." When he continued to gape at her, she flung a hand toward the stage. "I can't see! I want to sit on your shoulders."

He finally gathered his wits enough to shake his head at her. "No, too dangerous. If anyone here is on Job's payroll, it'll make you too easy a target."

She put on her most pitiful, pleading face. "Please? Nobody knows we're here and I can't see!"

Jack shook his head at his own weakness as he keyed his radio. "Deacon, how's it look?"

Deacon's voice came back clear as a bell through the handset. "All clear. Security sweep didn't pick up anyone or anything unusual."

"Keep your eyes peeled." He pocketed the radio, eyeing Rowan sternly. "One song only."

"Seven."

"Two."

"Six."

"Two."

"Jeez, fine. Two." She grinned at him as he knelt down. "This is so cool. I always wanted to do this at a concert but all my boyfriends were wimps and wouldn't let me."

She hoisted herself onto his shoulders, gripping his hair for balance as he stood again. "Man, you're tall—I can see for *miles*. Oooh look, they're starting!" She let go of his hair, hooking her feet under his arms and around his back for balance instead as the band took the stage. She flung her arms in the air, drew breath into her lungs and screamed her head off with the rest of the crowd as the music started with a roll of drums and the scream of a guitar.

He tried to make her get down after only one song, claiming rib dents from her feet pounding on him and spine distortion from her dancing on top of his shoulders but she wouldn't budge. She took pity on him halfway through the second song even though she didn't buy he was developing a hunch.

"Isn't this FUN?" She had to shout to be heard above the steady roar of the crowd and she couldn't see anymore — jeez, who'd have thought he'd be such a wuss about a little bruising, he'd heal in no time anyway — but she was so glad to be out of that dim little apartment she just didn't care.

"Yes. Fun." He had to admit he was enjoying himself immensely. The music was good — much better than he'd anticipated — and Rowan was positively glowing with happiness. Her eyes were shining, there was a flush in her cheeks and she was dancing her little heart out.

She wasn't a good dancer, he realized with mild astonishment. That lean, muscled, athlete's body so suited to running, and she danced like a giraffe on speed. Oh she had rhythm and enthusiasm to spare but not a heck of a lot of style and no moves at all. She was just all out there, rocking as hard as anyone, looking like a fool. And judging by the grin and the glow, not giving a shit.

He leaned down to speak directly into her ear, putting one hand on her bobbing head after he had to dodge once to avoid a broken nose. "You know you can't dance, right?"

She grinned at him. "Who cares?" she shouted back, and gave a quick little hip shimmy.

He looked down into her laughing face, the driving pulse of the music filling the air, and was suddenly so absurdly turned on he couldn't wait. He grabbed her hand and began dragging her though the crowd toward the castle.

"What are we doing?" she shouted, hurrying to keep up with his longer strides. "Did you see someone, is something wrong?"

He stopped so suddenly she slammed into his back and she had to grab his waistband with her free hand in order to stay on her feet. He turned to face her and she forgot to breathe at the look in his eyes. As she watched, he took a steadying breath, tried to battle back the tide of lust swamping him.

His voice when he spoke was a low, rumbling growl she had to strain to hear over the crowd. "If I don't get you someplace private, I'm going to end up fucking you right in the middle of this concert."

Rowan fought to steady herself. Not an easy task with visions of him throwing her down on the crushed grass and fucking her to unconsciousness, regardless of the several thousand people who would be bearing witness. The idea that he wanted her that much, that he simply couldn't wait to have her—it went to her head like one-hundred-proof vodka and suddenly she needed him just as badly, just as quickly.

"We'll never make it back to the apartment," she managed, and saw the flare of heat in his eyes as he realized she wasn't going to argue.

Jack gave her a feral grin that had shivers skittering up her spine and her pussy flooding with wet heat. "Don't have to. C'mon."

She clung to his hand like a lifeline as he barreled through the throng of gyrating bodies. Breathing shallowly, her own pulse pounding in her ears so loudly she barely heard the music anymore, she concentrated on putting one foot in front of the other and keeping up with him. He dragged her though the gates and back into the castle itself. This time she didn't even notice the ceilings or wall hangings or rugs, she was concentrating too hard on not fainting from lust.

He tugged her down a side hall, away from the main tourist areas of the castle and began turning knobs, looking for an unlocked door. She thought briefly that maybe she ought to be offended he was about to bang her in a utility room or broom closet, but the truth was, as long as there was room enough to spread her legs wide enough, she didn't care.

He found an unlocked door and hustled her in ahead of him with a firm hand on her back, shutting the door behind him. She waited in the pitch black for a moment, felt him fumbling around behind her for a light switch then the single bare bulb hanging from the ceiling clicked on and she looked around.

It was a utility closet, all right, the dim yellow light illuminating metal shelves holding cans of old paint and various cleaning supplies. There was a mop bucket tucked in the corner next to a "wet floor" sign, a stack of dustrags and a single low-backed chair whose upholstery had seen better days.

She was still processing the room when hard hands suddenly grasped her shoulders and spun her so her back hit the door. She barely had time to open her mouth to gasp—she sure as heck wasn't going to try and talk him out of it—when his mouth swooped down on hers to devour.

She moaned into the kiss, frantically sucking at his tongue as he thrust it deep into her mouth. Her cunt grew instantly wetter as she imagined his cock thrusting into her with the same feral hunger. He brought his knee up, wedging her thighs apart and forcing her feet up off the floor.

She began tearing at his belt buckle with trembling fingers, eager to fill her hands with the flesh straining behind his zipper.

Rowan nearly howled in disappointment when he snatched her hands and pressed them to the door on either side of her head. She wrenched her mouth from his. "Jack," she moaned, her voice almost soundless as she fought to drag in enough air to speak. "Let me touch."

"No." He growled it and gave her lip a sharp bite. "You don't get to touch until I say so."

"But I'm supposed to be in charge," she gasped, mildly panicked at the look in his eyes.

"Not this time, Rowan. I'm sorry, but I need you too much. Please, just let me have you."

She hung there, straddling his leg in the dim little room as he waited for her answer. She could see the hunger in his eyes, the barely restrained violence of his lust, and was oddly unafraid. She swallowed hard, knowing her answer would change the tone of their relationship, would somehow shift the subtle balance of power they'd shared these last two weeks. He was pleading with her for permission, holding himself back until he got it, and she couldn't not give it to him.

"Okay." She forced the word out, her throat suddenly tight with nerves. "But no biting."

His breath escaped in a rush and he crushed his mouth to hers. "Thank you," he said against her lips, the words so full of gratitude that she smiled. He kissed her again, his tongue thrusting deep as he wedged his knee firmly between her legs. She ground herself on it, struggling to find some relief from the pulsing ache between her legs. His hands released their grip on her wrists to grasp her hips and suddenly she found herself lifted up. Reflexively she reached up and grasped the bare pipes over her head. She felt her pants loosen, slide down her legs, taking her thong with them as she hung about a foot off the floor with only his hands on her hips helping to support her weight.

"Don't let go until I tell you," he growled, and she nodded frantically. *Once he gets permission to take over*, she thought, *he doesn't waste any time*. The wash of cool air over her wet, hot pussy made her shiver again and the ravenous look in his eyes as he ran his hands over her bare flesh was making her head swim. She was so close to coming already she wasn't sure if she could take whatever he had in mind.

She looked down. With his eyes holding hers, he reached up, pushing her shirt and bra over her breasts. He palmed them hard, squeezing, and she moaned as her cunt flooded with moisture. Her nipples were diamond hard, the skin puckered by excitement as well as the faint chill in the room. His face was level with her chest, so he simply leaned forward and started sucking. She gasped and bucked at the sensation, and he wrapped his arms around her back to hold her steady.

He sucked first one nipple then the other, nipping and biting and tugging on the tender flesh until she was whimpering. "Shhhh" he whispered. "Be careful or everyone walking down the hallway will know exactly what we're doing in here." She started, incredulous she'd forgotten they were in a public building and she froze as the voices in the hallway reached her ears.

He didn't give her time to think about it too much. He ran his fingers over the bare, damp flesh of her cunt, smiling when he felt how wet she was for him. He put her legs on his shoulders, forcing her to pull herself up higher and she felt him pull the lips of her pussy gently apart, exposing her hard clit. He blew on it gently and she nearly went flying over the edge but it wasn't quite enough. As she watched, fascinated, he bent his head and swiped his tongue from the bottom of her weeping cunt to the top, where her clit pulsed and throbbed, begging for release. She shivered convulsively, hips arching hard in his hands as she strained toward the orgasm hovering barely out of reach.

"Tell me what you want," he whispered, his breath teasing her overheated flesh and she answered mindlessly, heedless now of the voices in the hall.

"I want to come."

Immediately, he clamped his mouth over her clit and sucked hard. At the same time he pushed two fingers into her pussy, thrusting them deep and she exploded, crying and whimpering as the spasms went on and on, racking her body for long moments until she finally went limp in exhaustion.

Her body still shuddering from her orgasm, her mind still a fog of lust, and all she could think was that she wanted to return the favor. "Please," she gasped, panting for air.

"Please what?" he said softly, his breath on her still quivering flesh making her shiver.

"Please, I want your cock in my mouth," she moaned, and he chuckled.

"Whatever the lady wishes," he said, and helped her unwrap her legs from around his head. She clung to the pipes, mindful of him telling her to hold tight until he told her to let go. He smiled, apparently pleased she remembered. "Let go, baby," he said, and she uncurled cramped fingers.

He pushed her legs off his shoulders and helped her down, steadying her as she wobbled a little. As soon as her face was level with his, she grabbed his head, tangled her fingers in his hair and slid her tongue across his mouth. She could taste herself on him and it made her pussy shiver and clench again in renewed lust. But now she wanted to taste *him*, so with one last lick, she slid to her knees.

She unfastened his pants quickly, shoving them and his boxers to his knees. His cock was already hard, bobbing gently as she stroked it lovingly from the tip down. She loved his cock—thick and hard and oh-so pretty, she could look at it for hours. But right now she wanted to suck so she leaned forward and gently swiped her tongue across the tip. She tasted the pre-come gathered there and heard him groan her name. She shivered as she felt him slide his hands in her hair, gently tugging her forward to take more of him. With a grateful moan, she slid her mouth over the head and down the pulsing shaft, taking as much as she could before pulling back, using her tongue and cheeks to suck hard. She tasted more pre-come and set a lazy pace, sucking slowly up and down, up and down, feeling him nudge the back of her throat with every downward stroke.

He let her set the pace for a few minutes but soon he started thrusting back, holding her head steady, and she tried to relax her throat as he begin fucking her mouth in earnest. She could hear him talking, muttered words, telling her how good it felt, how he'd like to keep her and fuck her like this every day, punctuating his words with hard, heavy thrusts that almost made her gag as she struggled to take it all. It was making her cunt wetter, having him hold her head and force her to take his cock while she knelt on the floor, naked except for the shirt and bra still shoved up under her arms.

He started thrusting faster, harder, and she began gagging on every push as she struggled to take him into her throat. Sensing he was close, she reached around and grabbed his ass, sinking her nails into the resilient flesh, silently begging for his come, and with one final shove he gave it to her. She swallowed as fast as she could, his come pumping into her mouth so fast and hard she could barely keep up. He kept thrusting as he came and she kept sucking, not wanting to miss a drop.

He pulled out of her mouth and she sat back on her haunches, breathless and still unbearably aroused. Amazingly he was still hard and with his hands still on her head, he pushed her down until she was on her hands and knees. He knelt behind her, his clever hands stroking over her heated flesh until they found her swollen and sensitive clit. She moaned, feeling herself racing toward another orgasm when he stopped suddenly. She stifled her instinctive protest and stayed still, even when she felt him stand and move away from her. She concentrated on catching her breathing, knowing that whatever he was planning was going to cause her to lose it again. She was brought out of her thoughts by the feel of his hands on her head once again. Her view of the cement floor was suddenly blocked and she realized he must have slipped something over her eyes so she couldn't see.

Without her sight, her other senses begin to sharpen. She could smell the scent of paint and damp and she felt the rough floor under her palms and knees. She was shivering with anticipation now—his mood seemed to have turned playful now that he'd taken the edge off the hunger for both of them and she wondered what else he had up his sleeve.

She felt a light stroke across her shoulders from something other than his hand. The caress came again and she realized he must have found a feather duster amid the cleaning supplies on the shelf. She felt its softness brush her skin, made hypersensitive by her arousal, and she shivered.

"You like that," he murmured, and did it again. He spent long moments just brushing the duster back and forth across her back, raising goose bumps and bringing little moans of desire from her throat.

He brushed it down so the feathers tickled across her hips and ass, drifting low enough to barely tickle the upturned flesh of her pussy, and she couldn't control the backward surge of her hips. SMACK! His palm landed with a crack on her ass. "Keep still," he growl, "or we're done." She stifled a giggle and braced herself firmly on the floor, unwilling to do anything to make him stop.

The steady back and forth motion of the feather duster continued, gliding down across her ass and thighs, over her calves and to her feet. She was vibrating like a plucked guitar string, struggling not to move as he teased and tormented her with the feathers.

She felt a hand at the base of her neck, stroking down the length of her spine to rest on the upturned curve of her ass. Her position thrust her buttocks out and up, her cheeks spread, leaving her feeling open and vulnerable. She felt him glide his thumb into the crevice of her ass and she jerked, startled.

"Easy," he murmured, and she heard the feather duster clatter to the floor as his other hand settled on her hip, holding her in place. His thumb brushed back and forth over her anus, the pressure gentle but insistent. For long moments that was all he did, and despite her trepidation, she found herself pushing back into his hand, liking the darkly erotic sensation.

He increased the pressure, murmuring reassurances, and with a gentle push, slid his thumb into her sensitive opening. She whimpered, hips thrusting back convulsively, the sensation of being stretched and filled fogging her brain and making it nearly impossible to keep still. He toyed with her for a moment, pulling it almost all the way out before sliding it back in slowly, and she found herself unexpectedly on the very edge of a screaming orgasm.

She was whimpering and moaning, hips thrusting back into his invading hand. She began begging mindlessly, the words jumbled and barely intelligible for him to end the torture and he finally took pity on her. With his thumb still firmly embedded in her rear, she felt his cock probing the entrance to her pussy, and with a heavy thrust, it was buried in her to the balls. He didn't give her time to adjust but began a hard, driving pace that she met with fierce thrusts of her hips, wanting all of him inside her. The hand that wasn't busy at her ass stroked down her stomach to stroke her throbbing clit and she could feel her eyes crossing, the orgasm bearing down on her, and her knees gave way.

With a growl, he wrenched his thumb from the depths of her anus and the orgasm plowed into her, the explosion intensifying as he came down on top of her, pinning her with his weight. He continued thrusting heavily and she came again hard before the first orgasm had a chance to fade. He clamped a hand over her mouth to muffle her screams as her cunt clenched rhythmically around his cock and with a groan, he thrust once more and came with her.

She lay there, panting for breath and shuddering through the aftershocks, her mind spinning in circles. She was lying naked, except for a blindfold and the shirt and bra that was still caught under her arms, on the cold, hard floor of a utility closet in Slane Castle with two hundred and forty pounds of vampire on her back. The thought made her giggle, and once she got started, she couldn't stop.

"Excuse me," he said, lifting himself off her and turning her over onto her back. He peeled the blindfold from her eyes and she blinked into the light. When she could focus, she found him staring down at her with a bemused expression on his face as she continued to giggle.

"I don't think that's a very appropriate response to a very forceful and manly display of sexual prowess," he admonished, affecting a wounded expression that kicked her laughter into high gear.

"I'm sorry," she gasped, holding her stomach as the laughter rolled through her. "If you could see the look on your face!"

"Christ, keep it down, will you?" He rolled his eyes, covering her mouth with his hand. "We're not exactly supposed to be in here, you know."

Her eyes twinkled at him from above his hand. "Mff mmf ffflt!"

"What?"

She peeled his fingers from her mouth. "I said," she whispered in between giggles, "it's not my fault. I'm not the one who dragged us in here in the middle of a freaking concert with the whole world outside!"

He grinned at her. "Sorry," he whispered back. "I got a bit carried away."

She giggled again. "No apology necessary. The multiple orgasms more than made up for any inconvenience."

"I'm glad to hear it." He dropped a quick kiss on her lips. "Do you want to go back outside and watch the rest of the show?"

She nodded eagerly. "But later let's fuck like monkeys again. Deal?"

"Deal."

They put their clothes on as quietly as they could, Rowan grimacing as she brushed the grit and dirt from her knees. "The next time you get the urge to do me doggy style," she whispered, "please bring a pillow." She winced. "My knees are bruised."

"Hey, now you know how men feel," he whispered back. "We're always on our knees doing all the work and nothing but bitch, bitch, bitch."

She rolled here eyes. "Fine. Next time I'll be on top, and you can just lie there like third base."

"Excellent." He looked her over. "You ready?" he asked, one hand on the doorknob.

She nodded. "Oh but wait," she said, putting her hand on his elbow. When he turned back, she pointed to the light overhead. "Turn the light out first," she whispered, "so it doesn't spill out into the hall." When he looked at her oddly, she said, "What? I don't want everyone knowing what we were doing in here!"

"And you think turning out the light is going to make a difference? At least if the light was on, we could pretend we were looking for something. If the light's off, it's going to be pretty obvious we were in here fucking our brains out."

"You think?"

"I don't really care!" He threw up his hands, exasperated. "But the longer we wait, the greater the chance of someone in the hall hearing us and finding us out."

"Okay, okay, let's just go." She swiped her hands through her hair. "How do I look?"

He looked her up and down. "Like you've been rolling around on the floor, fucking my brains out."

She threw him a look. "Just open the door."

He grinned and did, reaching up to turn the light out as the door swung open. He glanced up and down the hall quickly. "All clear," he said, and grasping her hand, pulled her out of the closet with him.

They walked down the hall, turned the corner and nearly bumped into the couple coming the other way.

"Oh! Excuse me!" A rather matronly looking woman adjusted her hat. "I'm afraid I didn't quite see where I was going."

Jack smiled his most charming smile and bowed slightly. "Not at all, madam. The fault was completely mine."

"Well." The woman tittered, patting her breastbone and fluttering her lashes. "Do you work here, young man? We're trying to find the main hall. Our wedding planner is meeting us there."

"The main hall is just round the way," Jack said, gesturing back the way they'd come. He looked from the woman to the very bored-looking man with her. "Are you getting married then? Congratulations."

The woman laughed again and Rowan rolled her eyes at Jack's back. "Oh heavens no, young man. Edgar and I will have been married for thirty-seven years this December." She waved a hand at Edgar, who forced a sickly smile and looked as though he could use a stiff drink. "No," the woman continued, "it's our daughter who's getting married. To an earl, you know." She leaned in conspiratorially. "We didn't think she'd make such a good match—she had acne as teenager, you know—it only fully cleared up just this year."

"Is that right?" Jack asked, poking Rowan hard in the ribs when she choked on a laugh.

The woman frowned. "Are you all right, child?"

"I'm fine." Rowan cleared her throat. "Just have a little tickle in my throat."

"Well, these castles can be so drafty," the woman said. She frowned as she got a good look at Rowan's disheveled appearance. "You may be getting a cold, dear."

Edgar sighed and looked at his watch. "Eloise, we're going to be late. I want to get this over with—England's playing Spain this afternoon on the telly."

"Hush, Edgar. Can't you see this poor darling isn't well?" She turned back to Rowan. "You're awfully flushed, dear." She looked at the top of Rowan's head. "And whatever has happened to your hair?"

Rowan put up a hand to smooth it down. "Ah..." she looked to Jack for help and he winked. *Traitorous son of a bitch*, she thought, and worked up a smile for Eloise. "I lost an earring," she improvised. "In the main hall. I crawled under a settee to look for it, and well..." she gestured to her hair.

"Oh dear." Eloise frowned, staring at Rowan's ear lobes, bare of jewelry. "Did you lose them both?"

"Yes! Yes I did." Rowan sighed. "It's awful, they were my favorite pair."

"Yes dear, that's horrible," Eloise murmured her sympathy. "But your hair is so dusty...is that a cobweb?"

Edgar, who was losing patience fast and obviously didn't want to miss the football match on the telly later, grabbed his wife by the elbow and began towing her away. "Eloise, we're going to be late."

"But Edgar, her hair!" Eloise protested, looking back over her shoulder as she found herself dragged down the hall. "All that dust, just from looking for a pair of lost earrings! If that's the way they clean house around here, I don't know if I want to have Portia's wedding here..."

Her voice faded away as they turned the corner. Jack and Rowan looked at each other and grinned.

"Lost an earring?" he asked.

"Well, you were no help!" She punched him lightly on the arm. "What was I supposed to say, 'Oh tell your daughter if she wants to consummate her marriage on the premises, there's a really lovely utility closet just down the hall'?"

Jack laughed and took her by the hand. "Come on, we're missing the concert," he said, and towed her out the door.

* * * * *

Several hours later, Rowan sighed and wriggled deeper into the softest bed in the world. "I can't believe you did this," she said, turning her head to watch Jack emerge from the connecting bath.

"Well now, I couldn't very well bring you to Slane Castle and not treat you to a night in the King's Suite," he said, striding naked and damp from his bath to the giant four-poster canopy bed that dominated the room. He leaned over and kissed her, his lips clinging to hers in a sweet caress.

"Mmm." She licked her lips. "You taste salty."

"Salt water bath," he said, climbing into bed with her. He sat up against the headboard and she turned to her side to see him better.

"Why salt water?" she asked, idly reaching up to wipe a droplet of water from his chest.

"For some reason it helps me heal faster," he said.

"Heal?" She frowned then sat up and looked at him. "Your sunburn! It's completely gone," she marveled, stroking her hands over his skin. Even though it'd been overcast and he'd taken a melanin tablet, he'd still burned. But where before there'd been red, angry skin, there was now only smooth, supple flesh. "That's amazing."

"Just one of the benefits," he said, propping his hands behind his head.

Rowan propped her chin on his abdomen. "Do you like being a vampire?" she asked, looking up at him.

He grinned down at her. "Beats being dead."

She smacked his belly lightly. "Smart-ass. C'mon, I'm serious. Tell me what it's like for you."

"Okay." He slid down farther in the bed so they were face to face. "What do you want to know?"

She shrugged. "I don't know. Tell me how it feels to be immortal."

"I'm not actually immortal, you know. It's more like I age very, very slowly."

"Practically immortal then. Tell me what it's like."

"It's lonely," he said.

"Lonely?"

"Yeah." He gave her a rueful smile. "Think about it. You outlive all your family, all your friends. Don't get me wrong, it's nice to not have to worry about disease or doctor bills. But it can be tough watching the people you love disappear."

"Oh." Rowan chewed her lip thoughtfully. "I guess I've never thought about it before," she said. "How do you get through it?"

He shrugged. "I do what everyone does when facing mortality, I guess. I try to make the most of every day, appreciate my friends for the treasures they are. What makes it different is instead of facing my own mortality, I'm facing theirs."

Rowan nodded then frowned. "How old are you, anyway?"

He grinned. "You probably don't want me to tell you that, darling."

"Ew. You're really old, aren't you?"

"I was born in 1891."

She grimaced. "You know what—I really don't want to know."

He chuckled. "You look like you just tasted something particularly foul."

"Well yeah!" She made a vague gesture with her hands. "You're over a hundred years old."

"Just think of me as antique," he chuckled.

She just shot him a look. "Bureaus are antiques. Not people."

He grinned. "Is this really bothering you?"

"It's icky!" she protested, smacking him in the chest when he laughed. "It doesn't bother you that I'm young enough to be your granddaughter?"

"Darling, everyone I fuck is young enough to be my granddaughter." He laughed when she smacked him again.

Rowan felt a reluctant smile curve her lips. "Okay, change of subject. Tell me how you got to be a vampire."

He shrugged. "I was ill, was likely going to die and someone saved me."

Rowan waited a beat. "That's it? That's how you tell a story?"

He spread his hands. "It's the truth."

She sighed. "No, no, no," she said, sitting up in bed. She folded her legs under her and tugged the comforter up around her breasts. "You told me the facts but not the story. Tell me the story."

He quirked a brow. "You really want to hear this?"

"Yes."

He shrugged. "Okay. Well, it was nineteen eighteen."

"Which would make you, what—twenty-seven, right?"

"Actually, it was the spring, so I was only twenty-six. My birthday's the first of November."

She rolled her eyes. "Scorpio. It figures."

He grinned. "Anyway, I'd joined the army to fight in the Great War—"

"World War I, right?"

He shot her a look. "At the time there wasn't a World War II so we just called it the Great War."

"Right, that is what the old timers call it." She ducked the flying pillow, giggling. "Sorry, sorry."

"Anyway," he went on, "I was part of the Thirty-Sixth Ulster division, fighting in Germany."

"Oh my gosh," she breathed, putting her hand on her chest. "Did you get shot?"

"No, I got the flu."

Rowan blinked. "I'm sorry, what? You got the flu?"

He grinned at her. "Not very dramatic, is it? But yes, the flu. The American soldiers were kind enough to bring it 'cross the pond with them."

"Oh that's right, it was a whole epidemic." She grimaced. "Must've been awful."

"It wasn't pleasant," he allowed. "I was lying on the ground in a ditch, still trying to fight alongside my friends, delirious with fever. I couldn't stand, I couldn't even crawl. The infection had turned to pneumonia so breathing was horribly difficult."

"Jeez," Rowan muttered. "What happened?"

"I passed out," he said. "The last thing I remember is lying in a muddy trench, wishing I was back in my mother's kitchen."

He was silent for a moment, eyes clouded with memories. "Three days later I woke up in a warm bed, feeling ridiculously strong for what I'd been through and I had fangs." He chuckled. "It was unsettling to say the least and I'm afraid I wasn't very gracious to my hosts."

Rowan slid down to lie next to him, chin in her hands. "Who were they?"

"A man named Cedric Peabody. And his bride Penelope, who I'm very chagrined to say was the first person I saw when I awoke." He shook his head, still feeling the sting of shame nearly ninety years later. "Let's just say I was horribly ungrateful for her hospitality, a fact which Cedric lost no time in pointing out when he came in the room."

Rowan stared at him, fascinated. "What'd he do?"

Jack smiled at the memory. "Gave me what my Gran used to call a thorough tongue-lashing while sitting on my chest to hold me down. I was strong but Cedric was much stronger and he wasn't newly changed." At her blank look, he said, "Newly changed vampires are strong but they're fairly erratic. I wasn't used to the strength I had, hadn't had time to grow used to it or learn how to channel it. Cedric was much more controlled, ruthlessly so, and he had no trouble besting me physically."

"So once you calmed down, then what?"

"Then he explained to me what had happened. What I was." He shook his head. "At first I didn't believe him. After all, I was a good Irish Catholic boy. Vampires didn't exist in my world."

"Bram Stoker wrote *Dracula* in 1897. You hadn't heard of it?"

He smiled at her. "Not until Cedric gave me a copy. Good Irish Catholic boys didn't read about vampires either, at least not in my house." He chuckled. "My mother would've boxed my ears if she'd found it."

Rowan smiled at the obvious affection in his voice as he mentioned his mother. "So what happened after that?"

"Well, I wasn't very happy with my new lot in life and I gave Cedric and Penelope no small amount of grief over it. Never mind they'd saved my life. I didn't care. I was angry and confused and not inclined to be gracious."

"After a few weeks of my skulking around their home, Cedric had had enough. He told me I should use the brain God gave me, accept the truth staring me in the face and be grateful for my second chance at life. Or I could squander the gift and slice my own head off. Then he handed me a sword."

"Wow." Rowan's eyes were big, riveted on his face. "Well, you didn't slice your own head off, that much is obvious. What did you do?"

"I screamed at him for about five minutes. How it was so unfair, why me, blah, blah, blah. Then," he shrugged, "I ran out of words, and out of anger I burst into tears."

Jack settled farther into the pillows, stacking his hands behind his head as he stared at the ceiling. "He sat there with me, on the floor of his elegant home, and held me while I cried. I don't know how long it took but when I was done, I just sat there feeling drained and exhausted. And he started to talk to me."

He shifted, rolling to his side and propping his head on one hand to look down at her. "He told me about his pre blood-sucking days. He used to be a duke, second cousin to the Prince of Wales. Life was all parties and weekends in the country and nights at White's gaming table. It was a good life, except one day a viscount took exception to Cedric's interest in his youngest daughter." He raised an eyebrow. "Apparently they were caught in a torrid embrace in the gazebo of the viscount's country house during a summer ball."

Rowan grinned. "I take it papa wasn't happy about it."

"To say the least. Tempers flared, and despite Cedric's declaration of intent to marry the girl, he ended up facing the business end of a rapier. Sliced him open and left him for dead."

"Ouch." She winced. "If you're worried at all, I don't think my father owns any rapiers."

Jack grinned at her. "I know he doesn't—I'm in charge of security, remember? I know all of his weapons. And no, I'm not worried."

She frowned briefly at that but she wanted to hear the rest of the story too much. "So they left him for dead…"

"Right. So he's lying there on the back lawn of the estate and bleeding out from a dozen different wounds. He can hear the daughter screaming from inside the house and all he wants to do is get to her. But he's bleeding to death and passes out trying to crawl to the house. When he awoke, he was in a loft in the stable already transformed."

"By who?"

Jack winced. "And you call yourself a teacher. It's whom, darling. By *whom*."

She rolled her eyes. "They're kindergarteners. I teach them how to tie their shoelaces and not to eat crayons. Grammar comes later."

"Still, it couldn't hurt to start them early. America's youth has fallen behind the rest of the world, you know."

She waved that away. "Whatever. Just tell me who transformed him."

"Well the 'who' was one of the household servants. Apparently he'd worked for the viscount's family for years. In any case, he found Cedric bleeding to death on the lawn. So while the rest of the staff and guests at the house for the weekend were preoccupied with the distraught daughter and the rest of the family, he took Cedric out to the barn."

Jack paused, reaching across Rowan to snag the bottle of water resting on the nightstand. He took a long drink while she practically vibrated with impatience.

"Jack, I'm going to stab you with the very nice letter opener on the writing desk over there if you don't spit it out."

He licked his lips. "Well, the servant had to exchange blood with Cedric in order for the change to take place. Normally the easiest way is with a bite—"

Rowan interrupted. "Okay, why is that easiest?"

He tapped a finger on his teeth. "It's what they're designed for. Razor-sharp points, perfect for slicing into flesh."

She gulped, eyes wide. "Right."

"Vampire's have traditionally been predators, you know. All predators evolve to survive."

"Uh-huh. Can we not talk about the teeth anymore?"

He rolled his eyes. "Coward."

"Bet your ass," she said.

He grinned. "That's what I like about you, darling. You never pretend something you don't feel."

"I'm a teacher, not an actress," she said, and shrugged. "I can't pull it off anyway, so why try?"

"Well, it's one of your most charming qualities."

"Thank you." She waved a hand impatiently. "Can we get back to Cedric's story, please? You said a bite is normally the easiest way."

"Right. But Cedric was already bleeding so badly, there wasn't any need for the bite. The servant simply drank from one of his wounds then sliced open his own wrist and fed Cedric from the wound."

"Ick."

He grinned at the face she made. "It's not as bad as you'd think, actually. It doesn't taste to me like it does to you. When you cut your finger and you bring it to your lips to ease the hurt, the blood tastes sharp. Coppery and tangy. But to me," he drew her hand to his mouth and grazed the soft pads of her fingertips with his lips. "To me it's heavy and sweet, like the finest cognac and goes to the head twice as fast."

Rowan shuddered with desire despite the instinctive fear she felt and struggled to keep the conversation on track. "So then what happened?"

Jack retained his gentle grip on her fingers, keeping them close to his lips as he spoke. "Cedric was unconscious, so he didn't feel the change happen. I was delirious when it happened to me so the details are fuzzy. But your senses become heightened so you can feel your bones shift, your cells change and reform from the inside out. It's not a painful sensation, but if you don't know it's coming, it can be fairly frightening."

"No kidding."

"Anyway," Jack continued. "Cedric woke fully the next night and immediately went looking for the viscount's daughter. He found her in her bedroom, just as she was slitting her wrists."

"Oh my God!" Rowan's eyes went round with shock. "What the hell?"

"Well, she loved him. Since she thought he was dead, the only thing she wanted to do was follow him to the afterlife."

Rowan rolled her eyes. "Jesus, these people are so dramatic."

"Hey, most women would find this story very romantic," he protested.

"Most women a hundred years ago maybe," she muttered. "But anytime after nineteen fifty-four it's just stupid." She yelped, yanking her hand out of his grip. "Hey, you bit me!"

He sent her an innocent look. "What?"

She scowled at him and examined her fingertips. The skin was tingling where his teeth had nipped but the skin was intact.

"As I was saying," he continued. "Cedric found his lady love bleeding out from her wounds and tried to save her the only way he could think of."

"He tried to turn her into a vampire too?"

"Exactly. But he didn't quite know what he was doing being a novice and nearly botched the whole thing by giving her so much of his own blood that he nearly died himself. Thankfully his new mentor was close by and was able to set things to right with an impromptu transfusion.

"When his lady love awoke, they set off for London where Cedric collected what money he could. Then they essentially disappeared. Cedric's family believed him killed by the viscount's hand and all they ever found of the girl was a blood-soaked nightgown."

He stacked his hands behind his head, watching her face. "They traveled the world together, eventually settling back in London. After sufficient time had passed of course and anyone who might've recognized them was long gone. And that's where he took me when he found me on the battlefield."

"They're still together, after all this time? Penelope was the viscount's daughter?" Rowan sighed when he nodded. "Now that is romantic."

"Told you," he said smugly.

She swatted him lightly on the chest. "So after Cedric told you this story, you felt better?"

"Hell no," he scoffed. "I was still alone, with no family and no friends. Everyone thought I'd died, you see, so I couldn't go home. And no idea what the hell I was going to do with the rest of my existence. But he got my attention and made it pretty clear he wasn't going to put up with any bullshit."

"I'll say."

"So I pulled it together and started to figure it out." He reclaimed her hand, idly toying with her fingers as he talked. "Cedric kept me busy, teaching me how to survive in my new world. And Penelope, who'd never been able to bear a child because she was…you know…"

"Technically dead?" Rowan supplied.

"Right. Anyway, she treated me like the son she'd never had. Which was disconcerting, considering she was only sixteen when she'd been changed. Being scolded by someone who looked as though she should still be in the school room was odd, to say the least."

"It's sweet though," she said.

"It was great," he admitted. "I loved being with them, but after a time I grew restless. I needed to be out in the world. It's not in my nature to be idle. So I said my goodbyes and headed out."

He shrugged broad shoulders. "And that's how it happened."

Rowan slid down in the bed to snuggle against his side, tilting her head up to look at his face. "You miss them, don't you?"

He frowned at her. "What makes you say that?"

"They're your family," she said, as if it made all the sense in the world. "They are still alive, aren't they?"

"Alive's relative," he said, "but yes, they're still around. They're living in Budapest now."

"When's the last time you saw them?" she asked around a yawn.

"It's been about five years, I guess."

"You should plan a trip when all this is over," she suggested, settling her head in the curve of his arm and closing her eyes. "Go to Budapest and see them. You shouldn't neglect family."

She felt him brush a kiss over her forehead. "You're right."

She yawned again. "Of course I am," she said, and drifted off to sleep with his chuckles ringing in her ears.

* * * * *

"Hmmm," Rowan sighed. Her eyes fluttered open to find Jack watching her. Unsurprised, she smiled. "Hello."

"Hi," he said, smiling back. "What were you dreaming about?"

"Oh just a dream," she said, reaching her arms over her head to stretch. "One of those lovely, hazy dreams you don't really remember the details of, just the feeling."

He trailed a finger down the soft underside of her outstretched arm. "And what were you feeling?"

"Happy." She smiled.

He raised one eyebrow and she stifled a giggle. "Just happy?"

She sighed in mock exasperation. "Jeez, it wasn't that kind of dream. Get your mind out of the gutter."

His eyes went wide. "Out of the gutter? *Out* of the gutter? Whatever for when it's so happy there? In fact—" he reached up and locked his hands over hers, grinning wickedly when her eyes went wide and shocked "—why don't you join me there?"

He set his mouth to hers, nudging her lips apart and sliding his tongue past her teeth. His tongue tangled with hers in a playful tango, the thrust and parry delighting them both. She nipped at his lip, eliciting a muffled yelp. He pulled his head up and grinned wickedly at her. "None of that now, unless you're willing to invite the same."

She licked her lips, tasting his musky flavor with the lingering tang of salt, and sent him a sultry smile. "Sorry."

He lowered his head, once again taking her mouth and she bit his lip again. This time his head reared back and he pinned her with the intensity of his stare.

"Rowan, be sure," he said, his voice quiet and firm. "If you keep that up, I'm not going to be able to keep from biting you."

"I'm counting on it," she said, and smiled into his shocked eyes.

"You're sure?" he rasped, and Rowan felt her heart clutch at the cautious excitement in his voice. "I don't want to scare you, baby."

She shook her head. "I'm not scared. I'm not," she insisted when he looked skeptical. "I mean, I was at first. But I know you now. I know you won't hurt me." She licked her lips. "Besides, the idea of you biting me…it's kind of hot."

His eyes smoldered down at her. "It's not kind of hot, it's very hot."

Rowan felt her pulse quicken at the predatory gleam in his eye and let out a slow breath. "Yeah," she whispered. "Very hot."

"As long as you're sure," he rumbled.

She flexed her hands in his grip, smiling when he immediately turned her loose. She slid her arms up around his neck, twining her fingers in his hair. She tugged his mouth down until it was a breath away from hers. "I'm very sure," she whispered, flicking her tongue out to tease his bottom lip. "Now, are you going to talk all night or fuck me?"

She got a brief view of gleaming white teeth as his grin flashed then suddenly the room was spinning and she found herself flipped over onto her stomach with two hundred plus pounds of horny vampire on top of her.

"I'm confused," she managed, barely swallowing a moan as his hands came up to once more trap hers above her head. "Does that mean 'talk' or 'fuck'?"

His chuckle rumbled in her ear, sending shivers racing down her spine. "Oh I think if you pay close enough attention, the answer to that will come to you." He pressed her hands briefly into the mattress. "Keep your hands up there, love. Can you do that for me?"

Rowan's throat had closed off, making speech an impossibility, but she nodded her head in agreement and apparently that was good enough. He slid his hands from hers, dragging his rough palms along the smooth skin of her arms, up over her shoulders and down her back. She felt him move hair to the side, stiffening slightly despite her excitement when he nuzzled into her neck.

"Mmmm," he growled. "I can smell the blood flowing under your skin." His tongue flicked out, teasing the delicate skin under her ear and drawing a whimper from her lips. "It smells so sweet, so rich." He lowered his voice to a rough whisper. "I can't wait to taste it. But first," she felt him slide away from her neck and down her body, "I need to taste this."

She nearly screamed into the pillow when he delved his tongue into the soaked folds between her legs. For the next ten minutes she panted and whimpered and bit holes into the thousand thread count Irish linen pillowcase as he drove her crazy. He licked and sucked and nibbled every square inch of her pussy, taking his sweet time doing it and she thought she'd go insane if he didn't do it faster, harder, deeper. Nothing made him go faster — not threats or pleas for mercy or outright begging. He just kept on, savoring her at his own leisurely pace, a pace that conveniently seemed to slow considerably whenever she felt herself approaching orgasm.

After what seemed like hours of hovering on the ragged edge of release with her vision dimming at the edges and her pulse drumming a beat in her ears, she licked dry lips and rasped, "Are you tying to kill me?"

He chuckled against her damp flesh, the vibration bringing her agonizingly close to climax once again. He had her clit clamped between his teeth and he gave it a flick and a tug before letting go. "I don't want you dead, darling. But I need you turned on, as hot for me as I am for you. I want this to be so good for you."

She twisted her head on the pillow, restless energy building to a fever pitch in her body so that she thought she'd burst with it. "Trust me, if I get any hotter, I'll burst into flames!" She moaned and picked up her head, turning to look where he was crouched between her spread thighs. She could barely see him through the haze of lust and the tangle of hair in her way. "If you don't fuck me in the next thirty seconds, I'm going to go insane."

"I don't know, are you ready?" He slid one finger deep into her pussy, hissing in approval when her desperate muscles clamped down on him. "You are so wet, darling. And hot and tight. Maybe you are ready for me."

Rowan squealed when he added a second finger to her cunt, tossing her head back and staring with blind eyes at the bed canopy overhead. "Oh God, I'm so ready I'm about to get there without you. Please oh please hurry up and fuck me. I want you deep inside me when I come."

She felt the bed shift as he moved then he was looming over her, his elbows braced next to her shoulders. He slid one hand into her hair, turning her face to the side. He pressed his cheek to hers as he spoke. "I'll be so deep inside you, you won't be able to tell where you end and I begin."

He shifted his weight, sliding his free hand down her spine. She couldn't help the involuntary shiver as his fingertips trailed through the crease of her buttocks. They lingered there for a moment, exerting gentle pressure against the puckered, sensitive flesh there. The pressure increased, his fingertip seeking access to that forbidden entrance and she felt a flash of heat at the thought he might take her there.

He held the pressure a moment longer, chuckling as she grew tense and held her breath. "No, I think we'll save that for another time," he murmured, and with a last flick against her anus, trailed his fingers down to her pussy.

Rowan barely had time to wonder if it was relief or disappointment she felt that he wasn't going to take her ass. He pulled his hand from her hair and slid his thumbs into her cunt from behind, prying her lips apart and opening her to his gaze. Even though it was dark in the room, she knew his superior night vision would allow him to see her as though the room were fully lit. She felt her belly clutch, knowing he was looking at her, flesh spread and eager for him to fill it. Keeping her hands where he'd put them, she drew up her knees slightly and tilted her ass in the air. She felt the wash of cool air over her heated flesh as she raised her hips to him. She heard his hissing intake of breath and shivered.

She licked her lips. "Fuck me."

The words had no sooner left her lips when she felt him spear into her, driving her forward on the bed so hard she missed banging her head on the headboard by inches. She braced her hands on the headboard and dropped her face into the pillow as he began thrusting hard and fast. She felt him curl his fingers into her hips as he pounded into her, the bite of his grip only adding to the fire in the pit of her stomach.

Jack draped himself over her back, pressing her into the mattress until her knees slid out from under her. He immediately wedged his knees between hers, holding her wide open and unable limit the depth or strength of his thrusts. He began moving faster, slamming his hips into hers from behind, jolting her against her braced hands with every thrust. She was moaning constantly now, crying out as every push of his hips drove his cock deeper into her pussy. She could feel the spasms starting, the delicate flutters of her inner muscles as the orgasm built. He felt it too and redoubled his thrusts.

"Ah God!" she wailed, throwing her head back, eyes open and blind as the pressure built and built, threatening to tear her apart. She pushed her hips back, desperate for the orgasm she could almost taste, but he tightened his grip on her hips and held her down.

"What's the matter, baby?" he growled, his lips so close to her ear she could feel his breath. "You want to come?"

She turned her head to the side, his face so close she could see the sweat beaded on his brow. His eyes were glowing at her as if lit from within, the pupil's dilated so almost all the color was swallowed by bright black. She felt pinned by that look, like a bug on a board, and somehow more turned on than ever.

"Do you want to come?" he repeated.

"Yes, damn you!" she hissed, and tried to push her hips back. He countered with a heavy thrust, pressing her deep into the mattress. He held her there, pinned under his heavy weight.

Frustrated and unbearably aroused, she pulled her hands from the headboard, intending to push herself up and gain some leverage. But quick as lightning, he caught her hands before she could wedge them under herself and yanked her flat again, holding her arms out to the sides. She cursed, hissing and bucking, and he laughed as he effortlessly controlled her struggles.

"Now, that's not a nice thing to say," he admonished when she paused for breath. "You don't even know my mother."

"You miserable piece of shit," she snarled, glaring at him from behind a tangle of hair. She tried to close her legs to gain just a little bit of friction, but he settled his weight more firmly on top of her and held her legs apart with his knees.

"Ah, ah, ah," he chided. "Name-calling, Rowan? So immature."

She bucked again. "I'll stake you in your sleep if you don't let me come, you blood-sucking jackass!"

"That's not the magic word," he said, and still holding her motionless, pushed his hips hard into hers.

"Jesus!" Rowan's head flew back at the sensation, her body bucking mindlessly as sparks went off in her vision. She was wound so tight she thought she might explode if she couldn't get relief.

"That's not the magic word either," he said, laughter and strain evident in his voice. He lowered his mouth to her ear. "Say please, darling," he whispered, and had to move quickly out of the way when she tried to head-butt him. He let go of one of her hands and tangled it in her hair, pulling her head back so her neck arched. "That was not nice," he growled, giving her hair a sharp tug that made her eyes flare. "Let's try that again, shall we?" He put his mouth on her ear, flicking the lobe with the tip of his tongue. "Say please."

She had to swallow twice and lick her lips before she could speak. "Please don't make me kill you," she hissed, and bucked her hips hard.

He laughed, the sound darkly erotic. "You just can't give in, can you? That's fine," he said, shifting to his knees. "I'll just take what I want anyway." He let go of her other hand and slid his arm under her hips. Tucking his hand into the notch of her thighs, he scissored his fingers around her clit and began thrusting again, driving into her with pummeling force and she screamed.

Rowan felt her eyes roll back in her head as he started thrusting again. The tension in her pelvis began building again, twisting tighter and higher until she felt the spasms begin. "Oh God, yes, I'm coming!" she screamed. Her vision started to dim as her entire body clenched down and prepared for the implosion.

She felt his hand tighten in her hair, felt him pull her head even farther back so her throat formed a perfect arch. She felt the scrape of his fangs against her pulse, the heat of his breath against her skin as he growled into her neck. "Come!" he commanded, simultaneously twisting his fingers around her swollen clit and pushing himself deep inside her, and she did.

She cried out, screaming as the orgasm plowed into her. Her cunt clamped down on his invading cock, rippling with pulsing spasms, and with a snarling groan, he sank his fangs into her as he came.

Rowan screamed again, the heated slide of his teeth into her neck kicking her orgasm into overdrive. She felt overloaded with sensation. The dual penetration of his teeth and cock pushing her higher and higher until she thought her body would splinter into a thousand pieces from the pleasure. She whimpered as he began drawing on her neck, pulling her blood from the punctures his teeth made, and his moan of pure pleasure at the taste of her fogged her mind and she gave herself up to the whirl of pleasure.

He drew on her until she felt faint, dizzy from either loss of blood or the orgasm that seemed to go on and on. She felt his fangs withdraw, nicking her slightly as they went. She continued to shudder and spasm as he laved her wounds with his tongue, the sensation both soothing and searing.

"Are you all right?" he rasped, his breathing ragged in her ear.

She struggled to respond but she couldn't seem to catch her breath long enough to form words. She nodded instead and the action seemed to remind him that he still had his fist tangled in her hair.

"Sorry," he muttered, easing his grip so she could lay her cheek on the pillow then went about untangling the sweaty strands from around his fingers.

He eased off her, his cock sliding out of her with a delicious friction that sent aftershocks tumbling through both of them and collapsed next to her.

He wrapped one arm around her waist, tugging her limp form into the curve of his body. "Baby?" He swept his hand across her face, pushing her hair back. She kept her eyes closed and concentrated on breathing.

"I'm fine," she managed. "I just need…a minute. Or fifty."

"I guess you liked it then."

She popped one eye open to find him grinning down at her giddily. "You look pretty fucking happy with yourself."

He grinned. "Is it that obvious?"

She grunted, closing her eye and snuggling into his arms. "Just remember, I owe you one."

"One great orgasm."

"Actually, there were two great orgasms, but that's not what I mean." Her eye popped back open. "'Say please?' What was that all about?"

His grin got even wider. "You loved it."

"You're lucky I'm too tired to hurt you," she grumbled, a reluctant smile curving her lips.

"And why are you so tired?" he asked, teasing laughter in his voice. She stayed stubbornly silent even though her smile grew and she heard him sigh.

"Okay then. I'm going to have to torture it out of you." He dug his fingers into her ribs, making her squeal. "Come on," he said as she writhed and giggled, trying to get away. "You have to say it."

Rowan gasped, laughing so hard she couldn't breathe and struggled to get away from his dancing fingers. "Okay, okay!" she gasped, sighing with relief when he immediately stopped tickling. She lay there for a moment panting for breath then looked up at him with mischievous eyes. "What was the question again?"

Chapter Eleven

Late the next afternoon, Rowan was working on the New York Times crossword puzzle with a cup of tea when Jack came into the kitchen shirtless and barefoot in worn jeans. She looked up when he dropped a kiss on her forehead.

"Hey," she said. "How'd you sleep?"

"Great," he said. "But then I always do. How about you, when did you get up?"

"About an hour ago," she said, taking a sip of her tea. "You keep me up all night so I have to sleep during the day. Pretty soon I'll be keeping the same hours as you."

Jack leaned down and took her mouth in a lingering kiss. "All a part of my plan, darling." He tilted her chin to the side to look at her neck. "How are your bites?"

She arched her neck to the light so he could see. "All healed actually. I was surprised, there's hardly even any bruising."

He brushed his thumb over the faint bluish tint that lingered under her skin. "Something in vampire saliva," he said absently. "Promotes healing."

Rowan touched her fingers to the wound as he went to fill the kettle for his own tea. "I bet that came in handy during the old days."

He grinned at her. "Very handy. Would hardly do to leave evidence behind, especially when one went to all the trouble to make the whole experience seem like a slightly fuzzy dream."

Rowan frowned and shoved the newspaper aside. "How's that work, anyway?"

"What, the fuzzy dream bit?"

"Yeah. You said you can put your victim in a sort of dream state?"

Jack set the kettle to boil then came to join her at the table. "It's not really a dream state as they're not actually asleep. It's more like I'm able to tap into their conscious mind and...rearrange things a bit."

She grimaced. "That's awful."

He looked blank. "What is?"

"Tapping into someone's mind like that," she said. "It's such an invasion of privacy, such a violation."

He rolled his eyes then sobered when he saw how genuinely put off she was by the idea. "Well, what would be better? Letting them remember that not only were they a meal for a vampire—a creature believed not only to be mythical but also inherently evil—but that they enjoyed it as well?"

"They enjoyed it?"

"Didn't you?" he countered, and incredibly she felt herself blush as the night before came rushing back in a flood of memories.

"Well, yes," she admitted. "But that's different. We were...you know."

"Fucking like mad jackrabbits?" he suggested, and chuckled when her blush intensified. "I love that you can still blush after all we've done with each other."

"Glad one of us likes it," she muttered.

"But in any case, it's not so different. Except for the actual sex, the pleasure you felt when I bit you is pretty much the same for every donor."

"Donor?"

Jack shrugged. "We don't like the word victim," he said. "Too negative and besides, we don't use force. Seduction yes, but not force. Donors give us a gift and the pleasure we give them is our gift in return."

"So that," Rowan gestured with her hands, "kick of power I felt when you bit me. Everyone feels that?"

"Not in the same way but yes. You felt it as an amplifier, correct? A boost to the already intense feelings of your orgasm."

"Boy, did I," she said, and he grinned.

"You're welcome," he said.

"So you never fucked and bit before?" she asked.

To her surprise he looked decidedly uncomfortable and she started to laugh.

"Jack, you act like I'm going to stab you with my fork if you say that you have." She grinned at him, shaking her head. "I know you had a life before me — over a hundred years of life as it turns out. It's not going to freak me out to know you've done this before."

He let out his breath in a sigh. "I don't do it all the time," he said. "But the mental charge I get out of giving pleasure to a woman, well, it makes it better for me. Synthetic or donated blood just doesn't have the same kick."

She thought it over for a moment. "That makes sense," she allowed. She raised an eyebrow, appreciating the view as he stretched. "Feeling rejuvenated this afternoon, are we?"

"Infinitely," he agreed then frowned. "How about you? I didn't take too much from you last night, did I?"

She shook her head. "I don't think so, I feel fine."

"No dizziness?"

"Nope."

"That's all right then." The kettle began to whistle and he got up. He fixed his tea then brought his cup back to the table. "So physically you're fine. How about otherwise?"

She frowned at him, not quite understanding. "What do you mean?"

He sipped the tea, watching her carefully over the rim of the cup. "I mean, it's not every day you get bitten by a vampire. I'm just wondering if there's been any weird moments for you emotionally."

Rowan blinked, surprised he would ask. "No, of course not."

"You're sure?"

"Yes. Jack, I've been sleeping with a vampire for weeks. What makes you think being bitten by one would be so much different?"

"Because it is," he said simply.

She opened her mouth to refute that then shut it again when he just looked at her. "You're right. It is. But it isn't upsetting me."

He just watched her over the rim of his teacup. "What?" she asked.

"It was intense," he said quietly. "For me, at least. And I'm wondering how it was for you."

Whoa, she thought. *Moment of truth time.* "It was intense for me too," she said, wishing she could look away. But his eyes held her there, wouldn't let her hide. "Probably the most intense orgasm of my life."

Jack's brow furrowed in a frown and he made an impatient sound under his breath. "That wasn't what I meant."

"I know," she said quickly, and he quieted to listen to her. "I know that isn't what you meant." She paused, trying to gather her suddenly scattered thoughts. "It's just…that was part of what made it so intense for me."

"Because it's not easy for you to let go?"

His quiet question had her nodding, her eyes on her teacup again. "Sometimes it's hard to get out of my own head, you know? To shut off my mind and just be completely physical." She raised her gaze to his. "It sort of scares me how easy that is to do with you."

"I know," he said.

She felt her lips twitch at the wealth of satisfaction in his words. "Watch your ego, Jack. It'll crowd us out of the room if you're not careful."

He chuckled. "I can't help it if I'm happy that you're in much the same boat as I am."

She started visibly, making him chuckle again. "You didn't know? Darling, I've been chasing you for eighteen months. Did you think it was just basic lust?"

She blinked, completely nonplussed by the notion that he was as emotionally tangled in her as she was in him. "I knew you wanted me but I thought it was just the joy of the chase. The challenge, since I didn't fall all over you like every other woman within a ten-mile radius."

He grinned. "You're turning green, darling." He laughed when she stuck her tongue out at him. "No, it wasn't that. I'm not so ego-driven I need to seduce every woman I meet."

He set his teacup aside and held out a hand. Without thinking she rose, placing her hand in his and allowing herself to be tugged onto his lap. He smoothed her hair back from her face, his eyes intent on hers. "I just liked you, Rowan. I liked your humor, your sass." He grinned. "Do you remember the first night we met?"

She chuckled weakly. "God, the night of the barbeque."

"You were so cute."

"I was so ridiculous," she countered. "I'd been running around after those kids all day long, I was sweating like crazy and one of the little buggers had smeared sauce in my hair." She closed her eyes, the memory still painful. "And then I fell into the pool."

He laughed as she buried her face in his neck. "You were so pissed off when you climbed out and trying not to show it."

"I couldn't start screaming," she grumbled. "It was my father's party, how would it have looked for his daughter to throw a hissy fit over a dunking in the pool?"

"Of course not," he agreed. "So you smiled even though you were so royally pissed you had steam coming out of your ears—"

"And you tried to help me dry off," she said, looking at him now with amusement. "You were laughing your ass off too."

"I beg your pardon," he said with mock affront. "I thought I was being quite chivalrous."

"You were trying so hard not to laugh you were biting your lip."

"At least I was trying," he said. "Everyone else was laughing outright."

"True," she conceded.

"And for my trouble I got a withering glare and a face full of wet hair as you swept away." He grinned at her. "I remember thinking, 'Got spirit, that one has'. And I asked you to dinner as soon as you came back out in dry clothes."

She snorted. "Right. Like I was going to go out with you after you saw me like that."

"What's that got to do with anything?"

"Sweetie." She laid one hand on his cheek. "Trust me. No woman wants to go out with a man who's just seen her at her worst."

"Darling, if that was your worst, then I'd really like to see your best. You were beautiful—soaking wet and spitting mad." He tucked a stray lock of hair behind her ear. "It was instant lust."

"Really?" She couldn't help the goofy grin that spread across her face at the notion.

"Absolutely," he said. "And then I got to know you a bit—as much as you'd allow in any case—and I was even more smitten."

Despite herself, she felt her face begin to heat. His smile went gentle as he stroked a fingertip across her cheek. "And you spurned my every advance."

She shrugged. "It seemed like the right thing to do," she said. "You're one of those guys, you know."

"One of those guys?"

She nodded. "Yeah. One of those guys girls talk about when we're alone. The ones we look at and say, 'Yep, there he is. That's trouble.' Then we shake our heads, adjust our panties and go for ice cream."

He laughed, tugging her face down to his for a quick kiss. "I can't help but take that as a compliment."

"You should," she said. "I don't adjust my panties for just anyone."

"Indeed," he chuckled. "How did we get on this topic?"

"You were telling me you lusted after me."

He tweaked her nose. "I was not. I was telling you I like you and have from the first."

"Oh right." She smiled smugly. "That was it."

"Brat," he said.

She put her hands on his face, pressing her forehead to his and looked into his eyes. With her heart in her throat, she whispered, "I like you too."

"I know," he whispered back. "But thank you for telling me."

"You're welcome," she whispered. "Wanna make out?"

He laughed, giving her a kiss and a quick pat on the hip then shifted her off his lap as he stood. "I'd love too, darling, but I've got to check in with the lads back in L.A., do a little work."

She sighed. "Okay, if you have to. If you talk to my father, will you tell him I love him?"

He kissed her again, lingering this time. "Of course."

She watched him go out the door. "Jesus," she muttered. "I'm in love with a vampire."

And she could only shake her head and laugh when he called back, "I heard that!"

* * * * *

When the phone rang several hours later, Rowan looked up from her book with a frown. A quick glance at her watch told her it was after one in the morning. Jack hadn't returned to the apartment but she'd been rereading the latest *Harry Potter* and hadn't noticed.

The phone shrilled again but she ignored it. Jack had given her a pager to wear and would call it if he were trying to get in touch with her. The phone was off-limits, just one of the many rules he'd put in place to safeguard her. It had chaffed at the time, being so completely cut off from the world at large, but as time went on, she found she liked the freedom to ignore it.

The machine clicked on, Jack's voice bidding the caller to leave a message and she cocked her head to listen.

"Jack, it's Deacon. If you're there, pick up."

Rowan put her book down, her brow furrowed in concern. Deacon sounded horrible—his voice agitated and ragged, and she was reaching for the receiver to pick up the call when Jack burst through the door.

He spared her a baleful glance when he saw her hand hovering over the receiver. She pulled it back as he snatched it up.

"Deacon," he said then listened intently. Rowan could hear Deacon's voice on the other end of the line but couldn't make out any of the words. Unfortunately, the machine automatically stopped recording when someone picked up so she wasn't able to hear the whole conversation.

Then Jack asked, "Is everyone accounted for?" and she started to panic.

"Jack, what's going on?" she demanded, rising from her prone position on the couch to stand next to him. He shook his head at her, indicating he was listening to Deacon. He caught her hand in his, gave a reassuring squeeze and she forced herself to wait.

By the time he hung up the phone a few minutes later she was practically vibrating. He barely had the receiver away from his ear when she began pelting him with questions.

"Wait!" he said, and she stopped to take a breath. He framed her face in his hands and kissed her quickly. "Thank you. Now, first things—everyone is fine."

Rowan drew a deep breath at that, feeling the relief flood her tense muscles. "Okay. What happened?"

"Your father's house was broken into last night by a few Army of God henchmen."

Completely forgetting what he'd said about everyone being all right, she clutched at his arm. "What?"

"Rowan, calm down." He peeled her fingers off his arm and sat on the sofa, tugging her down to sit beside him. "The house was empty. Your father's been staying at a safe house and none of the regular staff were there. I had my own people in place, just in case something like this happened."

"Okay," she said, and took another cleansing breath. "So what happened?"

"Well, from what I can get so far they were sent in to either kill your father or kidnap him. There are some conflicting statements on that."

"So they were arrested?"

He nodded. "Two of them were killed in the process but the majority of them were rounded up by the local police and are being interrogated by both them and the FBI."

She frowned. "Will your security people be in any trouble for the dead ones?"

He shook his head. "No, the L.A. police and the FBI are well aware of the situation and all of my people are fully trained. Several of them used to work for the police or the FBI, so aside from the nightmare of paperwork there won't be any trouble."

"Have they arrested Job?"

"No, they haven't."

"Well, why the fuck not?" she exploded. "I mean, obviously they were working for him. Why don't they arrest him?"

He began stroking her hand in an unconscious bid to calm her down. "They do know the kidnapping attempt came from him. Some of his flunkies aren't very bright and they're singing a jolly tune to try to keep themselves from felony jail time. But they haven't arrested him because they can't seem to find him."

"Well, shit."

He grinned at her acerbic tone. "I can always count on you to drill through the muck to the heart of the matter, darling."

She ignored that. "Have you talked to my father?"

"Not yet, but I did talk to the man in charge of his security detail. He's fine and very eager to talk to you."

"I can talk to him?" she asked, her entire face lighting up at the prospect.

"The threat isn't completely over," he said, "not until Job is caught. But this bunch we have in custody is already singing to the FBI—apparently Job doesn't treat his minions very well. They're closing in on Job and should have him in custody within twenty-four hours, so yes, you can talk to your father."

"Can I go home?"

When he hesitated, she scowled. "I can't go home."

"I'm just not sure it's one hundred percent safe, Rowan."

"Jack, crossing the damn street isn't one hundred percent safe. Nothing is." He narrowed his eyes at her and she tamped down her exasperation. "Did you or did you not just say that it wouldn't be long before they caught Job?"

"Yes," he mumbled grudgingly.

"They're closing in on him."

"Yes."

"So why can't I go home?"

"Because I want to keep you here as my love slave a little while longer."

Immediately, her scowl faded as her face broke out into a smile. "Aww. That's really sweet." She waited until his mouth was within a breath of hers then said, "It's also bullshit."

He rested his forehead against hers. "Damn."

She grinned at the despair in his voice. "Come on, Jack. You know there's no reason to keep me here anymore."

"They're probably watching your house," he said.

"And so are you," she countered. "And so is the FBI. And they'll have Job in custody before we even get there."

"Fuck," he muttered, and she chuckled.

"You're cute when you're defeated," she whispered, and watched his head come up like lightning.

"Defeated?" he growled, scowling when she giggled. "Defeated? Woman, I do not get defeated."

"Oh," she said, trying without success to school her features into serious lines. "Well, maybe I'm wrong. It must be the heavy layer of desperation in your voice. That's what made me say defeated." She shrugged when he glared harder. "My mistake."

Jack shook his head slowly, his eyes lit with a predatory gleam. "Oh sweetheart. You've got five seconds."

She swallowed the laugh and looked him dead in the eye. "Five seconds until what?"

"Until I throw you over my shoulder, carry you back to the bedroom and fuck your brains out."

"Hmm." She licked her lips. "If you need a few extra moments — you know, in case you have to deal with the despair — feel free to take them."

The words were barely out of her mouth when he lurched to his feet. He was still holding her hand and he used it to yank her to her feet. He ducked as she rose, tucking his shoulder to her midsection and smoothly lifting her over a shoulder in a fireman's carry. She giggled, her head spinning as he started toward the bedroom.

"Was it something I said?" she asked as she bounced against his back, clinging to his belt for balance.

"Yes," he said, the terse answer making her giggle again. She opened her mouth to speak and squealed instead when she found herself suddenly flying through the air.

"Oof!" She landed in the middle of the bed with a whump, bouncing twice before settling into the mattress. She pushed herself up on her elbows, giggling again as she watched him strip out of his clothes with lightning speed.

"Remind me what it was later," she said as he crawled naked on top of her. "So I can be sure to say it again."

"Shut up," he said, and clamped his mouth on hers.

Rowan moaned into his mouth, sucking avidly on his tongue as he speared it past her teeth. She felt him tearing at the fastening on her jeans and in seconds she was as naked as him, her clothes lying in shreds across the bed. Later she was sure, she'd be upset or at the very least miffed at the sight of her favorite pair of perfectly worn-in jeans in tatters. Now however, the only thing she could think of was how perfect he felt against her skin. How delicious he tasted, how good his hands felt as they slid over her breasts, her belly, her —

"God!" she gasped, tearing her mouth from his and arching her head back as the pleasure speared through her. He twisted his wrist, sliding two fingers slowly into her cunt as she gasped for air. She clutched at him, fingernails digging into his wrist in an effort to slow him down, speed him up, she wasn't sure which. Whatever the plea, he ignored it, continuing the steady pump and plunge as his mouth slid down her neck.

She spasmed around his invading fingers when he nipped at the vein that throbbed in her throat and he chuckled against her skin.

"You like that," he murmured. He did it again, biting hard enough this time to draw the tiniest trickle of blood. She heard him growl, felt his cock grow impossibly hard and thick against her hip. And when she felt the warmth of his tongue lapping at her blood, she screamed and exploded.

When she could see again, she found him looming over her. His hands were braced by her shoulders, her legs caught over his elbows. She was spread wide, tilted up and open for him, but he didn't move.

She licked dry lips. "What're you waiting for?" she managed, her voice sounding harsh to her own ears.

"For you to be with me," he all but growled, and she felt her heart expand in her chest until she feared it might burst free.

She moved her hands from where they'd fallen limp, sliding them up to where his were braced against the mattress. She pushed her hands beneath his, palm to palm, their fingers laced together so he held her hands pinned to the mattress as he braced his weight over her.

"I'm with you," she whispered.

Jack blinked down at her, his eyes darting to where he held her hands captive and back again to the utter trust and love that shined in her face as she looked at him. He swallowed convulsively, opening his mouth to speak but no words came out.

"Jack," she whispered. His eyes locked on hers, brimming over with emotion she couldn't—or wouldn't—name. "Jack," she said again, "come inside me. Please, I need you inside me."

He lowered his head to hers, his breathing ragged and uneven. In a shaky voice, he said, "I do love you."

She smiled, radiant and sure. "I know you do," she whispered, and arching up, pressed her mouth to his.

The kiss seemed to break the chains holding him and with a groan, he sank into her, pushing deep, deep, deep, until it was impossible to tell where he ended and she began.

He held himself still, deep inside her, letting her body adjust to the invasion of his. Her mouth clung to his, her whimpering cries swallowed in his kiss. Unable to keep still, her hips surged against his and with a rumbling groan he began to move.

He shifted, lifting his mouth from hers so he could watch her face as he moved in and out of her. He kept his thrusts slow and steady, resisting her efforts to increase the pace and watching the pleasure wash over her.

Rowan tossed her head from side to side, the pleasure and the pressure building in her body as he thrust in and out. She strained to meet his thrusts, arching her hips as much as she could, whimpering in frustration when he refused to speed up.

"Jack," she gasped.

"What, baby," he breathed, ducking his face to her neck to lick and suck at the sweat and dried blood gathered there. "What do you need? Tell me."

She flexed her hands in his, gripping his fingers as tight as she could. "I need you to *move*," she cried.

"I am moving," he protested, and kept up his steady pace.

"You're not moving enough," she countered, pushing up with her hips in a frantic bid to jar him out of his lazy pace. "I want to come."

"I know, baby," he said, and nipped at the side of her neck again. "But I don't want you to."

Horrified, she shrank back into the pillows. "What?"

He chuckled at the panicked look on her face but didn't alter his pace one millimeter. "I don't want it to be over yet," he explained, brushing a kiss over lips still parted in shock. "I just want to feel you for as long as possible. Surrounding me with your heat, your cunt so wet for me. You're so wet for me, Rowan, so soft and hot and wet, I just can't get enough."

"Oh God," she breathed. "That's good, that's a good one and I love you for it but I still want to come."

He chuckled. "Not yet."

She made a sound halfway between a whimper and a growl. "Please!"

He growled into her neck and shifted his weight, moving up her body slightly so that every downward thrust dragged the shaft of his cock over her swollen and sensitized clit. She half screamed, the sudden sharpness of the sensation pushing her to the edge of orgasm. But he just continued the slow and steady pace, and she stayed poised on the brink.

"You cruel, heartless son of a bitch," she snarled. She tried to pull her hands from beneath his but he tightened his grip, chuckling while she hissed in frustration.

"You're adorable when you're angry," he all but cooed at her then had to rear back, laughing, to avoid her snapping teeth. "Keep it up and I'll slow down."

"Bastard," she gasped, groaning as he thrust deep.

"Mmmm," he said. "That's right. Heartless, cruel, concerned only with my own pleasure." He grinned fiercely and thrust again, wringing another gasping cry from her lips.

"I hate you," she moaned.

"Oh that's too bad," he said, licking the weeping wound on her neck. "Because I'm not at all finished yet. I guess you'll have to just lie back and think of England."

Rowan didn't think she could stand five more seconds of his slow, steady thrusting. With her legs pinned back practically to her ears and her hands trapped, she didn't have a lot of options left for moving things along. She tried shifting her hips, pumping them up to meet his thrusts, but he ruthlessly controlled her movements with his body weight. She tried to reach his neck with her mouth, intending to nibble and suck and drive him as crazy as he was driving her. But he simply shifted out of her reach, dragging his lips from her neck to her breasts, and she could feel a sob of frustration building in her chest.

She felt him smile against her breast as he ground himself into her, giving her just enough clitoral stimulation to make her insane. With little to no physical recourse to shift the balance of power, she decided to use the only weapon she had — her voice.

"Oh God," she breathed, pouring all of her arousal and yearning into the words. "God, I love it when you fuck me, Jack."

"Tell me," he muttered, and she noted with satisfaction the laughter was gone from his voice.

"Your cock feels so good inside my cunt," she panted, feeling the appendage in question twitch at her words. "It just feels so big, so thick, I get wet just thinking about you fucking me."

He lifted his head to look down at her with glittering eyes. She met his gaze unflinchingly and licked her kiss-swollen lips. "I can feel you so deep in me," she whispered. "Fucking me so good."

His lips peeled back from his teeth in a soundless snarl and the sight of his fully extended fangs had her whimpering in lust. "Impaled," she breathed.

"What?" he asked, his voice so deep and rough if she hadn't been watching his mouth, she wouldn't have understood him.

"That's how I feel," she explained, whimpering when he picked up the pace slightly. "Impaled on your cock. I can't move, I can't think, I can only feel you inside me. Stretching me, filling me, so I barely remember what it's like to not be full of you."

Her voice hitched as she felt his cock expand, chafing the walls of her sensitized cunt. He lowered himself, pinning her knees back even farther and settling his chest on hers so he rubbed tender nipples with his chest on every thrust.

"Oh God," she gasped, not bothering to stifle the whimpers and moans that slipped from her lips as he moved. "Oh God, Jack, I'm so close. I can feel every inch of you. Please, please keep fucking me, don't ever stop fucking me, oh my God!"

She nearly wailed the words as suddenly he began driving into her with blinding speed. She was spread wide open, unable to limit or control the depths of his thrusts and she fleetingly thought, *Be careful what you wish for.* Then she couldn't think at all because all the tension coiled so tightly in her belly suddenly burst free and she was coming hard around his thrusting cock.

"Oh God, Jack, oh fuck me, don't stop, don't stop, oh I'm coming, oh *yes!*" she cried, her head arching back instinctively offering her throat, and with a growl he sank his fangs into her neck.

The sharp, piercing pain penetrated the fog of her orgasm and she screamed, twin sensations of pain and pleasure triggering another explosion. The rhythmic convulsions in her cunt proved too much for Jack to hold out against and with a muffled shout into her neck, he came with her.

Rowan lay under Jack, dazed and wrung out until the ache in her hips began to leak through the post coital fog. She winced and tried to stretch her muscles but he was a dead weight and about as easy to shift a Buick.

"Jack."

"Glump," he said, not moving.

"Jack, I'm bent in half."

"I know," he muttered into her neck, and she could feel his tongue snake out to lave at the wounds his teeth had left in her flesh.

"I need you to move so I can move," she said, biting her lip in discomfort as the ache became almost unbearable.

"Mmmm," he mumbled, his breathing evening out, and she realized he was falling asleep.

"Hey!" When she got no response, she reared up, stretching her neck painfully and clamped her teeth on the tip of his ear.

"Ow!" he howled, and his head came up in a rush. He glowered at her, releasing one of her hands to rub at his ear. "What'd you do that for?"

"Hello!" she said, looking down at herself. "I can lick my own knee here."

"Oh." He grinned at her. "Sorry."

He levered himself off her, his still semi-hard cock sliding from her with slick friction that had her shuddering. He sat back on his haunches as she stretched her legs out, rubbing his hands along the outsides of her thighs to ease the cramped muscles.

She sighed with pleasure. "That's nice."

He kneaded her muscles until all the muscle cramps were gone then stretched out beside her.

"Dirty pool," he said, and she opened one lazy eye to peer at him.

"What?"

"That bit with the dirty talk. 'I love your cock in me, you're so big.'" He raised a brow. "Laying it on a bit thick, weren't you?"

She chuckled, turning to snuggle into his arms. "Hey, if you didn't move so I could come, I was going to kill you.

Besides, it's true. You are so big," she whispered, pressing a kiss to his collarbone, "and I *love* your cock in me."

He rewarded her for that with a long kiss. "But," she said when he lifted his head, "I'm still going home."

"Damn."

The utter defeat in his voice made her smile. "Did you think I'd forget?"

"No," he admitted. "That would've been too good to be true."

"I'll be fine, Jack." She tilted her head back to look at him. "I'll be smart, I'll stick with whatever security detail you want me to have but I need to go back. I miss my dad, I miss my job and I miss my home."

"I know," he said, rubbing her back. "I'm just not ready to let you go yet."

"So come home with me," she said.

His head snapped around. "What?"

"Come home with me." She laughed at his dumbstruck expression. "What?"

"I just…" He fumbled for a moment then finally said, "I guess I expected a battle."

She frowned, confused. "A battle for what?"

"To get you to let me into your life once we got home."

"Why would you think that?"

"Well, it was nearly a two-year struggle just to get you to admit you wanted me," he said. "I figured you'd be just as stubborn with the rest of it."

She propped herself on one elbow, the better to glare at him. "Just because I didn't fall into your bed at your whim doesn't mean I was stubborn."

He raised a brow, undaunted by her snippy tone. "Darling. Tell that to someone who didn't get frozen out by your cold shoulder for two years."

She stuck her tongue out at him. "Bite me, Fang Face."

"I did," he said with some satisfaction, "but I'll be happy to do it again."

She laughed and swatted his shoulder. "My stubbornness aside, did you really think I'd ditch you once we got back to the States?"

"The thought occurred to me," he admitted, and the uncertain vulnerability in his tone had her softening.

"Sweetie." She laid her hand on his cheek, looking into his chocolate eyes. "While I will admit to a certain degree of stubbornness—"

"Ha!"

"—I am not silly enough to cut off my nose to spite my face." She dropped a kiss on his smiling mouth. "I want to be with you. I'm not saying we don't have a few technical points to work through. There is that whole blood-sucking thing to consider. But I want to be with you."

"That's handy," he said, toying with the ends of her hair. "Because I wasn't going to let you go."

She rolled her eyes at his toothy grin. "What were you going to do, kidnap me again?"

"If necessary," he said, and her eyes narrowed.

"You know, I overlooked it the first time because I didn't really have any choice and you turned out to be good in bed."

He grinned. "Stop, you'll make me blush."

"But don't think you can get away with such behavior on a regular basis. Psychotic Christian fundamentalists aside, I can take care of myself and any attempt to undermine that will get you cut off."

"Cut off?"

"As in no more nookie, Fang. Persona non grata with the pussy. Denied entrance to the gates of paradise."

His eyes widened. "No sex?"

She smirked. "Bingo."

He blinked, astonished. "Well, that seems harsh."

"Doesn't sound great to me either," she said, "but if you piss me off enough, I won't want to fuck you anyway so it won't be that hard."

He was looking decidedly uneasy. "Is there anything else that might have the same effect on you?"

She shrugged. "Not really. I mean, I won't cut you off if you leave wet towels on the bathroom floor or forget to unload the dishwasher or anything else like that. No, it's pretty much just high-handed interference in my life without consulting me or taking my feelings into account. That's about it."

"Duly noted," he said. "But I will go on record by saying if you're in danger, there's nothing I wouldn't do to get you out of it. And that includes hurting your feelings."

"Understood," she said. "And same goes."

She snuggled back into the curve of his shoulder while he struggled to digest the notion of her protecting him. His arm came up to encircle her shoulder as she settled down with a sigh.

"So you'll come home with me?" she asked.

He kissed her forehead and hugged her tighter. "You couldn't keep me away."

Chapter Twelve

"I just don't understand why we can't take a boat."

"Because it would take two weeks and then we'd still have to get from New York to L.A."

Rowan frowned. "So? That's okay. I don't mind."

"Sweetheart." He took her hands gently, his tone soothing. "We have to get on the plane now."

She shook her head so hard she nearly gave herself whiplash. "No we don't. We don't!" she insisted when he opened his mouth again. "Look, it'll be really romantic, okay? We'll book one of those cruises, like on the Queen Mary 2. It's supposed to be a really nice boat and we can get a big room. I'll buy! And it'll be really romantic and we can just laze around all day. It'll be like a vacation!"

"The Queen Mary 2 isn't even in dock right now, darling." He patted her hand soothingly as he tried to tug her toward the private jet waiting to take them to Los Angeles.

Rowan dug in her heels. "Jack, I know it's silly and stupid and I really hate it but I really, honestly, for sure, don't want to get on the plane. If you don't make me, I'll be your sex slave."

He stopped tugging and looked at her appraisingly. "For how long?"

"Um…a month?"

He considered for a moment then shook his head. "Nope, not long enough." He moved behind her and began pushing her along. "On the plane, Rowan."

She tried to tamp down her panic as they approached the stairs. "Jack, I'm begging you. Can't you just drug me again?"

He chucked in her ear as he nudged her up the steps. "Wouldn't that fall into the category of undermining your ability to take care of yourself and thus get me cut off?"

She shook her head, bracing her arms on the either side of the open plane door. "Not in this case because I'm telling you it's okay. C'mon, don't you at least have an Ambien or two to take the edge off? Valium? Xanax?"

"Sorry, darling, no drugs." He pried her fingers off the doorframe and nudged her into the cabin. He guided her to one of the plushly appointed seats in the main area, sitting her down and fastening her seat belt around her. "You're going to be just fine."

She glared at him. "Sure, tell me that when I'm lying on the bottom of the ocean for the fish to feed on."

He chuckled and sat next to her, buckling his own seat belt. He nodded to the pilot. "We're set, David. The sooner we're in the air, the better I think."

David, who worked for Rowan's father and had been privy to her mid flight freak-outs before, nodded and closed the cabin door. "Try to keep her out of the cockpit, will you? The last time she broke through the door and almost killed my copilot."

Rowan scowled at him. "It wasn't that bad," she muttered. "And anyway, there was turbulence."

"Right." Dave shook his head and headed into the cockpit where they heard the copilot say, "He's keeping her back there, right?" before the door closed.

"That guy's a wimp," she sniffed. "A couple of scratches and he whined like a little baby girl."

Jack chuckled next to her and she whipped her head around to snarl at him. "What's funny?"

"Nothing," he said, making a valiant attempt to school his features into serious lines. "It's just that—you're so self-assured, so together, with everything else. It's amazing that a little thing like flying scares you this much."

"It's not a little thing," she protested, tensing even further as she felt the plane's twin jet engines fire up. "People are not supposed to fly. Birds fly, insects fly. They have wings. I have no wings, therefore, I should not be thirty thousand feet in the air!"

She squeezed her eyes tight as the plane began its taxi. "Are you sure you don't have any drugs?"

"I'm sure, and I'm beginning to regret it," he muttered dryly. "Just try to calm down, think of something pleasant."

She was silent for a moment, concentrating on not thinking of fiery, bloody crashes into the ocean but it didn't work. "I can't. All I can think of is fiery, bloody crashes into the ocean."

"Well, if we crash in the ocean, the fire will be out fairly quickly," he said.

"Do you think you're funny?" she spat. She started fumbling with her seat belt. "I'm so getting out of here right now. I don't know what I was thinking letting you drag me on to this deathtrap with wings."

She was half out of her seat and headed for the door when he snagged her hand, pulling her off balance and into his lap. He clamped his arms around her when she tried to push to her feet, holding her tight to his chest, her legs straddling his hips.

"You can't go anywhere, we're already moving."

She buried her face against his neck and tried not to think about how the plane was speeding up. "I know. I can tell by the way my stomach hurts." She lifted pleading eyes to his. "How about you punch me in the jaw and knock me out? I promise I won't hold it against you later."

"But I would," he said. "I'm just going to have to find a way to distract you."

She eyed his mischievous grin sardonically. "Oh please. You're good, but if you think you're going to be able fuck me for all thirteen hours of this flight, you're delusional."

"What, you don't think I can go for half a day?" He looked affronted. "You wound me."

"I don't think a tank could wound you, and even if you could go for thirteen hours, I know I can't. I'm not practically immortal and I will at some point begin to chafe."

"So we'll take a short break and play cards. Pinochle?"

She laughed then shrieked and grabbed at his shoulders as the plane lifted off the ground.

"Calm down," he soothed, stroking her back. "It's just the takeoff."

"I know." Her nails were digging holes into his shoulders. "Oh God, I don't want to die."

"You're not going to die."

"Don't make fun of me!"

"I'm not."

"You rolled your eyes!"

"I did not!"

"Well, maybe not," she grudgingly admitted. "But you wanted to, I could hear it in your voice."

He rolled his eyes now. "Well, the arguing is distracting you but it's not quite what I had in mind."

She smacked his shoulder. "What did you expect? I *told* you I was afraid to fly!"

"Okay, that's it." To her considerable panic, he began unbuckling his safety belt.

"What're you doing?" she squealed as he lurched to his feet, carrying her with him. She clung to his neck with a death grip. "The plane is in the *air*. We're supposed to be *sitting*!"

"I don't care," he muttered, walking toward the back of the cabin with her in his arms. "I'm not going to spend the next thirteen hours fighting with you. And since I don't want you to have a heart attack from fright either, that only leaves one choice."

"You know, it's not about *you*. And anyway, it's what you get for thinking you could just get me on an airplane with no trouble. And where the hell are we going, anyway?"

He strode through the narrow door at the back of the cabin she'd assumed went to the bathroom. Instead she found herself in a surprisingly spacious bedroom with a vanity, a small chest of drawers and a queen-sized bed with a satin coverlet.

She barely had time to take it all in before she was dumped unceremoniously on the mattress. She stared at him as he efficiently shucked off his shirt.

"That's nice," she said. "I'm having a nervous breakdown and you're thinking about sex." She looked around the room. "Does this mattress convert to a floatation device in the event of a water landing?"

He said nothing as he unbuckled his belt and toed off his shoes.

"These are not the actions of someone who is concerned for my state of mind," she continued, trying not to be distracted from her righteous indignation when he took off his pants. "These are the actions of someone who is horny. And I'm not, so you can just put your pants back on, put this plane on the ground and we'll take a damn boat back to the States."

He ignored her, tossing his pants across the vanity stool. He dropped his boxer briefs to the floor and started walking toward the bed.

She held up a hand when he put one knee on the bed and shouted, "Wait!"

He stopped immediately, half on and half off the bed. "What?"

Rowan chewed her lip, trying to think of a good reason why she'd stopped him. "What are you going to do?"

"I'm going to take your mind off the fact we've just reached our cruising altitude of thirty thousand feet."

She felt her head go light and she fell back on the bed. "I think I'm going to throw up."

She squealed when her sight was suddenly obliterated, panicking that she might have just gone blind from fright. Then she realized the tiny daisies across her vision weren't a fear-induced hallucination but the print on her peasant skirt— he'd flipped it up over her head.

She opened her mouth to blast him—what the hell made him think sex was going to distract her from the idea of crashing into a fiery ball in the ocean—when she felt his tongue snake under the edge of her underwear.

"Oh Jesus!" she cried, and forgot about imminent death. "What the hell are you doing?"

The mattress shifted as he moved and she blinked when he peeled back the veil of her skirt. "Just close your eyes," he advised with a twinkle in his own, "and pretend we're on a boat."

He flipped the skirt back over her laughing face and settled back between her thighs. She felt him tug her panties off then he was peeling her open, delving in with lips and tongue and teeth, and she forgot all about the possibility of a water landing.

Half an hour and three orgasms later, she flipped her skirt off her face. "Enough," she gasped, her voice gone hoarse from screaming out her pleasure.

His face appeared in front of hers, his mouth and chin glistening with her juices. "I've only been down here half an hour," he said, his own voice rough with passion. "We have twelve and a half hours to go."

"Oh God, you'll kill me!" she wailed, and grabbed his ears when he started to slide back down.

"Forget it," she muttered, dragging him up beside her and pushing him to his back. "It's my turn." She slithered down to his jutting cock, taking it in her fist and licking the head like an ice cream cone. She grinned over his groan and settled in for a lengthy blowjob.

She worked him until her jaws were aching, her lips nearly numb. Every time she felt him getting close, she'd back off, caressing him with a light touch until he cooled down just enough then started in again. By the time she finally let him come, he was thrusting his hips into the air, gripping her hair and shouting at the ceiling.

"For the love of the little baby Jesus," he gasped. "What was that?"

She smiled smugly into his bellybutton, darting her tongue into the little crevice and feeling his cock jump against her neck in response. "Payback?" she suggested.

"Bitch," he muttered without heat, and she laughed, dragging herself up to lie beside him.

"You sweet talker you," she sighed, closing her eyes. "Well, that's one hour gone. What now? Got anything good to read?"

She opened one eye when she felt him pop up beside her. He was staring at her, his expression intense and determined, and she felt the first stirrings of alarm. "What are you thinking?"

He reached out for the buttons on her blouse. "One of us is wearing too many clothes."

"Oh right," she smirked. "Like you can get it up again after that."

He smiled grimly. "I'm practically immortal, remember? I rejuvenate quickly."

"Yeah, well, I don't." She closed her eyes and lay there as he systematically peeled off her clothes. "So I can be naked but I'm just going to lie here. No funny business, got it?"

"Sure, got it. Whatever you say, darling."

"Good." She settled into the pillows with a sigh, not moving while he swiftly stripped the rest of her clothes. She frowned, eyes still closed, when he lifted one leg. Her panties were already off so was her skirt, why would he be lifting —

"Oh my God!" he eyes flew open, her back arching and her hips lifting in automatic reaction as Jack slid into her in one sure, slow thrust. Her eyes searched his face, her stomach clenching and her breath quickening at the naked lust on his face.

"Hey, I said no funny business," she gasped.

He withdrew and thrust again just as slowly so she could feel every inch of him, every ridge and vein of his cock in her sensitive, swollen sheath. "I'm not laughing," he said. "And you can just lie there if you want."

She moaned, her hands coming up to clutch at his wrists. He bent over her, lifting her leg to his shoulder to nuzzle her breasts. "Do you want me to stop?" he murmured. "I will if you want me to."

"If you stop, I'll kill you," she managed, and he chuckled.

"Then hang on, darling," he growled, and proceeded to drive her out of her mind, pushing her to two more orgasms before he let himself come.

They dozed after, a tangled, sweaty heap on top of the covers until she got chilly and tried to crawl between the sheets. He took that as an invitation to make love again, this time rolling her to her stomach and taking her from behind, sinking his teeth into her neck as she came screaming into the pillow.

By the time they reached Los Angeles, they'd made love on the bed, the floor, the vanity twice and in the narrow bathroom shower. Rowan couldn't believe his stamina. Dating a vampire certainly had its advantages.

"I don't know why you're so crabby," he admonished as they deplaned to go through customs. "You weren't scared the whole flight, you should be happy."

"I'm not crabby, I'm exhausted," she explained as she made her way across the tarmac to the terminal. "You fucked me into exhaustion."

"Didn't hear you complaining," he said, making her grin.

"I'm not complaining," she said, jumping up to give him a smacking kiss. "But don't touch me again until I get a bath and six hours of sleep."

He laughed, slinging an arm around her shoulders and tugging her into a swift hug. "We'll see about that."

They made it through customs quickly and within an hour Jack was pulling up in front of her house.

"Hey, my car's here."

He threw the car in park, letting the engine idle. "I had one of my guys bring it by. Marvin said he'd keep an eye on it and the house while you were gone."

"He's a doll. I need to go let him know I'm home."

Jack unbuckled his own seat belt, intending on coming around to help her out of the car but she stopped him with a hand on his arm.

"Don't get out, sweetie. You didn't take a pill, so you'll burn. And I used to think these tinted windows were strictly for show."

He grinned and tapped the almost completely blacked-out driver's window. "Functional and elitist. You can get the bags okay?" he asked, and she rolled her eyes.

"It's one little suitcase and a laptop case. I think I can manage."

"I have to go check in with the FBI and the local police, get the details on the arrests. They should have Job in custody by now and I'd like to be present for the interrogation. It'll probably take most of the rest of the day."

Rowan checked the display on her cell phone, which he'd given back to her once they'd landed. "It's already after four, so I'd say that's a pretty good bet. Do you know where my dad is?"

He nodded. "He's back at the house, or should be by now."

"I'm going to get cleaned up, grab a quick bite and go see my dad." A flash of unease lit Jack's features for a moment and she sighed. "Jack, it'll be fine. Stop worrying."

He shrugged, sheepish. "I can't help it. Something isn't feeling quite right. Which is why you've got a couple of sentries posted, just in case."

She swung around, scanning the front of the house. "What? Where are they?"

"They wouldn't be any good if you could see them. Trust me, they're there."

"Regular human guards or special vampire ones?"

"Regular human ones," he said. "There aren't too many of us special vampire ones. In any case, they'll be checking in with me every hour and I'll have one of them drive you to your dad's house and back."

She patted his cheek. "You're so cute when you worry. Like a little mama hen, fussing over all her little baby chicks."

He glowered as she'd meant him to. "I am not a mama hen and for the record, you're my only little baby chick."

"I better be," she warned, and kissed his cheek when he chuckled. "Come back over when you're done with the cops, okay?"

"It might be really late," he warned, and she laughed as she tugged the overnight bag from the backseat.

"I've been keeping vampire hours for weeks now. Anyway, by then maybe my delicate human body will have healed sufficiently for you to have your way with me again."

He grinned. "It's a date."

Rowan leaned over for one last kiss then got out and walked up the steps to the front door. She opened the door, giving a little wave over her shoulder as he drove off.

"Home," she sighed.

She realized Marvin must have been in regularly while she was gone. There wasn't a speck of dust and all her plants looked healthy and watered. In fact, they looked healthier than when she took care of them. "Maybe he talks to them the way he talks to his pasta sauce," she muttered.

She picked up the phone on her way through the house, dialing Marvin's number. His machine picked up and she frowned. He was usually home by now but maybe he had another hot date. At the beep, she said, "Hi, Marvy, it's me. Just wanted to let you know I'm home, safe and sound, and yes, I will give you the details. And I'd also like a few from you, Mr. I'll Pack An Overnight Bag For The Kidnappers. I'm going to head to my dad's in a little while, but if it's not too late when I get back I'll pop over. Bye."

She clicked off and laid the handset on the edge of the bathroom sink. She turned the water on in the tub, flipping the switch to plug the drain. She dumped in a handful of foaming bath salts and shed her clothes, dropping them where she stood. After pinning her hair up, not wanting to deal with drying it, she stepped into the tub.

"Oh that's the stuff," she sighed, sinking chin deep into the fragrant water. She used her feet to turn off the taps, hit the button for the jets and just lay back while the water swirled around her.

She eventually roused enough to grab a loofah and a bottle of body wash and lazily soaped her limbs. Her mind was as relaxed as her body, the relief of not worrying about her father's safety—or her own, for that matter—finally sinking in. And now that those worries were gone, an entire fresh set had moved in to take their place.

"Namely, how do I have a relationship with a vampire?" she wondered out loud. She soaped her arm thoughtfully. She didn't imagine it was much different than having a relationship with a human, except for the obvious quirks. "Probably won't be able to take him sailing," she mused, "unless it's at night. But who cares?"

She set the loofah down and lay back in the tub. There would be some changes to make, that much was obvious. She'd probably have to adjust her schedule a bit but that didn't pose too big of a problem. She taught during the day and that wouldn't change. She could hardly convince the school board to change classroom hours from eight to three to three to ten, but that was okay. It just meant that when she was coming home from work, he'd be waking up. It wasn't the most convenient arrangement, but they'd figure out a way around it.

"And now I'm getting mired down in the details," she decided, and toed the switch to open the drain. She stood, dragging a towel off the hook and briskly rubbing her skin dry before stepping out of the tub. She tossed the towel aside, wrapped herself in a robe and stared at her reflection in the mirror.

"I will not overthink this," she vowed to herself. "What happens, happens, and we'll deal with things as they come." Including, she thought, the possibility of her becoming a vampire as well.

She wondered if he'd thought of it. "He must have," she mused as she slathered on skin cream. At least, she hoped he had. It had occurred to her somewhere between New York and L.A. that he was going to seriously outlive her if he didn't turn her, an idea she didn't like at all. Still, it was a big decision, deciding to be practically immortal and drinking blood for the rest of her life, and she wasn't quite ready to talk to him about it yet.

There was also the terrifying possibility he *hadn't* thought of it. Which would mean he wasn't thinking Long Term

Relationship, or LTR as Marvin always called them. It had been a while since her last one—five years? Six? In any case, it had been a long time since she'd been with anyone who made her think of the future in terms of years rather than months or weeks.

"Years, hell," she muttered as she wiped her hands dry of cream. "I'm thinking decades. Maybe he put some kind of vampire mojo on me."

If he did, she'd somehow managed to put the same mojo on him because he was gone over her. She smiled at her reflection. Regardless of whether he'd thought over the possibility of turning her, she knew he was in love with her. He'd told her, but even more telling, he'd shown her.

Like when he'd freaked out about going back home because he was afraid of losing her. He'd been so cute, she thought, worrying she'd start giving him the cold shoulder again when they were back in the real world.

"Silly man," she said softly, her smile turning dreamy as she capped the jar of body cream. "I couldn't even if I wanted to."

Suddenly full of energy—the bath had been both soothing and rejuvenating—she decided to forage for something to eat. Anything she'd had in her refrigerator before her kidnapping was way beyond its expiration date by now but she had peanut butter and bread and was hungry enough to settle for a simple sandwich. *Or maybe Marvin's home by now and I can bribe him into feeding me with stories of my abduction by vampires.* Picturing his face when she told him that, she was laughing as she opened the bathroom door.

The laugh froze in her throat when she saw the figure sitting on her bed. "Hello, Rowan," he said, and before she could scream, something hit her on the back of the head and after a sharp burst of white-hot pain, everything went black.

Chapter Thirteen

※

"Ms. Evans, are you with us?"

Rowan frowned. The voice was unfamiliar and sounded far away. And her head hurt—why did her head hurt?

"Ms. Evans?"

This time the voice was closer and really shrill. She turned her head away with a whimper. God, her head was splitting in two.

"I think Ms. Evans needs a bit of incentive to join our little party, gentlemen. Isaac, please encourage her."

The cold water hit her face like a closed fist, stealing her breath as her eyes flew open with shock. She began coughing reflexively.

"There, there," the voice said, a hand patting her shoulder gently and she turned to look. And recoiled in horror.

The man standing next to her was tall, over six feet and pudgy. His face was round and ruddy, his dirty blond hair in a sad little comb—one that barely covered his scalp. He was dressed like a banker, in a dark suit and tie over a shirt so white it was almost blinding. He was smiling, a deceptively gentle curve of the lips, but when she looked in his eyes, it was like looking into a bottomless pit.

"Stephen Job," she breathed, and the smile widened.

"I'm so pleased to know you've heard of me," he crooned, lifting his hand to stroke her hair. Not wanting him to touch her, she tried to move away and couldn't.

"What the hell?" She swiveled her head around, biting back a moan at the pain that shot through her skull at the motion. She stared at the ropes holding her hands and feet down, realizing in horror that she was staked out on the floor, arms and legs spread-eagle, still wearing her bathrobe.

She looked back at Job and struggled to hide her fear. "What's going on?"

"Well, dear, as you may be aware, I'm having a bit of a philosophical difference with your father." He sighed and shrugged as though the weight of the world rested on his shoulders. "It distresses me it's come to this but I see no other way of getting his attention."

"You should try email," she suggested in a voice that barely shook at all. "He's real good at answering his messages."

The smile turned cold. "I'm afraid that's just not going to work."

"Why not? I promise, he's right on top of his email. Checks it even when he's traveling."

"No, I think for the point I'm trying to make, a more graphic message is in order." She saw him gesture to someone out of her line of sight and suddenly she was flanked by two men. They were both dressed in black with simple wooden crosses hanging on strings around their necks. Her breath strangled in her throat and she struggled not to whimper in fear as the one on her left bent down.

"What are you going to do?" she asked, and her eyes flew to Job's as he chuckled.

"We just need to set the stage, my dear." He patted her head while the man in black rolled the sleeve of her robe up. She watched with rising panic as he held up a syringe.

"Now don't be alarmed," Job said in a soothing voice that made her skin crawl. "He's just giving you something to help you rest. You have a very big evening ahead of you, after all."

That didn't sound good at all. She cringed away but she felt the needle slide under her skin. It burned and within moments she could feel her limbs grow heavy.

"What are you going to do?" she asked again, appalled at the way her words slurred and ran together. She fought to keep her eyelids open, blinking hard. His face was looming in her vision, the image splitting in two and merging again as her vision doubled.

"We have to get you ready," he explained, as the room faded to black, "for the sacrifice you're about to become."

* * * * *

Jack was on his way to meet with his security team when his cell phone rang. He reached for it absently, his mind on tying up the loose ends with the FBI so he could get back to Rowan.

"Hello."

"Jack."

He smiled at the breathless quality of Rowan's voice. "Hi, baby. Miss me already?"

"Jack, please…"

He frowned, panic blooming as he heard the distress in her voice. "Rowan? What's wrong?"

There was a rustle and his panic increased as her voice faded away. "Rowan! Are you there?"

Suddenly the connection was crystal clear, a low chuckle sounding in his ear and his blood froze. "I'm sorry, Mr. Donnelly. She's a little indisposed at the moment."

"Job," he growled.

"I'm flattered, Mr. Donnelly—or may I call you Jack?"

"If you've hurt her, you son of a bitch, I'll kill you."

"Well, I'd say death threats put us on a first name basis. As I was saying, Jack, I'm flattered you know who I am. I must admit, I had feared we hadn't made any impression on you or your employer at all. You've certainly done a good job of ignoring our demands."

Jack had to grit his teeth to keep from screaming out in rage. "Your demands don't concern us."

Job chuckled again, the sound scraping along Jack's nerves like steel wool. "Well, they certainly concern you now. Ms. Evans is a very lovely girl."

Jack's heart seemed to leap in his throat. "What do you want?"

"Such delicate skin she has, like a blushing peach." Jack tensed even further, his foot nearly pushing the gas pedal through the floorboards as he heard a whimpering moan from the background.

"What. Do. You. Want?" he ground out, and a heavy sigh came through the phone.

"Young man, I suggest you watch your tone. We're playing by my rules now. As I was saying, your little whore here really is lovely."

Jack bit back an angry retort, literally seeing red at the insult and took the exit to Simon's house at ninety miles an hour. "Yes, she is," he agreed, whipping the car up through the turn and gunning the engine up the road.

"That's better," Job said approvingly. "Yes, I think she'll do quite nicely."

He paused, expectant, and Jack obediently said, "Nicely for what?"

"Why as bait, of course."

"Bait?" Jack asked, bringing the Mercedes to a screaming halt at the top of the drive. He was out the door and running toward the house before the car stopped rocking on its wheels. "Bait for what?"

"For her father."

Jack was through the front door now, running silently down the corridor to the back of the house. "You're using Rowan as bait to lure her father. So you can do what exactly?"

"Kill him. At least, that was the plan. But now, after seeing the delicious and engaging Ms. Evans, we may have to adjust our plan slightly. Are you at the house yet, Jack?"

He silently cursed, wondering how in the hell Job could know where he was. He decided lying would be useless. "Yes."

"Good. Please let Mr. Evans know we have his daughter and he should follow the directions on the email coming through now on his personal account or we'll slice her up into cat food. Oh and Jack—please don't be tedious. You've enough of a hero complex to try some sort of rescue scenario. Believe me when I say it won't do you any good. She'd be dead before you got through the front door."

Jack cursed when the connection ended, flipping the phone shut as he burst through the study doors. "Simon!" he bellowed then skidded to a halt as he saw his friend sitting in front of his computer.

The look of pure horror on Simon's face had Jack's own stomach clutching in fear. "Simon?"

"They took her, Jack." The words emerged in a strained whisper, barely audible in the tomblike quiet of the room as he looked up from the computer screen. "They took my baby girl."

Jack came around the desk to look over Simon's shoulder. The email was already open and he read aloud. "Come to the Army of God House of Worship in Hollywood by eight o'clock and be prepared to answer for your sins. Or she will."

"There's a picture," Simon said, his voice hollow with shock, and Jack noticed the attachment. He clicked the icon to open it and after a second's delay the picture filled the screen.

"Son of a fucking bitch!" he snarled, his heart filled with rage at the image. Rowan was stripped naked, her hair still wet from her bath, and the look of confused pain on her face had his hands clenching into fists. She was on the floor, arms and legs tied down with rope, her limbs spread wide to expose her to the camera's lens.

"I have to go."

Jack jerked his head around. Simon was standing, pulling his suit jacket from the back of the desk chair and shrugging into it. He was moving with stilted, detached movements, as if his mind and body were strangely disconnected. He turned to pick up his keys from the desk and Jack saw his eyes, dilated wide with shock. He laid a hand on Simon's arm.

"Simon," he said quietly. "Simon, you can't go."

He looked up at Jack blankly. "I have to. They're hurting her. I have to go, I have to stop it!" His voice became agitated, his breath coming fast and harsh as the fear broke through the shock. "Look at what they're doing to her, Jack, because of me. Because of me! I have to go. If I go, if I give them what they want, they'll leave her alone."

"Simon, they won't." Jack took his old friend by the shoulders and gave him a careful shake. "They won't and you know it. They won't let her go because they can't. They never intended to. They'll use her to get you there and then they'll kill you both."

"I have to try!" Simon shouted, looking older and more haggard than Jack had ever seen him. "Look at what they're doing to her!" He knocked Jack's hands away, rage twisting his features as the last of the shock faded and white-hot anger took its place. "How can you stand here and be so calm while they're torturing my baby girl!"

"Because I have to!" Jack shouted, his own rage boiling over. "I can't help her if I get angry because they're going to kill her! They're going to kill her and if I'm not calm, I won't be able to stop them!"

"Dammit, I'm scared!" Simon slammed his fists down on the desk, making the laptop jump and toppling the Tiffany lamp. It hit the floor and shattered into a thousand colorful shards neither man noticed. "I'm terrified for her."

"So am I!" Jack's hands were clenched in bloodless fists at his sides. "I love her too, you know."

Amazingly that brought a glimmer of a smile to Simon's face. "I knew you did," he said, the anger drained out of his voice. Suddenly deflated, he sat heavily in the desk chair once again, putting his head in his hands. "How are we going to get her out of there, Jack? How are we going to save my baby?"

Jack swallowed the lump of fear in his own throat and put his hand on Simon's shoulder. "I'm going to find her, Simon. I promise. But I need you to work with me and I need you to try and stay calm. If we go off half-cocked, they'll kill her!"

Simon's hand came up to cover Jack's, his grip desperately strong. He took a deep breath then released it slowly. "What do we do?"

Jack squeezed his friend's shoulder before letting go. "First, I need to have a look at that email."

Chapter Fourteen

෨

Rowan kept her eyes closed and took silent inventory. Her head hurt, her body felt like she'd been run over by a truck and the greasy waves of nausea in her stomach had her breathing deeply though her mouth to keep it down. She'd woken up again when the same two cross-wearing henchmen who'd been in the room with Job had brought her wherever she was now, but she'd kept her eyes shut and her body limp so they'd think she was still knocked out from the shot they'd given her. They'd left as soon as they were finished securing her hands and feet once again, their voices fading as they'd walked away, and she'd waited a couple of minutes to be sure they were gone before opening her eyes.

When she felt it was safe, she slowly lifted her head, opening her eyes to look around the room. She winced at the light—there was a fluorescent fixture right above her head—and the room spun sickeningly but she blinked repeatedly until it came into focus.

It was round, the curved walls fashioned from cinder blocks painted a ghastly green. The only furniture in the room was a single ladder-back chair and whatever she was tied to. She looked down to see what it was and grimaced in distaste.

"For God's sake," she muttered, her voice echoing in the small chamber. "Can't they be the slightest bit original?"

She was on a large wooden cross in the middle of the room. As far as she could tell it was laid horizontal on some sort of platform that kept it raised about three feet off the floor. She was again tethered hand and foot with additional rope wound around her waist and torso for good measure. She noticed, unsurprised, they'd taken her bathrobe, leaving her naked.

"Of course they did," she said out loud, and struggled to tamp down the fear. She knew Job had called Jack—she had a vague recollection of that—and she knew it would only be a matter of time before he found her. She just had to hold on until he showed up with the cavalry.

"Which I hope is soon," she said, shivering. The room was cold and the bindings on her wrists and ankles were starting to cut into her skin. She shifted experimentally, trying to loosen the ropes but they were too tight and she couldn't reach the knots with her fingers. She tried until her wrists were rubbed raw from the rope and her head was throbbing from the exertion but got nowhere.

The throb in her head was making the nausea rise in her throat again so she closed her eyes and concentrated on breathing until it passed. She decided to conserve her strength for whatever was coming next and concentrated on relaxing her tense muscles.

She lay there for at least half an hour, getting colder and more uncomfortable by the minute. She tried to make the best of the time alone, carefully looking around and memorizing the contours of the room, searching out possible weapons or escape routes. There was only one door and the only weapon was the wooden chair. Which wouldn't do her any good if she was still tied to the cross.

"I feel like I'm in a bad movie," Rowan said aloud, her voice bouncing off the walls.

She shifted, trying in vain to find a more comfortable position on the plank of wood she was lying on. The ropes around her waist were too snug to allow for much movement so she only succeeded in scraping her spine along the rough wood. Frustration and fear were building inside her, making it hard to remain calm. She tried reciting the preamble to the Constitution in her head but couldn't concentrate. Her mind kept wandering back to Jack and her father.

They had to be going insane with worry. She vaguely remembered a flash of light going off while Job had been on the phone with Jack. It must have been a camera flash, proof they had her. She winced, hoping they'd only sent it to Jack and not to her father. She could only imagine how crazy her father would go if he saw her like this.

Her thoughts were interrupted at the creak of wood and she turned her head to see the door opening. Job stood in the doorway, his henchmen flanking him, all of them wearing identical serene smiles.

"Ms. Evans. It's good to see you again." He stepped in the room as the henchmen took flanking positions in the hall. He smiled wider and closed the door behind him. "Let's get started, shall we?"

Jack, where are you?

* * * * *

He was pacing Simon's study, growing more frustrated by the second.

"Goddamn it all to hell and back, Jacob!" Jack struggled to keep the snarl out of his voice. "I need that IP address and I need it now."

"I'm working on it, Jack." The young man at the computer never took his eyes off the screen. "I'll get further if you stop breathing down my neck."

Jack bit back a pithy retort and spun away to pace some more. When his cell phone rang, he had it open and answered before the first ring died away. "Donnelly." He listened for a moment. "I thought so. Okay, round them up, question them. Call me back with any developments."

He clicked off and walked over to sit next to Simon on the couch. "Simon, the address they gave you in the email was a trap—she wasn't there."

Simon looked up from his fisted hands. "You're sure?"

Jack nodded. "My people are there now. There were a couple of Job's men there, waiting to grab you and take you someplace else. They're being questioned," he added before Simon could ask.

Simon nodded. "Okay, so what now?"

"Now we find out where she is, either from the computer trace or from the men he had waiting for you, whichever comes first."

Simon nodded again. "Did you find out what happened to the men you had at Rowan's house?"

Jack's face turned grim, a fierce light coming into his eyes. "They were found, bound and gagged in her basement. Not dead," he said when Simon's face went ashen. "Drugged heavily though, they had enough barbiturates in their systems to push them into a drug-induced coma. They're on their way to the hospital."

Simon sighed in relief then frowned. "Were they taken by surprise?"

"It looks like they were nabbed before I even dropped Rowan off." He hesitated then said, "Her neighbor Marvin was with them. He may have been in the house when they showed up—he was keeping an eye on it for her while she was gone. He's fine," he hasted to add at the look of horror on Simon's face. "He's at the hospital, being treated for cuts and bruises along with the sedative. Apparently he put up quite a fight."

"Good for him," Simon said, his voice fierce.

Jack opened his mouth to reply when a triumphant shout came from behind him.

"Got you, you little bastard!"

Both Simon and Jack leapt up to race over to where Jacob sat at the computer, a maniacal grin spread over his face. "Little fucker was bounced all over hell and gone but I finally tracked it down." He gestured to the screen. "Check it out."

Jack clapped a hand on Jacob's shoulder. "Jacob, I could kiss you."

"You're not really my type, boss."

Jack grinned. "Same goes." He opened a cabinet to reveal a cache of weapons, kept on hand for emergencies. "Send that address to Michael and Corbin in the field, tell them to head there and wait for me."

Simon stepped forward. "I'm going too."

Jack tucked a pistol in the waistband of his jeans and a knife in his boot. "You can't. It's too dangerous."

"She's my daughter, Jack."

"And you're the reason she was taken." The spasm of pain on Simon's face had him reaching out to grip his friend's shoulder. "I'm sorry," he said quietly, "but the fact is they want you even more than they want her. If you go, I'm going to have to worry about protecting both of you."

Simon's face twisted with anguish and his voice was hoarse with unshed tears. "You find her, Jack. You find her and do whatever you have to do to keep her safe."

"I will. You have my word on it." He squeezed Simon's shoulder in reassurance then turned to Jacob. "Make that call."

Simon watched as he sprinted out the door, hope blooming in his heart for the first time since he'd gotten the email. "Jacob," he said, turning to the younger man, "I could use a drink. Would you like to join me?"

Jacob nodded. "I could do with a scotch, if you've got it."

Simon picked up a decanter from the bar. "Scotch it is."

* * * * *

Rowan scowled and tried not to throw up from fright. "Why are you doing this?"

Job looked surprised by the question. "Is it important?" he asked, coming to a halt next to her prone form, and she struggled to not be cripplingly humiliated at her nudity.

"Considering you're getting ready to kill me—and my father, if I'm not mistaken—yes, I think it's very important. Do you really think you've been given some divine directive, some mission from God to kill my father?"

He chuckled, his sagging chin wobbling. "Christ, no."

She blinked, startled. "Huh?"

"Of course not," he said, looking at her with reproach. "I'd thought you were smarter than that, darling girl. I couldn't give a flying fuck for all that religion bullshit. That was my father's calling, not mine."

"Excuse me?" Rowan started at him, incredulous. "Then what the fuck am I doing tied naked to a Goddamn cross?"

"Oh that's just a little bit of theater." He waved his hand vaguely. "One does have to keep up appearances, you know."

Rowan opened her mouth to speak then closed it. "I have no idea what's going on."

"I'm so sorry," Job said, laying a hand on her bare midriff. The feel of his hand, cold and clammy, on her bare flesh made her want to throw up again. "I can see where this may have been a bit confusing for you, what with all the publicity. Let me see if I can explain."

He lifted his hand and moved to the foot of the cross. Her vast relief at no longer having his hand on her was quickly replaced by trepidation when he picked up a control box from the floor. He hit a button and she barely muffled a squeal as the cross began to lift.

"You see," he began, raising his voice to be heard over the clank of the lift chain, "my father was shortsighted. All he cared about was God, God, God. What God wanted, what God intended. 'You must lead the flock, Stevie', he'd say to me. I hated it when he called me Stevie. 'Lead them where the Lord wills it.' Well, fuck that. I'll lead them where *I* will it."

Rowan listened with half an ear, concentrating on the movement of the cross. The pneumatics were lifting it, raising it, so it stood upright on its end. She winced as the ropes around her wrists dug in as her weight settled, gravity pulling her down against the bonds. The ropes around her torso kept her from falling forward, digging into her rib cage painfully and making it difficult to breathe.

The lift finally stopped moving, the cross settling into place with a clank and Job set the control back on the floor. "People are sheep, Father was right about that," he said. "But he wanted to lead them 'in the path of righteousness'! Please." He dismissed that with a sneer. "What's in it for me?"

Rowan swallowed heavily as he moved to stand in front of her. Her position on the cross elevated her above him so his head was level with her bare breasts and she barely controlled a tremor as he reached out to absently stroke one nipple. "I don't know," she managed.

He laughed, genuine humor mixing with the gleam of homicidal mania in his face. It wasn't a good look. "Nothing!" he chortled. Actually chortled.

"So maybe you should think of another career," she suggested. "I hear they're hiring at the airport."

"Nah, I've got a new career," he said with a smile. A very toothy, fangy smile. "I'm a vampire."

"Oh. My. God," she breathed.

"Isn't it great?" he enthused, literally jumping up and down with boyish glee. "Bet you didn't know there were really such things as vampires, did you?"

"Uh...no," she said, watching him spin in gleeful circles.

"Nobody does," he sighed, coming to a stop in front of her again. He reached out and put both hands on her breasts, squeezing until she winced in pain. "Nobody knows, nobody knows but me," he sang.

He's flat-out nuts, Rowan realized, biting her lip to keep from screaming as his fingers tightened even farther on her breasts. "What about the people in your church?" she choked out.

"Oh they won't find out," he said, giving her nipples a sharp tweak before releasing her. He tilted his head, a funny half smile on his face, and Rowan realized with horror that he was admiring the marks already forming on her bruised breasts.

"Lovely," he murmured dreamily then blinked. "Anyway, it's all part of my plan."

Rowan had to swallow twice before she could ask, "Plan?"

"Oh I didn't tell you about the plan! I'm so sorry." He shook his head. "I've been so busy lately, it just slipped my mind. Anyway, the plan is basically this—take over the world."

Rowan stared. *Not just nuts*, she decided, *but completely insane*.

He went on. "How, you may ask, do I plan to do this? It's quite simple really. All those religious fanatics my father surrounded himself with for all those years are finally going to come in handy."

"How's that?" she asked. *Keep him talking, buy some time. Where the fuck are you, Jack?*

"Oh the details are boring," he said with a dismissive wave. "You don't want to hear about that."

"Oh but I do," she protested, desperate to keep him talking instead of doing. She had a feeling when he started doing, the situation was going to go downhill fast.

"Well I don't want to tell you about it!" he snarled, and she flinched away. "I'd rather get on with the show," he continued in an almost normal tone of voice. "You're the star of the show, you know. You should feel very proud."

"But I'm not prepared," she squeaked out, trying to shrink back into the wood of the cross as he came closer.

"Don't worry about that," he said, madness glowing in his eyes as he pulled a knife from his pocket. He laid it against her breastbone and smiled. "I am."

And as he drew the blade across her flesh, Rowan started to pray.

*****

Jack crouched near the basement window of the house and signaled for the two men waiting in the shadows to join him. They moved quickly on silent feet and crouched beside him, taking care to stay out of the wash of light from the windows.

Michael, his surfer-blond hair hidden under a watch cap, snapped the wad of bubble gum in his mouth. "How's it look, boss?"

Jack kept his voice low. "The outbuildings are all empty, not in use. This is the main house and it's mostly empty. There are three people, all women, in the kitchen on the main floor at the back. They've got Rowan in the basement, two armed men guarding the door and one in the room with her."

Corbin gave a short, sharp nod, his no-nonsense, all-business demeanor in direct contrast to Michael's casual gum chewing. "How do you want to play it?"

"Take the women in the kitchen first. I don't think they're a direct threat but I don't want anyone raising an alarm."

"Take 'em hard?"

Jack shook his head at Corbin. "Soft—tranquilizer's only. I'm not looking for a high body count on this one."

Michael popped his gum again. "What about the goons in the basement?"

"They're armed. Use necessary force. But," he stressed, "we take them quietly. I'm not sure what's going on inside that room and I don't want Job to know we're here until the last possible second."

Corbin was checking his equipment methodically and didn't look up. "You're sure Job's the one in the room with her?"

"Yeah," Jack said grimly. "I can hear her screaming inside her head and she's screaming at him."

Michael sniffed. "Plus, you can smell him. It's like burning trash."

Jack was checking his own weapon. "You both set?" They both nodded, standing when he did. "Okay. Fast and silent, gentlemen."

He moved silently around the side of the house to the back door, using hand signals to gesture Corbin to one side of the door and Michael to the other. They'd worked together many times before and moved quickly and seamlessly into place.

Michael gave the doorknob a testing twist and finding it unlocked, gave a quick nod. Jack moved in front of the door, Corbin moving in behind him, and nodded. Michael drew the door open and they slipped in, Jack and Corbin first with Michael bringing up the rear.

There was a short hallway leading from the back door into the kitchen. They stayed close to the wall, inching along to the open doorway. They could hear the quiet murmur of female voices, the clank of dishes as they moved around the room. Jack sidled to the edge of the door waiting for Michael to fall in behind him and Corbin to move to the other side of the door. He took a quick breath, let it out slowly and swung into the room.

The woman standing by the sink turned in surprise, the sponge in her hand dripping soapy water onto the floor. She jumped a little when the tranquilizer dart hit her above the right breast then just stared at it jutting out of her flesh until she crumpled to the floor.

The other two women had their backs to the door and Michael and Corbin had each fired off a dart before they could turn around. The younger of the two, who looked to be no more than sixteen or seventeen, squeaked in surprise when the dart hit her hip. The tranquilizer hit the blood stream fast and they were out within seconds.

Jack checked the pulse of the woman by the sink while Michael and Corbin did the same with the other two, removing the darts as they did so. Even though he was reasonably sure there was no one else in the house, they swept it anyway, going room by room.

When they got to the basement stairs, Jack stopped. He turned to his friends. "We take the guards as fast as possible, I don't care if it gets messy as long as it's quiet. But I go into the room first." He waited for them both to acknowledge the command then nodded.

"Go."

Chapter Fifteen

☙

Rowan's head was swimming, her vision fading in and out as she struggled to stay conscious through the pain and the fear. She still hung on the cross, her hands long gone numb from the bindings and she was bleeding from too many to wounds count. While none of them were deep enough to cause major damage on their own, the combined blood loss was making her weak and lightheaded.

She saw the flash of steel in the corner of her vision and moaned slightly, not even bothering to try to move out of its path anymore. Struggling was useless and only put more pressure on her battered wrists, ankles and ribs as she fought the ropes binding her. She barely felt the knife slide into her skin, watching with a detached sort of horror as the blade sliced through the pale flesh of her breast.

"You've got pretty tits," Job remarked, his brow furrowed in concentration as he drew the knife. "They're not very big," he continued, pricking at the nipple with the point of the knife until little droplets of blood appeared, "but they've got a nice shape to them."

Rowan swallowed, her tongue feeling like a wad of cotton in her mouth. "I've always been attached to them," she managed, and grimaced as the knife dug in deeper.

"You might not be attached to them much longer!" Job laughed uproariously at his own joke, wiping tears of mirth from his eyes. "Oh that's a good one," he sighed. "But I think I'll let you keep them for a while longer, I like looking at them."

She swallowed again, nausea rolling in her belly. She looked down at herself and mentally cursed as despair overwhelmed her. She was covered in her own blood, little rivulets trailing down to drip onto the floor to pool there. The smell of it hung heavy in the air and Job seemed to be growing more and more agitated with every drop she bled.

He was focused on her breast, licking his lips as he watched the blood flow with glassy eyes. "I love this part," he breathed, leaning in to nuzzle the valley between her breasts. "I love it when they bleed." He looked up at her, his face smeared with her sweat and blood, and Rowan nearly lost the battle with her stomach.

"Do you know why the bleeding is the best part?" he asked.

She remained silent and his face twisted with rage so he pushed the tip of the knife into her ribs. She whimpered as he increased the pressure, feeling the blade begin to pierce the skin. "No, I don't know why," she cried, and felt a flood of relief when the pressure eased.

"That's better," he said, his face taking on a daydream quality once again. "It's the best because it means it's dinner time."

Rowan gagged, horror and revulsion battling inside her as he grabbed her ravaged breast and put his mouth over the cut. He squeezed hard, forcing the cut to bleed heavily and drank greedily from her torn flesh. She shrank away, instinctively recoiling, but there was nowhere for her to go, she only succeeded in digging her back painfully into the wood of the cross.

Job raised his head, his mouth glistening with her blood and licked his lips. "Yum, you are delicious." He gave her breast a final squeeze, purring in satisfaction as blood continued to well then turned away.

"You've been a very charming guest, Ms. Evans," he said. He pulled a handkerchief out of his pocket and wiped the blade clean then dabbed at the blood on his hands. "But unfortunately, you don't appear to have served your purpose.

You see, I only needed you to get your father here. I thought the pictures I sent would have brought him running—"

"Pictures?" Rowan asked. It was a struggle to keep her eyes open and focused but she managed. "What pictures?"

"Oh I took a few snapshots. A few candids for the album. Would you like to see?" He walked back to stand in front of her and drew a folded piece of copy paper from his back pocket. He unfolded it and held it up. "The quality here isn't very good, since it's only a computer printout. But I think you get the idea."

Rowan stared at the page. "You sent those photos to my father?" she asked, her fatigue and fear fading as rage set in. As violated as she felt in looking at the photos, she was even more horrified that her father had been subjected to those images of her.

"They're quite good, aren't they?" He turned the page around to admire the images. "I think they might have turned out better with a little more natural light to work with but one does what one can."

"You're a sick, sadistic motherfucker," she spat, her self-preservation instincts overridden by her anger.

He had the nerve to look affronted. "That's uncalled for. I'd never do anything so vile as to have sexual relations with my mother." His face twisted with distaste. "My mother isn't at all attractive."

"You're a pig," she snarled.

Job's eyes narrowed. "You're not being very sociable. I don't like rude guests."

"Well, I don't like knife-wielding, blood-sucking hosts so I guess we're even."

"You've outlived your purpose, Rowan," he said, letting the paper drop. It fluttered to the floor to settle in the pool of her blood. "Your father isn't coming to your rescue and I doubt anyone else is either. You'd be smart to be nicer to me, I might let you live a bit longer."

Rowan could feel her body failing her. She'd lost enough blood to feel extremely weakened and she knew if she didn't get medical care fairly soon, she could very well bleed out from the dozens of small cuts he'd inflicted. Logic was telling her to prolong the conversation, keep him from dealing his final blow as long as she could to give Jack time to find her. She knew he was looking for her and she trusted him to find her in time. But the rage rolling through her felt good, it felt right. It was such a welcome relief from the pain and fear that she couldn't think straight.

She snarled at him. "You're just a pathetic little man trying to get out from under daddy's shadow."

His eyes lit with savage hatred and he pushed his face into hers. "I am *way* better than my father! He was a religious nut with no vision! I'm making something of his church, something great!"

"He might have been a religious nut but he was doing something he believed in. You're just on some power trip, a quest to prove you're a big man. Well I've got news for you, Stevie. If you have to prove you're a big man, then you aren't one."

"*Don't call me Stevie!*" he screamed. He had the knife clenched in his fist, she hadn't seen him pick it back up again. Or maybe he'd never dropped it, she didn't know. He shook it in her face, the blade glinting in the light. "I'm a better man than my father ever was!"

"You're not a better man than anyone," she spat at him, and on a howl of rage, he plunged the knife into her side.

Rowan gasped in shock. The pain hit a second later, rolling in and swamping her like a tidal wave. She felt him jerk the knife out and looked down to see a flood of blood pour out of the wound in her side. She could feel the warmth of it running over her hip, down her leg, and she knew she'd bleed out if she didn't get help right away.

"You bitch," Job sobbed, his face streaked with tears. "You made me do this. I wanted to keep you alive, I was going to let you go but you had to ruin it!" He stomped his feet like a petulant child. "You ruined it!" He raised the knife and Rowan could see in his eyes he had gone over, beyond reach, and closed her eyes and braced herself for the killing blow.

Then she heard the crash and her eyes flew back open.

Job pivoted away from her as the door burst open with such force the wood splintered. He never even had time to squeak in surprise because with an odd-sounding pop, the man who'd burst through the door shot him, leaving a neat, round hole in his forehead. Rowan watched as he toppled backward without a sound, still holding the knife clenched in his fist.

Rowan looked toward the doorway and smiled feebly. "Where have you been?"

Jack ignored the question, shoving his weapon into his waistband and leaping toward her so fast she barely saw him move. "Jesus, Rowan, look at you." He lifted his hands to touch her and then stopped, his hands hovering over her as if he were afraid to touch her. "What the fuck did he do to you?"

"I've looked better, huh?" she managed.

"I should have killed him slower," he growled.

"That's nice," she whispered, "but can you get me down now?"

"I'm sorry, sweetheart." He pulled a knife out of his boot and knelt, slicing through the ropes at her ankles. She whimpered as they fell slack, the feeling returning to her numb feet painfully and her rib cage taking the full weight of her body. He started to cut the ropes on her waist then stopped.

"If I cut you loose you're going to fall."

"I don't care," she moaned, clinging to consciousness by the skin of her teeth. "Just get me down, I really need a doctor."

Jack looked up into her ashen face and the blood still flowing sluggishly from the wound in her side. He cursed. "Michael, Corbin! I need your help!"

Rowan turned her head, noticing for the first time the two men in black fatigues by the door. "More vampires?" she murmured as they came forward.

"They work for me," Jack said. He turned to the men. "I need you to hold her up while I cut her loose. One on each side and be careful of the wounds."

The men moved in to flank her, each putting a bracing hand on her abdomen and another just under her armpit. As Jack began to saw through the ropes at her waist, she smiled wanly down at the man on her left.

"I'm Rowan," she said, and he grinned at her.

"Michael, ma'am. Pleased to meet you." He snapped his chewing gum loudly and nodded to his companion. "That's Corbin."

The other man nodded. "Just hold on a few more minutes, we'll have you down and out of here."

"I'm pleased to meet you both," she said. She jerked a little in their grip as the ropes around her waist finally fell to the ground and she heard them grunt as they took her weight. "Sorry," she managed, breathing carefully to try to control the pain. "I keep meaning to loose those pesky ten pounds."

Michael grinned up at her as Jack moved to release her wrists. "Don't you worry about it, sugar. You're like a feather—we can hold you up all day here if we have to."

"That's sweet...of you to say," she managed. She cried out, her vision hazing and her stomach roiling with nausea as her wrists were freed. They'd been numb for so long it was like hot needles driving into her flesh as the feeling came back. She didn't even realize she was crying until she felt Jack's hands come up to wipe them from her cheeks.

"Shh, baby, please don't cry. It's going to be okay, I'm going to get you out of here." He gathered her up as gently as he could, his words tumbling over themselves as he whispered apologies and reassurances. She bit her lip to keep from crying out again in pain as they moved her, Michael and Corbin helping to ease her down from the cross and into Jack's arms. "We're getting out of here right now."

Fine by me, she thought, biting her lip to keep from howling in pain as he began walking. Then a thought struck suddenly. "Wait. Jack wait, we can't leave yet."

"What? Why not?"

"Job," she said, gesturing to the body lying on the floor. "He isn't dead yet."

"Sweetheart, he is," he soothed, and started for the door again. "Trust me, he can't hurt you anymore."

"No!" she shouted. "He's a vampire!"

Jack stopped again, looking at her with stunned surprise. "Are you sure?"

"He said he was and he had fangs," Rowan said.

Jack looked over her head to Corbin. "Check it out."

He waited while the other man crouched over Job's body, prying his jaw open to look at his teeth. "Yeah boss, we've got fangs." He looked up at Jack. "And the bullet hole in his forehead is starting to heal quick."

"Shit. I wasn't expecting this. I didn't bring a long enough blade." Jack jerked his chin at Michael. "See if you can find something in the kitchen."

"You got it, boss."

Rowan groggily watched Michael lope out of the room then turned to Jack. "What's he looking for?"

"Something to cut his head off with," Jack explained.

"Can't you just stake him with a chunk of the door?" she asked, and bit back a moan as he shifted her in his arms.

"Decapitation is cleaner. If you don't get the stake in just the right spot, there's a chance for regeneration." He looked at her sharply and swore. "I'm getting you to the hospital. Corbin, you and Michael handle cleanup."

"No problem, boss."

Jack hardly waited for the answer before he was out the door and hitting the stairs at almost a dead run. Rowan grimaced, feeling the renewed flow of blood from a dozen wounds at the jostling. He sped into the brush, his feet flying over the ground, and they made it to the Mercedes he'd hidden in an orange grove in about thirty seconds. He bundled her into the passenger seat, getting a blanket from the trunk to tuck around her and buckled her in.

"Just hang on, you'll be okay." He came around and climbed in, starting the car and out onto the long driveway.

"Where are we anyway?"

"About an hour outside L.A.," he said, "at an estate Job's church just purchased last week. I think he was planning his own Branch Davidian-style compound."

"Jack." She let her eyes drift shut. "I really don't think I'm going to make it to the hospital."

"Don't say that." She heard the panic in his voice, felt the tremble in his hand as he reached over to clasp hers. "You're going to be just fine."

"No," she said, "I'm not. I lost a lot of blood, Jack. I'm still bleeding and it's going to take too long to get to the hospital."

"If I have to break every traffic law on the books, I'll get you there in time."

She smiled at the grim, fierce determination in his voice. "Jack."

"Dammit, Rowan, I'm not letting anything happen to you!"

"Then you're going to have to turn me."

Chapter Sixteen

☙

Jack couldn't believe his ears. "What?"

"You know you have to."

"No." He shook his head, panic threatening to grab him by the throat. "No, it's not that bad. We can make it to the hospital and you'll be fine. You'll be fine."

"Jack."

"You'll be fine!"

"Jack." She turned her hand so her fingers gripped his. "Look at me, baby." He flicked his glance her way to find her staring at him with quiet surety. "You know I'm not going to make it to the hospital. You know it," she said again when he opened his mouth to speak. "We're in the middle of nowhere, the nearest hospital is probably at least an hour away. It's the only way."

Jack slowed the car, pulling to the side of the drive. He cut the engine and turned to face her, his throat closing with fear when he saw her face. She was ashen, her eyes dulled by pain and shock, and the blanket he'd tucked around her was already soaked with her blood.

"Baby." He reached out to cradle her face in his hand, a shudder going through him at the cold, waxlike feel of her skin. When he struggled to speak, she turned her lips to his palm.

"I know," she murmured, her lips brushing his skin. "It's okay. I want you to."

"Are you sure?" he choked out through the emotion clogging his throat. "You can't change your mind later, it's permanent. I don't want you to hate me for this."

Her eyes had drifted shut again, the fatigue dragging at her, but she smiled at his words. "I couldn't hate you for it," she chided. "I've been trying to figure out a way to ask you to do it without making you feel trapped."

"Trapped?" he said incredulously. "How could I feel trapped?"

"Well, it's forever," she said, prying her eyes open to look at him.

"Forever's what I want from you, Rowan." He leaned over, pressing his forehead to hers. "But I want you to think. If you're not sure that's what you want from me—"

"I'm sure," she interrupted. "Really, really, sure and not just because I'm dying." She licked her lips. "I just want to be with you."

"Okay, baby, then hang on." He slid back into his own seat and started the car.

"Where are we going?"

"There's a caretaker's cottage at the front of the estate. We can go there."

"Okay," she whispered, and he looked over to see her eyes had drifted closed again. "Just hurry."

Jack squeezed her hand in reassurance then put both hands on the wheel and concentrated on driving.

They were at the cottage within two minutes. He ran ahead to the door, found it locked and with one swift kick broke it down. He came back to the passenger side of the car and carefully lifted her out. She didn't stir but he could see her chest move with her shallow breathing. "Hold on, baby, we're almost there."

He carried her in, kicking the ruined door closed behind him and headed to the back of the house. He found the bedroom, still with an old iron bedstead with a bare mattress on it and placed her gently on the bed. He unwrapped the blanket from around her, wincing when the blanket stuck to her wounds. He pulled it free as gently as he could but the fibers had become embedded in the dried blood that was caked on her skin and she moaned in pain as it pulled free.

"I'm sorry," he whispered, hating that he was causing her more pain.

"Let's just...do this," she whispered, her eyes opening. She focused on his face with visible effort. "What's first?"

"I need to take a little bit of your blood," he said.

"Haven't I lost...enough?"

"It makes the transition easier for you," he explained. "Having some of your blood in my system makes it easier for you to accept mine. Don't worry, I'm not going to bite you."

She frowned in confusion. "Why not?"

"Because you've been through enough and you're already bleeding. I can just take from one of the wounds—"

"No!" She grabbed his hand, her grip trembling and weak. "No, I don't want you to do that."

"Why not, baby?" He gripped her hand and swept a lock of hair from her forehead. "If I bite you now I'll hurt you, and I'm afraid to tap into your mind to ease the pain. You're already so fragile, I just don't know what that would do to you."

She shook her head violently. "No, I don't want you to drink from where he did. I don't want to remember him when we do this, I don't want—"

"Okay, okay," he soothed, stroking her forehead. Her body was starting to shake, fine tremors that made her look like she was lying on a vibrating bed and her lips and fingertips were starting to turn blue. He needed to move quickly before she lost much more blood.

He reached over, pulling the knife from his boot and setting it beside her head on the pillow. He leaned forward, placing his lips gently on hers. "You're sure?"

She nodded, almost imperceptibly. "Yes. Sure. Do it."

He pressed another kiss on her lips. "Okay, baby, here we go." He tilted her chin up and to the side, exposing her neck. He could see the pulse that beat feebly under the skin. He sent up a quick and fervent prayer that this would work and sank his fangs into her throat.

She cried out as his teeth pierced her skin, the sound feeble and weak to his ears. Her blood flowed into his mouth in a slow trickle, warning him she was closer to death than he'd realized. He had to time it just right, taking just enough from her to leave her hovering on the brink of death then use his blood to bring her back.

He took only a few swallows, his instinct telling him that taking more than that could push her past that delicate edge. He could feel her pulse beneath his lips slowing, becoming more sluggish, and he hurriedly reached for the knife. He sliced into the sleeve of his sweater, ripping it open to bare his arm while still keeping his lips on her throat, monitoring the ever slowing beat of her heart.

When he felt her pulse stutter and hesitate just a little longer than normal between beats, he lifted his head and quickly drew the knife across his own wrist. His blood welled up thick and dark and he brought it to her lips.

"Come on, baby, you have to drink," he said, pressing his wrist between her parted lips. She swallowed convulsively as her mouth filled with blood and he sighed with relief. "That's it, sweetheart."

His blood continued to flow into her mouth and she swallowed again, less feebly this time. He kept his eyes on her face, watching for any sign that she was beginning to regenerate. Her skin was still ashen but she was losing the waxlike appearance. He kept his wrist at her lips, encouraging her to drink, and he felt her lips flutter against his skin.

"Yes," he hissed. He pressed his wrist harder to her lips and was rewarded with answering pressure. He nearly wept with relief when she began to tentatively suckle his wrist, drawing his blood into her mouth. She made a noise, somewhere between a whimper and a moan and her eyes fluttered open.

"Keep drinking, baby," he urged, and her eyes sought his. "A little more sweetheart, you need a bit more." She obediently sucked harder, her hands coming up to hold his arm in place.

He let her drink for a few minutes more then tried to pull away. She whined a protest, her hands clinging to his arm with stunning strength, and he had to hold her head down with one hand while wrenching his wrist free. Immediately, the cut on his wrist began to heal over.

She tried to get up and he pressed his palm more firmly onto her forehead. Her skin was flushed now, the ashen pallor having been chased away by the rush of new blood. "Want more," she said, and he laughed.

"Greedy," he accused teasingly, feeling almost giddy with relief. "You need to wait a while for the transformation to be complete before you can have any more." He moved his hand off her head and grasped her hands. "Can you try to stand up?"

She swallowed, breathing heavily. "Okay," she said, and allowed herself to be pulled to her feet. The room tilted dizzyingly and she sat back down hard. "Whoa," she muttered. "Dizzy."

"Yeah, that's pretty normal. You've been mostly dead all day."

She ignored the way the room spun and narrowed her eyes at him. "Are you quoting *The Princess Bride* at me?"

He grinned. "Just call me Miracle Max."

"The miracle part feels right," she admitted. She looked down at her nude form and grimaced in distaste. "Ew."

He followed her gaze. "Yeah, you could use a shower. But the good news is, your wounds have almost fully healed," he said, touching a finger to the faint pink line that was all that was left of the gash in her breast. "You might not even scar."

She swiped at the dried blood between her breasts. "I'm just glad I didn't die."

He tilted her head up to kiss her. "Me too. Let's get out of here."

"Good idea," she said, and tried to stand again. She started to fall as the room spun dizzyingly again and with a curse, he swept her up into his arms.

"I won't always be this dizzy, will I?" she asked as they walked out of the house.

He shook his head. "It's part of the transformation, it'll fade once your system has had a chance to adjust. In fact, I'm surprised you're still conscious. Usually, newly turned vampires have to sleep for a while…" He trailed off as he looked down at her face and saw she *was* asleep. He chuckled and tucked her into the car, tucking the blanket around her naked form. He'd better stop on the way home and lay in some supplies, he was going to have a very hungry vampire on his hands when she woke up.

Chapter Seventeen

Rowan woke feeling hungry, amazingly well rested and horny as hell. The hungry was probably due to the fact she hadn't eaten since before the plane and that was God only knew how long ago. She wasn't sure how long she'd been asleep but instinct told her it was at least a day, which would definitely account for the well rested. And the horny as hell was likely due to the man pressed up against her back with his morning wood poking her in the ass.

Or evening wood, in this case. The window curtains were open and she could see the dark blanket of the sky settled over the city. A quick glance at the bedside clock told her it was just after midnight. *So technically, middle-of-the-night wood,* she thought, and wiggled back against it.

"Morning," he rumbled in her ear, and with a surprisingly girlish giggle she twisted in his arms to face him.

"It's the middle of the night," she pointed out.

"Is it?" He pressed a kiss to her lips, humming with satisfaction as her mouth opened automatically. "Who cares?"

"Not me," she said, and moved in for another kiss. "How long was I asleep?"

"Just about forty-eight hours," he said, sliding his hands into her hair to hold her still. He kissed her until she was practically purring under his hands. "How do you feel?"

"Like I could take on the Marines," she said, and he laughed.

"Do you mean in combat or in bed?"

"Both," she said, and placing her hands on his shoulders, rolled him to his back. She climbed on top of him and grinned. "Problem with that?"

"I don't share," he said. He swept his hands up to her breasts and palmed them with a firm touch, making her groan. "But you can beat them up if you want."

"Nah," she said breathlessly. His touch was shooting her arousal level to critical. "I'll just work out all this extra energy with you." She smiled into his eyes, loving the lust and love she saw there. "Problem with that?"

"Not at all."

"Good," she said. "Because there's this thing I have to do. It won't take me but a minute." She slid down, kicking the sheet to the foot of the bed and took his cock into her mouth in one smooth motion.

"Jesus!" he growled, his hips thrusting up off the bed and shoving his cock farther into her mouth. She adjusted quickly, angling her head so he slid into the back of her throat, and he growled again when she swallowed around him.

She pulled her mouth off him in surprise. "Wow. I never did that before!"

"You don't have to breathe as often now," he said through gritted teeth.

"That is cool as hell," she marveled.

"Yeah, it was," he agreed, tangling his hands in her hair. "Can you do it again?"

She grinned, giddy with discovery. "I don't know. Let's see!"

She engulfed him again, sliding him all the way back and down her throat. He hissed and pushed up, thrusting himself farther into her mouth. She pulled back, using her tongue to stroke and swirl before swallowing him down again.

She lifted her head to grin at him. "I really like this," she said, and he laughed.

"I can tell," he murmured, trailing his hands from her hair to stroke her face. "You're gorgeous, you know that? Beautiful."

"I feel beautiful," she said. She gave his cock one last lingering lick, swirling her tongue through the moisture pooled at the head before crawling back up his body. "I feel beautiful and strong and I want you so much."

She licked at his mouth, diving in when he opened for her. "I want to take you, Jack, the way you've taken me so many times. I want to make you beg and scream and forget what it's like not to be with me."

He groaned, his cock getting even harder at her words. "Then take me," he growled, his eyes lit with a fierce light.

Rowan kissed him again—hard—then moved back to straddle his hips. She slid her hand over his cock, up and down, spreading his own moisture over the shaft and using it to ease the friction of her hand. He growled again, pushing his hips up to spear into her but she held herself just out of his reach.

"What do you want, Jack?" she whispered, her tongue flicking out to wet her lips and her eyes watching him.

"You," he moaned.

"How bad do you want me, Jack? Bad enough to beg?"

"Yes," he hissed, pushing his hips up so fast he almost caught her off balance and sent her sprawling on the bed. She steadied herself, brushing her dripping cunt over the head of his cock, and he gritted his teeth against the urge to push into her.

"I don't hear you begging," she admonished, and a giggle escaped her lips.

"Laugh it up," he muttered. "Just remember, sweetheart, paybacks are hell."

"Blah, blah, blah," she said in a bored voice then spoiled it by giggling again. "I'll worry about later—later. Right now," she said with an eyebrow quirk, "I'm in charge. And I'm still not hearing you beg."

"I want you so much, Rowan," he said, holding her gaze with his. "I want you in my bed, in my life, in my heart, forever."

"Oh," she said, her face softening. "That's so sweet."

"And if you don't fuck me now," he continued, "my heart will explode and I won't be much good to you. So please, for the love of the little baby Jesus, fuck me!"

She tossed her head back and laughed, the sheer joy in the sound echoing in the room. "Not quite what I had in mind, but good enough," she said. She shifted, positioning herself and slowly impaled herself on him.

They both groaned at the sensation. Rowan reached out for Jack's hands, gripping them hard enough to grind bone as she began to move.

"God!" she gasped. "This is so unbelievable!"

He grunted as he pushed up to meet the thrust of her hips. "Heightened senses?" he asked.

"Yeah," she moaned. She ground her hips down on him, purring at the sensation. "Everything is sharper, clearer. Brighter, like a light's been turned on. Jesus, I can feel every little bit of you inside me!"

Jack watched her face, loving her expression as she rode him. She was so giving, so amazingly open it blew him away. "That's how I feel you," he said. "Every little ripple, every pulse. God, I love you!"

"I love you too," she gasped, her hips pumping faster. "I really, really do." Suddenly she felt something happening in her mouth. "Jack," she gasped. "Jack, my teeth."

He picked up his head, noted the elongated eyeteeth emerging from her gums. "Fangs," he growled. "They're coming in."

"Oh God, I want to bite," she breathed, her nostrils flaring as she caught the faint coppery scent of blood. "What do I do, I don't know what to do."

"Come here," he said, raising up and reaching for her. He wrapped his hand around the back of her neck and pulled her down, tucking her face into the hollow of his throat.

"You want to slide them in," he instructed, "not push or punch through. Your teeth are sharp enough to tear through steel, so take it slow and easy."

Rowan struggled to hold back, listen to his instructions. This close, she could smell the blood as it flowed under his skin. She could actually hear it, the rush of it like a river to her enhanced hearing. She licked out over her lips, her tongue getting caught on the tip of one fang. The taste of her own blood made her all the hungrier for his and with a delirious moan, she put her mouth to his neck.

He went still, his strong hands pinning her in place, and she opened her mouth and gently, oh-so gently, pierced the skin over his carotid artery. Even though he'd warned her, the ease with which her teeth pierced his flesh took her by surprise. The skin parted like butter under a heated blade and her mouth was flooded with sweet, warm liquid.

She felt his hand clench on the back of her head, felt the vibration of his vocal chords in her own mouth as he growled. "Suck," he commanded, and she did. She moaned in sheer pleasure as the liquid flowed, swallowing convulsively as she fed.

Her hips began moving again of their own volition, pumping frantically as she felt the orgasm building inside her. The taste of him went straight to her head, making her dizzy and frantic for more. Her cunt clamped down, the orgasm barreling through like a freight train and she ripped her mouth from his throat with a roar.

"Oh God, Jack—I'm coming!"

Her head went back and she stared blindly at the ceiling as her body imploded, pulsing and shuddering and vibrating around him. The orgasm went on and on, pushed higher by the constant drive of his hips. She screamed out again as she felt him grow impossibly harder, bigger inside her.

Jack reared up with a savage snarl. He wrapped his arms around her, latched a hand in her hair to drag her head back and sank his fangs into her neck.

Rowan howled, the piercing pleasure-pain pulsing through her and sending fresh waves of spasms through her body, and with a muffled roar, he followed.

* * * * *

"This has been the weirdest month," Rowan said, her mouth full of rare roast beef. They were sprawled on her living room rug having a two a.m. picnic. Rowan was bundled in her bathrobe and Jack just had on a pair of silk pajama bottoms that he'd had someone bring over, along with the rest of his clothes. "I get kidnapped, kidnapped again and turned into a vampire. Tough to beat for strange."

Jack grinned at her. "I can beat it," he said. "There was that July I was in Berlin with those two milkmaids—"

"Whatever!" Rowan held up a hand. "I don't want to know."

He chuckled into his wineglass. "Spoilsport."

"Damn right," she said. She took a sip of her own wine and hummed in appreciation. "This is amazing. I love how I can taste all the little flavors so clearly."

"One of the side benefits," he commented.

"This life is going to be pretty cool," she decided, sitting back with a satisfied sigh. "I'm really glad I can still eat real food. I'd have hated to give up cheesecake."

"You just have to be careful," he told her, topping off her wine glass. "Too much regular food can upset your system and you have to make certain you feed regularly."

"Right. By the way, that bit in the bedroom—"

He raised an eyebrow. "Bit? Or Bite?"

She grinned. "Both, I guess. Can we feed off each other or will we need to have other sources?"

"We can feed off each other for fun," he told her, lying down on his side. He propped his head in his hand so he could watch her. "But we will have to supplement that with synthetics."

"Wow." She blinked as though trying to clear the cobwebs from her vision. "I'm not human anymore."

"So dramatic," he chided, and rolled his eyes when she stuck her tongue out at him. "You're still human, you know. Your species can't change, although your DNA has gone through a bit of a transformation. It would be appropriate to say you're a little more than human now."

"It's going to take me a while to get used to this." She stared into the fireplace sipping her wine and Jack felt a cold trickle of dread crawl down his spine.

"Are you sorry?" he asked quietly, and her head snapped around to look at him with surprise.

"What? No, of course not." She set her wine aside and stretched out next to him. "Why would you say that?"

He shrugged, feeling horribly vulnerable and not liking it. "It was a big decision, made under duress. It'd be natural for you have some regrets."

She laughed, a deep belly laugh that had him turning to her in surprise. She was grinning at him. "You ass," she said with affection. "It was not a decision made under duress."

He frowned at her. "What're you talking about?"

Rowan reached out to flick the hair off his forehead, loving the way the light from the fire played over his features.

"I'd already decided I wanted you to turn me," she explained patiently. "So really the only thing that was decided on the fly was the timing."

"You'd already decided." She nodded. "And you didn't think maybe this was something we should discuss? You didn't think it was something you should tell me?"

"There wasn't a lot of time, Jack. I got kidnapped, if you'll recall."

"Yeah, I recall," he said sardonically. He reached out to grip her chin firmly, his eyes searching hers. "You're sure you don't have any regrets about this?"

"The only regret I could possibly have," she said quietly, "would be if you didn't want me any longer."

"Oh darling," he murmured. He pressed a gentle kiss to her lips. "That's never going to happen."

"Good," she sighed with satisfaction. "Then we've got no problems. Although I will have to find a new job," she mused. "Kind of hard to teach kindergarten when sunlight's a no-no."

"You could do it, if you wanted," he told her. "You'd just have to be very, very careful."

"I think it'd be too much trouble," she said. She turned to face away from him and scooted back into him so they nestled like spoons in a drawer. His arm came around her and she took his hand in hers. "I still want to teach though," she mused, toying with his fingers. "Maybe I'll get a job teaching night school. You know, to adult students going back for their GED? That might be interesting."

"You'll miss the kids," he said, and she shrugged.

"Sure," she said. "But it's okay. Maybe in a few years I'll decide it's worth it to go back. Either way, I'd rather be with you."

"Speaking of kids…"

She turned to look at him over her shoulder, frowning at the hesitant tone in his voice. "What about them?"

"Do you want to have children?"

"No." She shook her head. "Why, do you?"

"No, not really. In fact, I'm pretty sure I can't have children."

"Oh. Then why are you asking me?"

"I thought you should know, in case you wanted to have some. Don't most women want to have kids?"

"I don't know, but I never did." She shrugged again. "Just not the mom type, I guess."

"Oh. Okay."

She grinned at his relieved expression. "What would you have done if I'd said, yes, I want to have kids?"

"I have no idea," he said honestly.

She was giggling, shaking in his arms. "Well it's good to know you had a plan."

He dug his fingers into her ribs, making her shriek and wriggle. "Smart-ass." He settled his chin on the top of her head, inhaling her scent as they watched the fire.

She sighed. "I guess we have some stuff to figure out, huh?"

"Yes." He kissed her shoulder where her robe had slid off.

"I have to talk to my dad."

"I already did," he said, and that had her twisting around to look at him.

"You did? Of course you did," she realized, and turned back to face the fire once again. "He'd have been worried sick. What did he say when you told him?"

"He wasn't thrilled," Jack acknowledged. Actually, Simon had been more than a little concerned about the life his little girl was going to be leading from now on but he'd been remarkably calm about it. "He's going to need to hear the story from you, I think."

"I'll call him in the morning," she said then frowned. "Or rather, the evening. Yeah, this'll take some getting used to."

"You'll figure it out," he said, snuggling into her again. "And I'll be right there with you."

"Thanks, baby."

"Welcome. Listen, how do you feel about taking a trip?"

"You are NOT getting me on another plane! I swear to Christ if you drug me, when I wake up, I'll kick your fucking ass. And I bet I could do it now too. I'm sure I'm way stronger than I used to be."

He was shaking with laughter. "No, no plane. I was thinking more along the lines of a cruise."

"Really? That sounds like fun. But honestly, I'm not real big on the idea of being stuck on a boat with a couple of thousand strangers. Especially with my new diet."

"I have a friend with a yacht," he explained. "I have a standing invitation to use it so I thought we might go to Europe sometime soon."

"Why Europe? You've been there enough in your life, I'd think you'd want to go someplace new."

"Well, you didn't get to see much of it while you were there and I thought we could swing by Budapest while we were there."

She smiled. "You want to visit Cedric and Penelope."

"Yeah." He laid his cheek against hers. "You were right, I've been neglecting my family."

"I'm always right," she said smugly.

"Lord, are you going to be hard to live with for the next thousand years."

"Tough titties, Fangalicious, because you're stuck with me."

"I wouldn't have it any other way." There was a slight pause then he asked, "Did you just say tough titties?"

"Hey, I'm a child of the eighties," she protested while he laughed.

"I do love you," he said, amused.

"I love you too," she sighed, and closed her eyes.

"Hey, you're not going to sleep on me, are you?"

"I've had a hard couple of days," she murmured. "I'm catching up on my rest."

"You can rest when the sun comes up," he told her as he got to his feet. "For now, we have a few things to settle."

"Like what?" she said. She squealed, her eyes flying open as she was hoisted over his shoulder. He started for the bedroom and she eyed his silk-covered backside with interest as he walked.

"Like you making me beg." He swatted her on her robe-covered backside, distracting her from the very fine picture his ass made and making her squeal again. "Remember that?"

"Umm…I do have a vague recollection," she mused, grinning when he swatted her ass again. "Did you want to do it again?"

He growled low in his throat as he walked into the bedroom and tossed her on the bed. She bounced twice, laughing while he loomed at the foot.

"You're going to be the one doing the begging, darling. It's payback time so I'd start practicing my pleas if I were you."

Rowan got to her knees, letting the robe drop off her shoulders to pool around her. She saw his eyes flare at her nudity and barely suppressed a giggle. "Oh you mean to make me beg, do you?"

"Absolutely," he rumbled. He hooked his thumbs in his pajama pants and shucked them down. His cock was already hard, standing out from his body and pulsing with the rhythm of his blood.

"Well, I'm sure you can make me beg," she whispered, sliding off the bed and walking toward him. "But before you do, there's just one thing."

"What's that?"

She trailed her hand down his chest, down over his cock and reached underneath to cuddle his balls. His head dropped back and his breath hissed out in pleasure.

She leaned close to him, flicked her tongue over the faint marks her fangs had left on his neck, and whispered, "You have to catch me first."

She waited half a beat, just enough time for his eyes to snap open, then sprinted for the door. She heard his roar of laughter behind her and the pounding of his feet as he gave chase, and thought, *Yeah. This life is going to be good.*

Why an electronic book?

We live in the Information Age—an exciting time in the history of human civilization, in which technology rules supreme and continues to progress in leaps and bounds every minute of every day. For a multitude of reasons, more and more avid literary fans are opting to purchase e-books instead of paper books. The question from those not yet initiated into the world of electronic reading is simply: *Why?*

1. ***Price.*** An electronic title at Ellora's Cave Publishing and Cerridwen Press runs anywhere from 40% to 75% less than the cover price of the exact same title in paperback format. Why? Basic mathematics and cost. It is less expensive to publish an e-book (no paper and printing, no warehousing and shipping) than it is to publish a paperback, so the savings are passed along to the consumer.
2. ***Space.*** Running out of room in your house for your books? That is one worry you will never have with electronic books. For a low one-time cost, you can purchase a handheld device specifically designed for e-reading. Many e-readers have large, convenient screens for viewing. Better yet, hundreds of titles can be stored within your new library—on a single microchip. There are a variety of e-readers from different manufacturers. You can also read e-books on your PC or laptop computer. (Please note that Ellora's Cave does not endorse any specific brands.

You can check our websites at www.ellorascave.com or www.cerridwenpress.com for information we make available to new consumers.)
3. ***Mobility.*** Because your new e-library consists of only a microchip within a small, easily transportable e-reader, your entire cache of books can be taken with you wherever you go.
4. ***Personal Viewing Preferences.*** Are the words you are currently reading too small? Too large? Too… ANNOYING? Paperback books cannot be modified according to personal preferences, but e-books can.
5. ***Instant Gratification.*** Is it the middle of the night and all the bookstores near you are closed? Are you tired of waiting days, sometimes weeks, for bookstores to ship the novels you bought? Ellora's Cave Publishing sells instantaneous downloads twenty-four hours a day, seven days a week, every day of the year. Our webstore is never closed. Our e-book delivery system is 100% automated, meaning your order is filled as soon as you pay for it.

Those are a few of the top reasons why electronic books are replacing paperbacks for many avid readers.

As always, Ellora's Cave and Cerridwen Press welcome your questions and comments. We invite you to email us at Comments@ellorascave.com or write to us directly at Ellora's Cave Publishing Inc., 1056 Home Avenue, Akron, OH 44310-3502.

COMING TO A BOOKSTORE NEAR YOU!

ELLORA'S CAVE

Bestselling Authors Tour

UPDATES AVAILABLE AT
WWW.ELLORASCAVE.COM

Cerridwen, the Celtic Goddess of wisdom, was the muse who brought inspiration to storytellers and those in the creative arts. Cerridwen Press encompasses the best and most innovative stories in all genres of today's fiction. Visit our site and discover the newest titles by talented authors who still get inspired - much like the ancient storytellers did, once upon a time.

Cerridwen Press
www.cerridwenpress.com

Discover for yourself why readers can't get enough of the multiple award-winning publisher
Ellora's Cave.
Whether you prefer e-books or paperbacks, be sure to visit EC on the web at www.ellorascave.com
for an erotic reading experience that will leave you breathless.